J.C.FIELDS

THE LAST INSURGENT

VINCI
BOOKS

By J.C. Fields

The Michael Wolfe Saga

Vinci Books

vinci-books.com

Published by Vinci Books Ltd in 2026

1

Copyright © J.C. Fields 2021

A CIP catalogue record for this book is available from the British Library.

Paperback ISBN: 9781036706555

The EU GPSR authorised representative is Logos Europe, 9 rue Nicolas Poussion, 17000 La Rochelle, France

contact@logoseurope.eu

Part I

Chapter One

Los Nuevo drug cartel Capo Juan Castillo remained still, his hands behind his back, staring into the darkness beyond the glow created by the bonfire's flickering flames. Shadows danced on the mountain wall behind him. He tapped his right foot to the rhythm of a tune only he heard. His first lieutenant, Salvador Montreal, stood one pace behind him, listening to a message from scouts somewhere out in the darkness. There were six Sicarios behind him armed with MAC-10 automatic pistols.

Montreal leaned in to speak into Castillo's ear. "They are coming. One hundred yards out."

The drug overlord nodded and remained quiet as he continued to stare into the darkness. The men behind him stiffened, their MAC-10s held at ready.

Minutes ticked by without anyone emerging from the darkness. Finally, Castillo saw two men appear out of the gloom and stop. Raising his hand, Castillo smiled and yelled, "We cannot negotiate from this distance. We will not fire. Come ahead."

The two men surveyed the area beside them and stepped aside as a short man with muscular shoulders and a droopy black mustache became illuminated by the fire's glow. This was the overlord of a competing cartel called Niños Perdidos. His real name remained a mystery, but he was known as El Capitan.

He approached the flickering fire and stopped ten feet from Castillo, the bonfire to his left. He said, "I am told you have a proposal."

With a slight smile, Castillo nodded. "Yes, we are wasting precious resources in this senseless back and forth competition between our two organizations."

El Capitan did not respond. But the furrows on his brow deepened.

"Would you agree?"

The shorter man shrugged. "I might or I might not agree—it depends. What do you have in mind?"

"A consolidation of sorts—a combining of resources."

"And you as the head of this consolidation. I think not."

Castillo laughed out loud. "No, my friend, not that type of consolidation. Instead of working against each other, we consolidate resources. We both have a common determent to expanding our markets. Correct?"

An icy stare was his answer.

"We both know who that determent is. What if we had a resource that could create fear and panic within the minds of our common enemy? Would that be worth discussing?"

El Capitan tilted his head. "It would depend on…"

Castillo's head disappeared in a cloud of gray and red mist. Before his body slumped to the rocky floor, the six Sicarios behind their Capo raised their MAC-10's and fired the weapons on full-automatic.

The MAC-10s firing continuously masked the report of

a sniper's rifle arriving two seconds after the head of Juan Castillo disappeared.

Ex-Marine sniper Michael Wolfe returned the scope mounted on his Barrett M82A1 sniper rifle to his aim point and watched the carnage as ten men fired automatic weapons at each other from point-blank range.

The now mortally wounded El Capitan fell sideways. Sparks from the disturbed embers sprayed everywhere as the cartel lord crashed into the middle of the large bonfire. An agonized scream could be heard above the echoes of gunfire. The sound of automatic weapons ceased as the last man fell.

Sweeping his scope over the carnage, he saw one man stand to survey the scene. The man was known to Wolfe from pictures provided by his control in Washington, DC. This was Salvador Montreal, the man responsible for setting up the meeting between the two cartel leaders. He was also the man who contacted an undercover DEA agent to arrange for the ambush. Wolfe suspected the man's real motive, in setting up the meeting, was not to rid the world of two bloodthirsty predators, but to give himself the opportunity to be the leader of both cartels.

Centering the crosshairs of the scope on the back of the survivor, Wolfe applied pressure to the trigger. It broke and the Barrett sent another .50 BMG round into the gap between the two mountains walls. The bullet traveled the 1500 meters in 1.758 seconds and arrived with enough inertia to knock Montreal to the ground, a gaping hole in his chest just to the right of his heart.

Although Wolfe could not see this from his position high above the scene, Montreal blinked once and then exhaled for the last time.

Wolfe's expression did not change. He stood from his prone position high above the scene below. With his Barrett in hand, he flipped his night vision goggles down, turned and started the one-mile hike back to his rented Jeep.

———————

In the darkness beyond the bonfire illumination, a shadowy figured crouched and watched the mayhem caused by the brief firefight, his short red hair hidden by a black watch cap and his face smeared with black camo face paint. Wearing black jeans and long-sleeve black T-shirt, he was invisible in the dark mountain ravine. With a Sig Sauer MPX K posed in his hands, he searched the hills above the fire for any sign of the sniper. He saw none. He turned his head back to the gruesome scene as Salvador Montreal stood. Almost immediately, a massive bullet wound opened in his chest and he jerked forward.

The sound of the high-powered rifle shot echoed off the canyon wall as Montreal's body hit the ground. Looking up at the mountain, the man smiled with admiration of the sniper's audacity and planning. With slow, cautious steps, he backed up, turned and melted into the nighttime landscape.

Chapter Two

Retired CIA agent Jerry Griggs observed the twin-engine Beechcraft B55 Baron circle the runway on its final approach. He glanced at the windsock atop the metal building next to where he stood and noted a gentle breeze out of the northwest. The Baron would land into the wind.

The woman next to him also watched the plane as it circled the property. Griggs turned to her. "You two have really done a nice job with this place. It was old and rundown when I first saw it."

"Thank you. Michael is extremely proud of his runway and hangar."

Griggs glanced over his left shoulder at the almost-completed new home one hundred yards from the hangar. He also noted the three-foot-wide strip of bare dirt extending from the side of the hangar to the house. "When's the house supposed to be done?"

Nadia Picard-Wolfe smiled and looked at the tall man standing next to her. "Two weeks."

He pointed to the long strip of dirt. "What's that?"

She smiled. "Utilities."

With a nod, Griggs said, "Joseph tells me you've been working with Alexia Gibbs to improve your computer skills?"

"I have. She has been patient with me. We have also become friends. She is from Spain and speaks fluent French. It is fun to be with her as we only speak French when we are together."

"An added benefit."

"Yes, we also share something else in common."

"What's that?"

"Husbands who are not, as you Americans say, nine-to-five office workers."

Griggs chuckled. "No, Jimmy Gibbs and Michael Wolfe are not your average nine-to-fivers."

She returned her gaze to the Beechcraft as it touched down.

With a smile, he saw the beautiful woman, who was born in France and raised in Israel, make a quick and subtle sign of the cross before she started walking toward the open hangar door.

Michael Wolfe parked the Beechcraft inside the hangar and finished his shutdown routine. When he completed his tasks, he glanced up and saw Nadia next to the plane, a smile on her face.

As soon as he stepped down from the plane, they embraced.

She looked up. "I'm glad you are home. I've missed you."

"I missed you too." He paused as they held each other. Eventually, he said, "Was that Jerry Griggs I saw waiting?"

"Yes. He said he needed to talk to you."

"I just completed one of his, 'I need to talk' assignments."

"This one might be different. It sounds like both of us will be involved."

Taking a deep breath, he sighed and said, "Very well, let's go see what he has to say."

The original house on the property, having been built in the late forties, was small compared to the larger home under construction thirty yards to the west. However, after some extensive remodeling it was a comfortable two-bedroom cottage. It would be torn down once the main home was completed.

Once inside, Griggs sat at a round table in the dining area while Wolfe prepared a pot of coffee. Nadia asked her husband, "Did you eat anything before you left this morning?"

He shook his head.

"Then I will make you one of my French omelets." She turned to Griggs. "Would you like one, Jerry?"

"Yes, ma'am. Michael's told me about them."

Wolfe placed a cup of coffee in front of the taller man and smiled. "Why do you think I didn't eat before I left?"

Nadia shook her head and started preparing the omelets.

Wolfe asked, "Nadia said you needed to talk to me."

Taking a sip of coffee, the ex-CIA man said, "How'd your trip go?"

Tilting his head, Wolfe frowned and took a sip of his own coffee. "Fine, nothing out of the ordinary. Why?"

"Good."

"Nadia said you might have something for us."

Griggs watched as Nadia sat a plate with the omelet in front him. She returned to the stove to make one for Michael.

"That looks delicious."

"They are." Wolfe tapped the table. "Stop stalling, Jerry."

"Have you been keeping up with the news lately?"

"I've been out of town and I try hard not to pay attention. You know that."

Griggs paused and took a bite of his omelet. He said, "This is excellent."

"Jerry?"

"Okay. On the Fourth of July, an appellate court judge from San Francisco died in a boating accident on Lake Tahoe."

"Those things happen." Wolfe paused as his wife sat another omelet in front of him.

Griggs nodded. "Yes, they do. However, a month later, a judge from the Phoenix area was found dead from an overdose of opioids. The man didn't have a prescription for them."

Without comment, Wolfe placed a fork of omelet in his mouth and chewed, not taking his eyes off his guest.

Griggs said, "Don't you find that odd, Michael?"

"No. Not particularly. It happens."

Silence fell between the two men as they ate. With the last of his omelet consumed, Wolfe pushed his plate away and placed his arms on the table. "Now you're going to tell me how these two incidents are related, aren't you?"

Griggs nodded.

"Go on."

"Three weeks ago, a sheriff in Santa Fe, New Mexico died when his department-supplied Ford F-150 failed to make a turn in the mountains and tumbled down a ravine."

Wolfe remained quiet. His gaze fixed on Griggs.

"It turns out the brakes on the Ford were tampered with and a newly hired mechanic disappeared the same day."

Wolfe grinned. "Let me guess—the mechanic was Hispanic."

"No, he wasn't." Griggs extracted a folded piece of paper from a pocket inside his jacket and slid it across the table. "That's a copy of his ID badge. While the department ran a background check, which he passed with flying colors, they discovered the guy used a stolen ID to apply for the job. The real mechanic was located in Wichita, Kansas and hasn't been out of the state for two decades."

Wolfe stared at the picture. "He's Caucasian. Okay, you have my attention. What do the judges and the sheriff have in common?"

"That's why I like you, Michael. You're a quick study."

Wolfe rolled his eyes.

"All of them were heavily involved with curtailing Mexican drug cartel activities in their respective state."

Studying the picture again, Wolfe kept silent.

"Any questions?"

"I take it the fake mechanic has been identified."

"He has, to an extent."

"Why are you telling me this, Jerry?"

"CIA and NSA believe the guy's an import. NSA picked up chatter out of Mexico to a cell phone inside the United States discussing the sheriff."

"And?"

"The US side voice had a Northern Ireland accent. Male. Mid-forties."

"Mid-forties?" Wolfe glanced at the picture. "This guy could be mid-forties."

With a nod, Griggs said, "Yeah, that's what the agency thinks, too."

"Isn't this something they should handle?"

"One would think so, but higher ups want you to find this guy."

Wolfe folded his arms and waited.

The younger man cleared his throat. "There's a reason they want you to look into it."

"Figured."

"If the FBI gets involved, regardless of how quietly, there's always a chance they'll spook him and he'll disappear until things calm down. You and Nadia are stealthy and make zero noise when you start a search."

"Okay, I get that." Wolfe stood, gathered the two empty plates and took them to the sink in the kitchen. He remained quiet as he rinsed them off. When he was done, he turned and leaned against the cabinet. "What exactly are you not telling us?"

With a grim smile, Griggs said, "One of the phone calls NSA intercepted mentioned the Irishman's ultimate target."

Wolfe waited. His arms folded again.

"No details were discussed during the phone call—just the target."

"Spit it out, Jerry."

"The ultimate target is the President of the United States."

Chapter Three

"Jerry, isn't that the Secret Service's area of expertise?"

"It is, and they've been given a heads up. But we need to find him before he has an opportunity."

Wolfe was quiet for a few moments as he focused on a spot on the wall above Griggs' head. "Elections are in November."

A nod from Griggs.

"The President will be making a lot of campaign stops and speeches."

Another nod.

"The Secret Service won't let just anyone get close to a president, so whatever he has planned will have to be from a distance."

Griggs remained quiet for a few moments. "How would you do it, Michael?"

"I'd have to give it some thought."

"But there is a way to do it?"

"There's always a way. It depends on this Irishman's skill set."

Griggs shook his head. "Nothing came back on voice-print match."

"Have you checked with MI5 or MI6?"

"We're trying to keep this quiet. No, we haven't asked them."

"Jerry, it would help if we knew who he is and what he's capable of. You have an intercepted cell phone call and a voice with an Irish accent. If this guy is a holdover from the Troubles, he could be dangerous."

"What do you mean?"

"You just told me the NSA identified him in his mid-forties. The Good Friday Agreement in 1998 was the official end of the conflict between the Provisional Irish Republican Army and the British. That was just a little over twenty years ago. If this guy was a teenager when they trained him and the conflict ended when he was in his mid-twenties, he'd be the right age. Have MI6 check his voice."

Griggs drummed his fingers on the kitchen table. "How dangerous?"

"Some of those guys were highly trained as terrorists. Who do you think developed the terrorist bombing techniques used by the Taliban and Al Qaeda in Afghanistan?"

"The IRA?"

"Correct."

Still drumming his fingers, he looked up at Wolfe. "Shit."

"Like I said, you need to have MI6 run an analysis of the voice."

The fingers stopped drumming. "When you were active with the CIA, did you ever hear of IRA holdouts?"

"All the time. But not so much toward the end. I think it's because they either outgrew their passion or the radical ones aren't alive any longer. Being a terrorist can result in a short career."

Griggs stood and went to the coffee maker. As he poured a fresh cup, he said, "Do you two still have any contacts with MI6?"

"Nadia and I are supposedly dead, remember?"

"Ah, that. Sorry."

"Jerry, I'm sure Joseph still has contacts within MI6 he can ask. The man knows everybody."

"Yeah, I know. I was just hoping we wouldn't have to get him involved."

"If anyone can do it quietly, it will be Joseph."

———

Later in the afternoon, after Jerry Griggs left, Michael returned to the hanger to service his Beechcraft. He also needed to retrieve his duffle bag and secure several tools of his trade. After locking the Barrett M82A1 and another rifle in the gun room on the second level of the hangar, he returned to checking the starboard engine.

As he worked on the aircraft, Nadia walked up and said, "You've been quiet ever since Jerry left."

"Thinking."

"About?"

He stopped, grabbed a hand towel, wiped his hands and turned toward her. "Before I say anything, what are your thoughts about looking for this Irish ghost?"

She shrugged. "I am apolitical, Michael. I don't care who the president is or who our local politicians are. From what I have observed about your federal government, it's Kabuki theater."

"I agree with you. Elaborate production without a lot of content."

She sighed, "But I do care if someone wants to kill the president."

"So, do I."

They were both quiet as Wolfe continued to wipe grease off his hands. Nadia finally said, "Whose idea was it for you to go to Mexico?"

"We're never told, you know that."

"Yes, I know, but someone made the request. Who?"

"I would assume it was the president or someone who consults with him."

"Joseph?"

"I'm sure he was involved in the decision. Why are you asking?"

"Think about it for a second. They knew about this Irishman before you left. They were hoping he'd be at the meeting."

Wolfe stared at his wife for several moments before he responded, "I was told it had to do with an intercepted phone call."

"Exactly, but no one gave you any details, right?"

"No."

"I think we need to ask Jerry more questions."

"I agree. He's staying at Joseph's place tonight."

The house was a modern two-story rustic log structure with a wraparound wooden deck. A massive oak door, with iron accents, featured prominently as the focal point of the front. Rock pillars supported the deck with rough-hewn railings. From previous visits, Wolfe and Nadia knew the sleeping quarters were on the second floor with the living and kitchen areas on the first. A gazebo-like structure containing a breakfast nook rounded out the right side of the house. Sitting on a lot of over twenty acres, the isolated property provided its owner seclusion and privacy.

Jerry Griggs' rental car sat parked in the circle drive close to the ascending steps. Wolfe set the parking brake on their Jeep Grand Cherokee and looked at the structure over the steering wheel. He said, "Jerry's on the back-deck, grilling."

"How can you tell?"

"I saw a whiff of smoke floating over the house as we pulled up."

"Think he'll have enough for three?"

"Let's make sure he feels bad if he doesn't."

The two climbed the seven steps leading to the wrap-around deck and walked toward the rear of the house. When they reached the expansive rear portion of the deck, they were pleased to see Joseph, crystal highball glass in hand, attending his large Weber gas grill. Griggs stood beside him sipping on a beer.

When Joseph saw them, he raised his glass and said, "I was wondering when you two would show up."

"Why didn't you tell us you were in town, Joseph?" Wolfe took a pull on the beer Griggs had handed him.

"It was a last-second decision and I'm not officially here." Smoke bellowed up as Joseph opened the lid. "The threat to the president is real, Michael. We're taking it seriously. What we are not doing is making it a topic of public discussion. That's why you are now involved."

Wolfe set his beer on the deck railing and leaned against the wood. His arms folded. "Who's the Irishman?"

"You were correct to ask if our friends at MI5 could identify him. They contacted me this morning—another reason I'm here."

Remaining quiet, Wolfe kept his gaze on Joseph.

"He's forty-seven years old, born during the height of the Troubles. His father worked on the docks and his mother disappeared when he was only ten. With his father working long hours and no supervision, he started hanging out with a group of boys who encouraged him to join the IRA. He supposedly killed his first British soldier as his initiation at the age of fifteen."

"What's his name?"

"Daniel McCaffrey. He goes by Danny."

Griggs said, "I didn't know most of these details when we spoke this afternoon, Michael. But you were asking the right questions."

"No problem, Jerry." Wolfe turned back to Joseph. "What happened to this guy after the Good Friday Agreement?"

"As you know, hostilities didn't end right away, but MI5 believes McCaffrey and several of his more violent brethren took off for Libya and worked for Gaddafi for a few years until the US invaded Afghanistan."

"Let me guess, McCaffrey was trained as a bomb maker."

Joseph nodded. "One of their best, according to my source. MI6 took over keeping track of him when he went overseas but lost his trail in 2002. They think he ended up in Iraq sometime in late 2003, six months after the US went into the country."

"Do they know where he is now?"

"No. He completely disappeared. There was speculation he died in a drone strike on the Pakistan and Afghan border in 2010. That assumption ended this morning when his voice was matched by MI5 to an intercepted phone call we recorded six months ago."

Wolfe grinned. "How many phone calls, Joseph?"

"We have now identified a total of ten."

"Why was I sent to Mexico?"

"Several of the calls indicated he was supposed to be at the meeting you interrupted."

"Ah…" Wolfe grew quiet as he sipped his beer. "What's this guy look like?"

Griggs said, "The only picture MI5 could send us is from his early school days. The CIA did a quick age progression analysis, and they think he looks like this." A sheet of paper was handed to Wolfe.

He looked at it and handed it back to Griggs. "He wasn't at the meeting I—uh—interrupted. Unless he was in the shadows. There's a vague resemblance to the mechanic's ID Jerry showed me this afternoon."

"Facial recognition software agrees with you." Joseph used tongs to remove four steaks from the grill and place them on a serving plate. "Hope you two are hungry."

Chapter Four

Wolfe pushed his plate away and leaned back. "As always, Joseph, your steak was excellent."

Raising a glass of old vine Zinfandel to his lips, Joseph nodded and took a sip.

Nadia asked, "Exactly what are you asking Michael and me to do?"

With a slight smile, Joseph set the glass down. "When McCaffrey and his buddies took off for Libya, an MI6 operative was tasked with knowing everything about him. We want you two to recruit that MI6 agent to help find the Irishman."

With his glass halfway to his lips, Wolfe stopped and stared hard at Joseph. "What's this MI6 operator's name?"

"Geoffrey Canfield."

Wolfe shot a quick glance at Nadia. She sat straighter in her chair and kept her gaze fixed on Joseph.

Jerry Griggs said, "Relax, you two. We've known about Canfield ever since your last trip to Grand Cayman."

"Michael, Jerry and I are the only ones who know

Canfield is still alive. We have no intentions of letting his former employer know otherwise."

Finally, after taking a sip of his wine, Wolfe narrowed his eyes. "How did you know we went to Grand Cayman?"

Joseph shrugged. "I, like you, have my sources."

"I don't know if Geoffrey will be a willing partner."

Griggs asked, "Doesn't he owe you a big favor?"

Wolfe frowned and stared hard at the two men sitting across from him and Nadia. "Maybe."

"Canfield can give you a more detailed background on McCaffrey. The man was his only project during the early 2000s."

"Didn't know that." He paused. "Why do you think McCaffrey started working with the Mexican cartels?"

After taking another sip of wine, Joseph set his glass down. "I would only be speculating."

Smiling, Wolfe said, "Joseph, your speculations are probably more informed than most. Indulge me."

"I think McCaffrey is an unrepentant insurgent who is trying to show the world he's still relevant."

Nadia tilted her head slightly. "What do you mean, relevant?"

"Men like McCaffrey thrive on creating chaos. Statistically, terrorism has been declining worldwide for the past few years. ISIS is a ghost of its former self, Al-Qaeda has been reduced to a few angry old men shouting about jihad, and terrorist attacks in Europe are down."

With a nod, Wolfe said, "If we know what drives this guy, we might be better able to predict his next move."

"Exactly." Joseph paused, smiled, and said, "That's why you two will need to utilize your US Marshal IDs to find the Irishman. It gives you legitimacy. Plus, Canfield might know the key to understanding the man and how to locate him."

———

Wolfe lay on their bed with his hands behind his head, staring at the ceiling in the dim light. He heard the shower shut off and Nadia singing softly in French. Five minutes later, she exited the bathroom but before she turned the light off, he noticed her normal sleeping clothes were absent. In their place she wore a long silky nightgown. A smile came to his lips when she slipped under the covers and snuggled against him.

"Aren't you going to be cold wearing that tonight?"

"No."

'It's a little chilly, you sure?"

"Yes." She paused and put her arm over his chest. "I have you to keep me warm."

He chuckled and pulled off his T-shirt.

———

As they lay in each other's arms, savoring the intimacy of the past hour, Wolfe said softly, "I called Chief of the Boat Rufus Carroll while you were in the shower."

"Will he take us to Grand Cayman again?"

"Yeah. He said business was a little soft right now, so he could take us whenever we need to go."

"Good, I like the solitude of that trip." She rose to one elbow and looked at him in the darkness. "You will have to make love to me while we are sailing in the gulf."

He grinned. "I'm sure that can be arranged."

She lay back down and pressed against him, her head on his chest. "Do you think we could go to Israel someday soon?"

The question gave him pause and he did not answer immediately. "What brought that on?"

"I haven't been there in almost three and a half years. I'm getting homesick."

"Won't that cause problems?"

"Yes. But I miss the simple things, like the aroma of rosemary in the spring, sunsets on the beaches of Tel Aviv and street vendors selling Falafel. While I am not particularly religious, I do miss the culture and the festivals we celebrate in Israel." She paused and remained quiet for a while. Wolfe let her reminisce. Finally, she said, "I'm glad I live here in the United States and that I'm your wife. This is my home now."

"There's a *however* in there."

"Yes. I should not feel this way, but I felt forced to leave Israel."

"You weren't. Circumstances made it necessary."

"I know. Is it silly for me to think that?"

"Not really. It's how you feel."

She grew silent as Wolfe held her tight. After a few moments, her body shook with a silent sob.

"Nadia, those circumstances were due to one individual, an individual who can no longer keep you out of Israel. We'll go whenever you want." He felt a tear touch his chest where her head lay.

The next morning Wolfe woke to the smell of coffee and fresh pastries. He glanced at the digital clock on his nightstand and saw the time was eleven minutes after eight. Nadia's side of the bed was empty. Normally an early riser, he felt a momentary pang of guilt for sleeping this late, but quickly dismissed it as he heard Nadia singing. She only sang when she was happy.

She entered the bedroom and stood at the foot of their bed, her arms folded. "It's about time you woke up. I must have exhausted you last night."

Rising to sit on the side of the bed, he nodded. "Yes, you must have."

She laughed and sat next to him. She then leaned over and kissed him. "Thank you."

"For what?"

"Listening."

He smiled and wrapped his arm around her shoulders. "What smells so good?"

"Fresh croissants and coffee. We will use the homemade raspberry jam we bought at the farmers market several weeks ago. It is my favorite breakfast."

"I thought omelets were your favorite."

"I am French. I can have more than one favorite."

He chuckled and followed her to the kitchen.

Wolfe finished filling the dishwasher and closed the door. He turned to lean on the cabinet and looked at Nadia, who took a sip of her coffee.

He said, "The croissants were excellent. Where did you learn to make them?"

"The last summer I stayed with my grandmama in Paris. She was a classically trained chef who worked for Eugenie Brazier and knew Julia Child. She also is the one who taught me how to properly cook."

"She did a great job. You're a wonderful cook." He paused for a second. "You've never told me this before."

She shrugged. "It was no big deal in my family." A faraway look came over her as she took another sip of coffee. "Did you know croissants are originally from Austria, but we French perfected them?"

"Nadia, you are avoiding the subject of your family."

"Yes. Like you, Michael, I am an only child. My father worked for a shipping company and was transferred to Marseille right after he married my mother, about two years before I was born. They loved Paris, but hated Marseille. There was a lot of anti-Semitism in the southern half of France at that time. I understand it still exists today."

"So, I've heard."

"When I was fourteen, we moved to Israel. I was told it was because of my father's job, but I think it was because they wanted to escape the hatred." She hesitated, looked at Michael and then returned her gaze to the coffee in her mug. "I never saw my grandmama again after we moved."

Michael asked, "Is she still alive?"

Nadia shook her head.

"I'm sorry."

"I had a trip planned to Paris the summer after I graduated from college, but she died in the spring. I never did go back to Paris."

"Do you want to?"

"No, she was the only person I knew there. I would rather go to Israel."

Wolfe smiled. "When? This coming spring?"

Her eyes grew wide and her solemn demeanor dissolved. "Oh, Michael, can we?"

"I think we have to."

Chapter Five

Chief Carroll watched as Wolfe parked the Beechcraft Baron outside a hangar in the general aviation section of Key West International Airport.

The man known as Chief to everyone who knew him hated his first name, Rufus. He seldom used it except on official documents. In his late-fifties and standing just under five-foot-ten, he still possessed broad shoulders and a trim waist. His habitual blue jean overalls and a sleeveless white T-shirt contrasted with his deeply tanned arms. A lifetime of tattoos, collected from different locales around the globe, adorned his well-defined biceps and forearms. Seldom trimmed, gray-streaked hair was swept back and restrained in a ponytail. A battered and well-worn Miami Dolphins ball cap kept the sun off a weathered face and gave him the appearance of a man ten years older. He and Michael had met while Marines and maintained their friendship over the ensuing years.

Wolfe waved to his old colleague as he exited the Baron. Nadia followed and also waved. As the two men shook hands, Chief said, "Nice plane. Why don't you just fly it down to the Caymans?"

With a grim smile, Wolfe opened the storage compartment and pointed at two rifle cases. "Because I don't believe the Cayman Island Airport Authorities would understand why I'm bringing these to the island."

With a laugh, Chief said, "No, I don't suppose they would. Let's get you two loaded and we'll head to the dock."

"As soon as I have the plane squared away, we can leave."

———

By sunset, Chief's boat, *Escape*, had cast off and navigated southwest to skirt the western side of Cuba. Their voyage toward the Cayman Islands would take forty-eight hours at fourteen knots per hour. Wolfe liked the name of the boat and thought it a good metaphor for him, Chief, and Nadia. As the lights of Key West fell behind them, the Milky Way ribbon grew in brilliance.

"I know we should have covered this before we set out, but what am I getting paid this time?"

Wolfe smiled. "What's your going rate?"

"I get twelve hundred for an eight-hour charter, Michael."

"My employer will be good with thirty-six hundred a day."

"Your employer?"

Turning to his old friend, Wolfe nodded. "He has deep pockets."

Keeping his focus on the horizon, Chief smiled. "I should have told you more."

The two men stood in silence on the helm and gazed

upon the calm waters ahead. Stars reflecting off the Gulf waters kept both of them mesmerized. After ten minutes, Wolfe broke the silence. "Do you ever get tired of this, Chief?"

"No, it's one of those mysteries I haven't figured out. I get bored easy, but never with this."

"I can see why."

More silence ensued as *Escape* slipped through the water on its heading toward the island. "What's in Grand Cayman this time, Michael?"

"I'm recruiting an old friend to help me find a man."

"You're always looking for someone, aren't you?"

"Seems that way."

"Who is it this time?"

"A ghost."

"That's not an answer."

"I know. To be honest, I only know his name and that he was involved with the Irish Republican Army in the late 1990s."

Chief gave a low whistle. "On my last tour in Afghanistan we heard rumors that some of those older IRA guys were training the locals on how to build IEDs."

"Wasn't a rumor. They were. The guy I'm looking for is supposedly one of the best bomb makers the IRA ever produced."

"Any idea how to find him?"

"That's why we're going to Grand Cayman. I know someone there who might be able to point me in the right direction."

"Your wife planning to sunbathe tomorrow?"

"Yes."

"Think she'll take her top off this time?"

Wolfe chuckled. "No, Chief, she won't be taking her top off this time."

Chief Carroll laughed. "Damn, I figured she might."

The trip to Grand Cayman took just under forty-eight hours. By four p.m. on their arrival day, Wolfe sat at a table in the back of a dingy bar listening to a multitude of conversations conducted in the Queen's English. As he waited, a glass of beer in front of him, he kept his attention on the screen of his cell phone, waiting for a text message. At ten minutes after four, the message from Nadia arrived. *On his way.*

Putting the cell phone in his back-jean pocket, he watched the front door of the noisy bar. At exactly 4:15 p.m. Geoffrey Canfield entered and waved as his mates raised their drinks to him. He strode purposefully to the bar, leaned over and spoke to the bartender. When she handed him the gin and tonic, she nodded toward the ex-MI6 operative's regular table. While taking a sip, Canfield turned to see what the bartender indicated.

Wolfe raised his glass and smiled.

Canfield hesitated, took a large gulp of his drink and walked slowly toward the table. "Never figured I'd see you again, mate."

"Time's change. How've you been, Geoffrey?"

"Fine, until about thirty seconds ago."

"Relax. I'm not here to settle any score."

After pulling the chair out across from Wolfe, he sat. "That's good to hear. To what do I owe this visit?"

"Want to be legit again?"

"Not following you, Michael."

Wolfe leaned over the table. "I need information."

Canfield took another sip of his gin and tonic. "Will that help you forget my past transgressions?"

"Not completely, but my memory might fade a bit."

With a smile, Canfield said, "What do you need to know?"

"I'm looking for a man you tried to find at the turn of the century."

Canfield sipped his drink and studied the tabletop.

"Do you know who I'm talking about?"

Looking up, the ex-MI6 operator said, "You're talking about Danny McCaffery, aren't you?"

Wolfe nodded.

"Dangerous man, Michael. You sure you want to piss off someone like him?"

"I can be dangerous myself."

"Yes—I know."

"Will you help me?"

"Are you sure he's still alive? Last I heard, he was in Afghanistan and hadn't been seen or heard from in a decade. MI6 considered him dead."

"He's alive. His voice was intercepted by the NSA talking to someone in Mexico recently."

The Englishman's eyes widened. "Mexico?"

"The FBI and the CIA believe he's working for one of the Mexican drug cartels and is planning something inside the US."

Canfield noticed his drink was empty and raised it so the bartender could see. She saw it, nodded and pulled a fresh glass from the shelves behind the bar. Returning his attention to Wolfe, Canfield asked, "What do you want from me?"

"I need background on the guy."

"That I can do."

"It's also time for you to come in from the cold and find him."

A waitress breezed by and deposited a fresh gin and tonic in front of Canfield. He studied the contents of the glass for several moments before raising it to his lips to take a sip. "I like being out in the cold. But old habits die hard. I tell you what— drop by my house, let's say, after six. We'll have dinner and discuss it further. Is Ms. Picard with you?"

"Yes."

"Then by all means, bring her too. Marilyn was most intrigued with her during their last conversation."

Wolfe stood. "Thanks, Geoffrey. We'll be there at six."

Back in their hotel room, Wolfe asked Nadia to download an app to his phone. When she completed the task, he made a call.

"Hello."

"Is this Jerry Griggs?"

"Who's calling?"

"Good phone security, Jerry. Never say yes or no on a call from a strange number."

"Michael?"

"Yes."

"This isn't your number."

"I know. We've made a discovery and I need some information. Are you near your computer?"

"I can be. Why?"

"I really don't want to discuss it on a cell phone. How long do you need to get to your laptop?"

"Five minutes."

"We'll call back."

He ended the call and turned to Nadia. "Guess you get to practice your computer skills."

She smiled and opened her laptop.

Using techniques taught to her under the tutelage of Alexia Gibbs—a computer hacker they met before their marriage—Nadia made the call and waited for Griggs to answer.

"Where the hell are you guys?"

Wolfe smiled. "I can tell you we're not in Nairobi, if that's what you are asking."

"Is this call secure?"

"More than you can imagine."

"Good. Where are you?"

"Grand Cayman."

"Did you make contact with Canfield?"

"Yes. Nadia and I are having dinner at his house tonight. He seemed willing to help."

"Then why the call?"

"Obviously, you guys knew he was still alive, so I'm guessing you've been keeping up with him."

"Guilty."

"Good, I'm glad you didn't lie to me. Geoffrey has never been one to sit around all day with nothing to do. Since you're keeping tabs on him, what's he been doing, besides going to a local bar at four in the afternoon every day?"

"He's not getting mixed up in the politics of the island, if that's what you mean."

"No, he's never been political. But my bet is he's developed a network of police officers and government functionaries who keep him abreast of anything that happens on the island."

Griggs chuckled. "Very good, Michael. He and his lady

friend have tea at a small café every morning at precisely eight. Sometimes they sit alone and other times they don't."

"When they have company, are they the same individuals?"

"Yes."

"What else have you guys observed?"

"He takes the same path every day to the pub. Around 3:30, he sits on a park bench overlooking the beach. He's normally joined by one of three individuals. They will sit there for about ten to fifteen minutes, not looking at each other and pretending to talk on cell phones."

"Yeah, that sounds like Canfield."

"Not terribly sophisticated if you ask me."

"No, but in his mind, he's still in the game."

"Other than that, Michael, he leads a pretty mundane life."

"Okay, Jerry. That's what I needed to know."

Wolfe ended the call and turned to Nadia. "As I suspected, Geoffrey is still active. Not sure for who, but he's still in the game."

Chapter Six

Canfield's small bungalow sat half a kilometer from the beach in Camana Bay. Tucked away in a grove of trees, other houses were close, but not enough to be claustrophobic. Wolfe and Nadia arrived in the area an hour early and explored the terrain with the purpose of determining escape routes, should they be needed.

At ten minutes to six, they stood one hundred meters down the street from the home, and Wolfe asked, "What do you think?"

"I don't believe I would want to live here."

He chuckled. "Not what I meant, but why not?"

"I have grown to like the four seasons in Missouri. This would be boring."

Wolfe smiled and nodded. "Yes, I would have to agree. My question was more about having to make a quick exit."

"I know. I'm still thinking about it."

They continued to survey the neighborhood for several more minutes. Finally, Nadia said, "Out the back and west toward the beach."

"I agree. We could be near the shops and restaurants in a matter of minutes then disappear into the crowd."

"Yes. Think we'll need to?"

"Don't know. At one time I trusted Geoffrey with my life, but now…"

Nadia looked at him and smiled. "Let's hope he can regain your trust."

"We'll see. Let's go knock on the door."

The patio behind Geoffrey Canfield's bungalow smelled of the sea and overgrown bougainvillea. The full sun and heat of the island helped the plant create an impenetrable thickness secluding them from prying neighbors. Canfield, crystal tumbler in hand, nodded toward Nadia and said to his partner, Dr. Marilyn Dawson, "You remember this lovely lass, don't you, my love?"

Marilyn offered her hand. "Yes, we had a most spirited conversation the last time we met. How are you, my dear?"

Nadia shook the woman's hand. "I am fine. Thank you for having us to your lovely home."

"It's a shack, dear." She turned to Wolfe. "And you must be the mysterious Michael Wolfe."

"Not sure about the mysterious, but yes I am." Wolfe shook the woman's hand and took in what he saw. She, like Geoffrey, was in her early sixties. Several inches taller than Nadia, she held herself with regale charm. Silver hair, cut short and professionally styled, contrasted with the deep tan her sundress revealed. Intense green eyes studied him with a hint of amusement.

"Geoffrey has told me about you for years and you are

indeed mysterious, Mr. Wolfe. And I might add, quite handsome."

"Call me Michael."

"Very well." She turned to Canfield. "Our guests are without refreshments, Geoffrey."

"I've taken care of that, my love."

As he spoke, a pencil-thin woman with tightly curled black hair and dark skin appeared on the patio with a silver tray of drinks. Wolfe thought she looked familiar, but out of place in this locale.

She handed a glass of wine to Nadia and said, "I'm told you prefer Chardonnay, ma'am."

"Yes, thank you."

The woman offered the tray to Wolfe keeping her back to Canfield and Marilyn. She said, "I'm told you like this brand of beer, Mr. Wolfe."

Wolfe saw the label and shot a quick glance at the woman's face. Sudden recognition of the woman's identity caused him to smile and take the offered bottle. "Yes, I do. Thank you."

The woman returned to the interior of the house.

Canfield raised his glass. "To old acquaintances and the prospects of renewed friendships."

Everyone raised their drinks and nodded.

Marilyn smiled. "Carla is a wonderful cook. We will have a marvelous meal. Why don't Nadia and I retreat to the living room and you two can conduct whatever business you need?"

Wolfe turned his attention to Marilyn. "Nadia and I are a team. She needs to hear what Geoffrey has to say."

The woman showed no hint of being rebuffed. She nodded and sipped the glass of wine she now held.

Turning his attention to Canfield, Wolfe took his first sip of beer. "Geoffrey."

"Ah, yes. Danny McCaffrey. What do you know about him?"

"Not much, just that he was trained by the IRA at a young age to be a bomb maker and that he left Ireland after the Good Friday Agreement in 1998."

Canfield nodded. "That he did."

"I was told he went to Libya and worked for Gaddafi."

"That was the general consensus among my colleagues at MI6. He might have passed through the country, but he didn't stay long. Instead, he offered his services to the Izz-al Din al-Qassam Brigades, which is the military branch of Hamas."

Wolfe and Nadia remained quiet. They were aware of what al-Qassam Brigades was and its capabilities.

After a sip of his gin and tonic, Canfield continued, "In September of 2000, the Second Intifada against Israel started with suicide bombings and other military activities. From that time through August of 2005, forty percent of the suicide attacks on Israeli civilians were carried out by members of the al-Qassam Brigades. And guess who taught them how to make bombs?"

"Danny McCaffrey."

"Yes. With the exception of a few who went to the United States, his pals had returned to Ireland by that time. He did not. I was tasked with trying to find him. I could never confirm his presence in Libya, but several sources spotted him on the streets of Gaza City in 2001." Geoffrey hesitated for a moment, took a sip of his cocktail then gave Wolfe a sad smile. "I hate to bring this up, but I believe you should know. The bomb that destroyed the bus your wife rode was made or at least designed by Danny McCaffrey."

The corner of Wolfe's mouth twitched. He stared hard at Canfield but kept silent. Nadia glanced at her husband and touched his arm.

Canfield continued, "Nasty business, this bomb making. And I might add, McCaffrey excelled at it. We lost track of him in 2002, around the same time the US invaded Afghanistan. No one saw him or heard from him until another one of my sources spotted him on the streets of Bagdad in 2003. He'd grown a beard, grayish red, I'm told. Kind of hard to hide in an Arabic country with red hair.

"My search for McCaffrey continued for several years without much success, I'm sorry to say. He was more of a ghost than anything. With my lack of progress and Britain's deepening involvement with the Afghan war, my duties changed." Canfield stared at his glass and drained the liquid in a long drink. "One would think the lessons of history would tell the world that Afghanistan is a tough nut to crack. The crown's attempt to change the politics of the country in 1839 became an embarrassment. The Russians tried it again in late 1979. They walked out in 1989 broke and their tails between their legs. Then the Americans invaded after 9/11 and are still involved to this day. Few nations have had success in trying to change Afghanistan."

"I'm aware of all this, Geoffrey. What about McCaffrey?"

"Part of the tale, my boy. Part of the tale." He paused for a moment with his now empty crystal tumbler. The black-haired woman appeared on the porch and handed Canfield a fresh gin and tonic.

Wolfe locked eyes with her for a brief moment and a slight grin came to his lips. He noticed Nadia's eyes following the woman back into the house.

With fresh drink in hand, Canfield continued his narrative. "Into the mix of the Taliban opposing the US and its coalition came Danny McCaffrey. Much like the CIA's support of the Mujahideen during the Soviet Union's invasion of the country, Danny McCaffrey single-handedly taught the Taliban how to defeat the Americans. Or at least bring the conflict to a bloody standoff."

"How?"

"With his bomb making skills and his experience as a guerilla fighter."

Nadia said, "The Mujahideen already knew how to be guerilla fighters. They honed their skills during their war with the Soviets in the 1980s."

"Yes, but Danny brought them something they didn't have before."

She replied, "What's that?"

"The innovation of remotely detonated IEDs."

"I thought they already knew about those."

Canfield turned his attention to Wolfe. "They did. But most of the IEDs they used were recycled mines obtained from your CIA. Boobytraps and buried mines caused most of the Soviet army's casualties during the ten years of their occupation."

Wolfe nodded.

"Like I said, MI6 lost track of Danny, and I went on to do other things."

With narrowed eyes, Wolfe said, "Yes, I'm aware of those other things."

Looking away from Wolfe, Canfield said, "Yes, I know you are." He inhaled deeply and continued, "After that, I heard on occasion about him being spotted in Iraq and Afghanistan until 2010. Some have speculated he died in an American drone strike on the Pakistan-Afghan border that year because afterward, he was never seen or heard about again, until now."

"Where do you think he was?"

"I think he was in Somalia."

"Why?"

Canfield shrugged. "Because in 2012, Al-Shabaab joined with Al-Qaeda and grew to prominence in the region. The group started using tactics similar to what Danny taught the Taliban in Afghanistan."

"But you've no proof?"

"None whatsoever. Just speculation."

"So, Danny McCaffrey has spent the last two decades training terrorists and no one has tried to find him since 2010?"

"It's hard to convince the higher-ups to commit pounds and personnel to find someone they believe to be dead."

Wolfe pursed his lips. "Yeah, I can see that. What about his childhood? I was told his mother disappeared and the father worked all the time."

"She did. But the father worked regular hours on the docks. There's more to the story."

Nadia sighed. "Well, then tell us."

"The mother went missing in October of 1984. On the twelfth of that month, the IRA bombed the Grand Hotel in Brighton. Members of the Conservative Party and their families were staying there for a conference. A total of five individuals were killed in the explosion. It would have been more, but Danny's mother supposedly told someone about the plan. She disappeared that same night. Her body was never found. MI6's domestic counterpart, MI5, believes she was thrown into the Irish Sea. Whether she was alive at the time will never be known."

"I take it Danny's father was a member of the IRA." Wolfe took a sip of his beer.

Canfield nodded. "One of the reasons he was never around the house after work. He spent most of his time plotting against the British as a radical member of the IRA. Probably where Danny got some of his ideas. The boy was only ten at the time of his mother's disappearance. The father never really cared for the kid and left him to fend for himself. MI5 thinks someone within the IRA took him under their wing and started training him."

"So, Nadia and I will be dealing with someone who's had to rely on themselves since childhood and has been eluding every intelligence agency in the world for two decades."

"Yes, Michael, I would say that's a correct assessment."

"Shit."

Canfield raised his glass. "Sucks, doesn't it?"

Wolfe and Nadia walked back to their hotel room, enjoying the warm evening and the gentle breeze coming across the island. She looked at her husband. "What do you think?"

"I think we should tell Jerry to get someone else to find McCaffrey."

"But you're not going to do that, are you?"

He shook his head. "No."

They walked a few more minutes in silence. Nadia asked, "You acted like you knew the woman who cooked dinner."

"I did."

Nadia smiled. "Who is she, an old girlfriend?"

Wolfe returned the smile. "No, she works for Jerry."

Chapter Seven

"I thought she looked familiar when she brought out the drinks, but the location and situation weren't right. So, I dismissed it. But then she turned her back to Geoffrey and Marilyn and mentioned the brand of beer on her tray."

"I didn't recognize it."

"I did. It's called Lech—it's brewed in Poland. How they got it to Grand Cayman is beyond me."

"She said she was told you liked the beer."

"I can't stand it. That's when I knew something was up and she was giving me a message."

"I noticed you only drank one. Am I missing something here?"

"I didn't even finish that one. I poured it out when I went to the rest room. Last time I had the stuff was in Poland on an assignment for the Mossad. Joseph surprised me with a visit, and we had dinner in a small restaurant in some obscure corner of Poznan. The stuff is brewed there. Anyway, I mentioned something about how horrible the beer was."

Nadia chuckled. "Leave it to Joseph to figure out an obscure way to send a message you."

"Yes, but it answers the question of how Joseph and Jerry knew about Canfield."

She nodded. "Do you think Geoffrey will help us?"

"I think he will. There was a hint of unfinished business in his narrative tonight."

"Such as."

"He referred to the drone strike several times and how MI6 thought it killed McCaffrey. My guess is Geoffrey helped the CIA plan the strike and now he knows it wasn't successful. He'll want another crack at the guy."

"So, where do we start?"

As they approached their hotel, Wolfe shrugged. "Not sure." He glanced at his watch. "It's late. Let's get some sleep and call Jerry in the morning."

As they approached their hotel room, they both noticed the door slightly ajar. Wolfe looked at Nadia and withdrew his Walther PPK from its inside the pant-waist holster. Nadia extracted her Glock 43 from the small handbag she wore over her shoulder. Both held their weapon with two hands, pointed down. Wolfe moved to the right side and Nadia covered him on the left. He pushed the door in and bolted inside.

Carla Webb sat on the edge of the bed and looked up as Wolfe rushed into the room with Nadia close behind. She said, "About time you two got back. What'd you do, take a stroll around the island?"

With the PPK still pointed at her, Wolfe tilted his head and stared at the diminutive woman. "How…" He stopped and holstered his gun. "Good way to get shot, Carla."

"That's what Jerry keeps telling me. Good to see you again, Michael." She stood and offered her hand to Nadia. "Sorry the Canfields were rude and didn't introduce us. I'm Carla Webb, Ms. Picard."

"Wolfe. Michael and I are married."

"Good for you." She turned back to Wolfe. "If you're wondering if Canfield is plotting against you, don't. He really wants back in your good graces. He's terrified of you." She paused and tilted her head. "Geoffrey's a tough nut. How did you achieve that?"

"Product demonstration."

She smiled. "Ah, that." She walked over to the sliding glass door that lead to a small covered balcony and local tropical foliage. With the curtains open, she could see stars reflecting off the surface of the Caribbean Sea in the distance.

"Why did you break into our room, Carla?"

"Because you weren't here, and I didn't think the hotel management would appreciate a scruffy black chick hanging out in the hallway."

Nadia folded her arms. "You have information for us, don't you?"

"Very good, Nadia. Your husband didn't pick up on that." She turned to Wolfe. "Did you, Michael?"

Without comment, Wolfe went to the sliding glass door and closed the curtains. He turned back to the woman. "If you have something to tell us, let's hear it."

"I've always liked that about you, Michael. You don't cater to social niceties. You get right to the point."

"Carla!"

She gave him a half-smile. "An image of McCaffrey was captured on CCTV in Tel Aviv two days ago."

Both Nadia and Wolfe shot quick glances at each other. Wolfe asked, "Where?"

"Walking past Carmel Market."

"How sure are they?"

"Positive. Facial recognition software made the match."

Wolfe wrinkled his brow. "Do they think he's planning something?"

"No one knows. Once the image was identified, they back tracked his path. He's apparently extremely adept at knowing where security cameras are at all times, because the one image that identified him was the only one with a clear picture of his face. After they knew what to look for, they found various CCTV cameras shots of him. His destination was a parked white Toyota Corolla. He drove north on Highway 2 to Haifa and then to a checkpoint and entered Lebanon. After that…" She shrugged.

Nadia asked, "Does Canfield know any of this?"

"No. To him and Marilyn, I'm just a cook."

With a frown, Nadia studied the woman. Fashion-model skinny, she wore loose clothes, which hid any trace of her gender. Her black curly hair hung loosely over an oval face, upturned nose and hazel eyes. "When did you start working for the Canfields?"

"About three weeks ago. My job was to make sure Geoffrey didn't have a surprise waiting for you when you visited."

Wolfe tilted his head. "We didn't make the decision to visit Geoffrey until earlier this week."

Carla smiled. "You've worked for Joseph for a long time. Something like this shouldn't surprise you."

He gave her a knowing grin. "No, I'm not surprised."

He paused for a brief moment. "How much longer are you going to stick around?"

She glanced at a nonexistent watch on her wrist. "Carla, the cook, just walked off the job. I've got a few other things I would rather be doing." With a bright smile showing her perfectly white teeth, she continued, "As I said before, Geoffrey is not a threat. They put up a good front tonight, but both he and Marilyn are scared shitless of you."

"Good. They should be."

The woman walked to the hotel room door. "When you decide to go to Israel, let Jerry know. He'll tell Joseph. I think the man wants to be there when you two are resurrected from the grave."

She opened the door and left.

Nadia turned to Wolfe. "I think it's time to go to Israel."

"Yeah, so do I."

"When?"

"We'll leave the island tomorrow. While you're helping Chief get the boat ready, I'll visit Geoffrey."

Canfield poured tea into the cup sitting in front of Wolfe. "Tel Aviv, you say?"

With a nod, Wolfe said, "Three days ago."

"I take it you and Nadia are going."

Another nod.

"Won't that be a bit awkward, considering you are both dead in the eyes of the Israelis?"

Wolfe shrugged.

"Ah…"

"What about it, Geoffrey? Are you interested?"

"Interested, yes. Willing, maybe. You have to understand, Michael, Marilyn and I have not left the island for almost five years. My former colleagues at MI6 believe me to be quite dead."

"You've been living under the name Greyson Collins. I assume you have identification proclaiming that?"

"Yes."

"I'm not asking you to go to England, Geoffrey. My guess is you probably know more about McCaffrey than any other living soul on the planet."

"Possibly."

"At one time, you were one of the best trackers MI6 ever produced."

"I've been out of the game for a while, Michael. My contacts are either dead or believe I am."

"Doesn't matter. If you decide to help, you'd be in the States. How about it?"

Canfield stared at a cup of tea he rotated clockwise then counter-clockwise. Wolfe waited patiently.

After several minutes, the older man looked up. "Oh, bloody hell. Why not?"

Chapter Eight

Uri Ben-David sipped coffee as he stared west through the window in his office. He could see dots of lights, off in the distance, moving horizontally across the Mediterranean Sea. Soon, as the first light of dawn brightened the land, those lights would become the silhouettes of ships approaching the harbors of Israel. Ben-David ran the counter-terrorist division of the Mossad. He wore his thinning gray hair short and he viewed the world through rimless glasses sitting on a prominent nose in front of brown eyes he inherited from his mother.

The day promised to be interesting. His appointment with the American National Security Advisor would not occur for another three hours and at this time, he did not have a clue about the meeting's purpose.

A knock at his open door brought him out of his thoughts. He turned and saw his assistant, Daniella Wiener, standing in the open-door frame, clutching a manila folder to her chest.

"Ah, Dani, good, you're here early. Come in, come in."

"I apologize for interrupting, but I thought you might want to see this." She offered the folder.

Taking the folder from the young woman, Ben-David opened it. After skimming the first page. He looked back up at her. "When was this intercepted?"

"About an hour ago. Could that be why the American NSA requested a meeting with you?"

"Very possible. Although, I have known Joseph a long time. If the purpose was about something like this, he would have mentioned it. No, there is another reason he requested the meeting."

The tall woman stood silently as she watched Ben-David read the remaining pages. When he finished, he said, "We do not hear anything about this Danny McCaffrey for almost a decade and suddenly his image is captured on the streets of Tel Aviv. Then we intercept a cell phone call with his voice on it. All within the span of a week. Why?" He paused and turned back to the window. Dawn had given way to full morning sun as the intense blue of the Mediterranean Sea provided a serene backdrop to the intense discussion. "Have you ever met Joseph Kincaid?"

"No, sir."

"Then I believe it is time for you to do so. You will accompany me this morning."

A slight smile appeared briefly on the woman lips. She quickly recovered and said, "Very well, when do you wish to leave?"

Glancing at the various clocks on his wall, which depicted the numerous time zones across the world, he smiled. "We will leave in time to be early. Joseph is a man of many talents, one of which is preparedness. He will already be at our meeting site getting ready."

The large man escorted Ben-David and Daniella through the courtyard of the US ambassador to Israel's residence. His biceps stretched the fabric of his untucked black linen shirt under which Ben-David could just see the outline of a gun in a holster on his hip. Dark aviator-style sunglasses hid the security man's eyes. His deeply tanned weathered face depicted a history of being outdoors in the wind and sun. He constantly swiveled his head, searching for hidden dangers along their path as they walked toward the front door of the structure. It opened as they approached and a smiling Joseph Kincaid offered his hand to Ben-David.

"Uri, good to see you again, my friend."

Ben-David shook it and said, "It is good to see you as well, Joseph." He turned to the woman beside him as their escort took a few steps backward, continuing to hunt for any potential dangers lurking about.

"Joseph, this is Daniella Wiener, the Assistant Director of Counter-Terrorism. She will probably take my spot as Director, someday."

The woman hesitated for a brief moment before shaking Joseph's offered hand.

Noting the momentary hesitation, Joseph turned to the large man, "Thank you, Sandy." He returned his attention to Ben-David. "Both of you, please come in. I have something to show you."

They retreated into the interior of the house as the front door closed and their escort stood outside making sure no one disturbed them.

Toward the rear of the home, they entered a room with floor-to-ceiling bookcases lining three walls. The shelves were filled with volumes of books on a variety of topics. In front of this backdrop stood a man of average height, slim of physique, hazel eyes and slightly wavy brownish-gray hair. His arms were folded and he wore a slight smile on his lips. Beside him was a woman three inches shorter. Her long dark brown hair fell provocatively over her shoulders and her green eyes stared at Uri Ben-David as he entered the room.

The Director of Mossad's Counter Terrorist Division immediately stopped when he saw the man and woman. His now wide eyes darted back and forth between them. Tilting his head to the side, a slight smile came to his lips. "Nadia Picard. Why am I not surprised to see you still among the living?"

"Because you trained me, Uri."

"Ah, that. Yes, I did." After the two embraced, he turned toward the man. "Michael Wolfe, also among the living."

Ben-David offered his hand. The two men shook as Wolfe nodded slightly. Uri glanced at the man's left hand and his smile widened. Nadia had an identical slim gold band on her left ring finger.

The Mossad director folded his arms and gave Joseph an accusatorial glance and then returned his attention to the man and woman. "Sometime in the future, you will need to explain how you two fooled the entire Israeli security network into believing you were dead."

Wolfe ignored the comment. "What do you know about Danny McCaffrey?"

"That's what I have always admired about you, Michael. You get to the point." Ben-David paused. "I do not hear this man's name for a decade, and all of a sudden, I hear it mentioned three times in less than a week."

Joseph asked, "Three times?"

A nod preceded Ben-David's answer. "Three days ago, one of our CCTV cameras picks up his image in a crowded market in Tel Aviv. Then this morning, Dani hands me a report of an intercepted phone call with his voice, clearly identified, talking to someone in Mexico. Now a ghost stands in front of me asking what I know about Danny McCaffrey."

Frowning, Joseph asked, "When was the phone call intercepted?"

Daniella, who had not stopped staring at Nadia since entering the library, turned her attention to Joseph and said, "About three o'clock this morning, Israel Standard Time."

Nadia asked, "What was the conversation about?"

"McCaffrey was demanding payment for a service rendered. The nature of that service was never mentioned. But the discussion got heated toward the end."

Wolfe and Joseph glanced at each other, which Ben-David noticed. "What do you two know about this?"

The National Security Advisor said, "That's the reason we're here. It appears McCaffrey has been commissioned by the Mexican drug cartels to disrupt the American government."

"Disrupt it? How?"

"By assassinating the President of The United States."

Ben-David laughed out loud. "That would be quite the accomplishment, since he is the most protected individual on the entire planet."

"But there are ways, Uri." Wolfe gave Ben-David a sly smile. "What about Yitzhak Rabin?"

"Our protection protocols are far more stringent now."

"But it happened."

A nod was Ben-David's response."

Joseph took over the conversation. "Uri, has the Mossad determined why McCaffrey was in Israel?"

"Not at this time. We have our suspicions, but nothing we can prove."

With a slight smile, Joseph said, "I like suspicions."

After pursing his lips, Ben-David nodded at Daniella. She stopped staring at Nadia and turned to Joseph. "We believe he is trying to acquire drone technology."

Wolfe's forehead furrowed. "Drone technology is commonplace. Why would McCaffrey take a chance on traveling to Israel for…?" He stopped. "He's after new technology being developed here, isn't he?"

"That's what we suspect."

Nadia put her hands on her hips. "Uri, I've seen the look before. What is he after?"

Ben-David took a deep breath and let it out slowly. With a sigh, he said, "We have been developing drones that are invisible to radar and can fire laser guided missiles."

"The US has drones with those capabilities." This from Joseph.

Shaking his head, the Mossad director said, "Not ones capable of being controlled by one person from a mobile site. All of your big drones are flown by anonymous pilots stuck somewhere in your Nevada desert."

"There are other sites, many not in the US."

"I know that, but they still require a pilot and a weapons officer."

Wolfe and Joseph nodded.

"We have developed the capability to launch drones from anywhere and control them with a single operator."

"That's a game changer, Uri."

"Yes, I know Joseph. But we do not believe he was successful in obtaining information about the system."

Folding his arms, Wolfe said, "What did he obtain?"

Ben-David looked at the floor and then back to Wolfe. "We are not sure, but we think he was able to obtain plans to a new laser-guided rocket we have developed."

"You think?"

With a nod, Ben-David remained quiet. Daniella said, "Most small guided missiles have a limited range of up to ten to fifteen kilometers. This one can hit a target over fifty kilometers away."

"It could be launched well outside a presidential protection zone." Wolfe unfolded his arms. "With his explosives experience, McCaffrey would have a weapon he could use against any thorough plan to protect the president."

Chapter Nine

Daniel McCaffrey sipped on a small cup of bitter coffee while he waited for the Palestinian to arrive. The small café stood in an older section of Damascus. Ceiling fans turned slowly above his head, circulating the smoked-filled air. Limited sunlight and low whispered conversations provided the backdrop for the coffee shop as he stared at the front door.

McCaffrey's normal reddish blond hair and newly grown beard were dyed black. He wore a black leather jacket over a black long sleeve T-shirt and faded blue jeans. Secured to his belt, covered by his jacket, was an Iraqi made Beretta 951 Tariq. Access to the weapon could be fast and swift. Brown-tinted contact lenses hid his crystal blue eyes.

The lines on his weathered face belied his forty-seven years. The stress of spending the vast majority of his adult life on the run in numerous Middle Eastern countries had not been kind to his appearance. Over the years, he'd learned to speak Arabic, Hebrew and various dialects of Persian fluently.

He glanced at his watch and noted the Palestinian was ten minutes late, a common occurrence for this particular individual. As McCaffrey sipped the last of his coffee, the front door to the small café opened and his contact entered. The man surveyed the room and his eyes locked on McCaffrey. Taking his time, he moved toward the table.

After sitting across from McCaffrey, he said, "As-salam alaykom."

In perfect regional Arabic, the former IRA terrorist said, "Why are you late?"

A shrug was his answer. The smaller man stood four inches shorter than the Irishman's six-foot frame. Short black hair and a neatly trimmed beard bestowed a metropolitan façade to his round, pockmarked face. He said, "And you are not Arabic, Irishman. You have changed your looks again. Why?"

"Occupational necessity. Do you have the information?"

The smaller man reached into an inside pocket of his linen jacket and extracted a small flash-drive. "It is all on here, Irishman." He held it so McCaffrey could see, but not touch it. "Do you have my money?"

A nod was his answer.

"Let me see it."

McCaffrey placed an envelope on the table out of reach of the man across from him. "Slide the device across and you can have your money."

"I have to count it first."

The Irishman stiffened and rubbed the back of his neck. After taking a deep breath and letting it out slowly, he pushed the envelope across the table. Still holding the flash-drive, the smaller man glanced inside the envelope and then slid the flash-drive across.

It disappeared into a pocket inside McCaffrey's jacket.

He stood without saying another word and walked out of the café entrance.

It took the Palestinian twenty minutes to emerge from the coffee bar and start walking through the alleys of this ancient section of the Syrian city. As he approached a darkened alcove, McCaffrey stepped out and stood in front of him, blocking his forward path.

The smaller man's eyes widened as the Tariq from the Irishman's belt holster was now pointed at his face, a metal tube protruding in front of the barrel.

No words were exchanged as McCaffrey pulled the trigger. Two muffled pops were heard in the alley and the smaller man collapsed to the brick pavement. The Irishman bent over and found the envelope with the cash in an inside pocket of the dead man's jacket. As he removed it, he muttered in his native Irish accent, "Should have been on time, laddie."

The twenty-year-old Iranian-made Peugeot 405 bumped along the pothole-strewn streets of an older part of Aleppo. The area still bore the effects of the Syrian Civil War with few intact buildings and fewer residents. While many sections of the city were being rebuilt, this was not one of them.

McCaffrey glanced over at his driver and said, "When do we get there?"

In clipped Arabic, the man behind the wheel said, "Soon. Around next corner."

With a frown, the Irishman returned his gaze to the street ahead, his right hand firmly holding the grab bar above the passenger window.

Five minutes later, the car turned a corner and parked in front of a relatively intact building. The driver nodded toward the entry. "There."

McCaffrey opened the door and stood outside the car. He swiveled his head to assess the area. It appeared abandoned. He extracted two US hundred-dollar bills from his pocket and tore them in half. He handed the driver the two left halves of the bills. "Stay here. The other halves will be yours when I return."

The man gave McCaffrey a toothy grin and nodded.

Before entering the building, he placed the Tariq in his jacket pocket with his right-hand firmly gripping the weapon. He opened the door with his left and entered the dark interior. At one time, the place had been a thriving carpet shop with the best Persian Rugs for sale. Now it was an empty dusty show room with only a few dirty samples remaining on the floor. A short barrel-chested man stood next to a counter. He wore a tan colored kaftan with a checkered Palestinian keffiyeh covering his head. With a nod, he gestured for McCaffrey to follow him.

The room they entered bore little evidence of the devastation of the surrounding neighborhoods. The area was clean and bright, expensive rugs lay on the floor and a traditional Arabic tea service could be seen in the middle of the room surrounded by floor pillows.

The barrel-chested man said, "Sit, Daniel. We will enjoy tea before we conduct our business."

McCaffrey knew better than to argue. This was Faheem al-Vaziri, the current leader of the Palestinian Islamic Jihad movement.

Ten minutes later after listening to al-Vaziri wax poetically about the current state of affairs in Syria and the

Middle East, he took a sip of tea. "Now, Daniel, why did you wish to see me."

McCaffrey withdrew the flash-drive from his jacket pocket and held it so the man across from him could see the object. "The information on this is pure crap. Where is the information I requested and paid for?"

A sly smile appeared on al-Vaziri's face. "Daniel, first of all, we have never received payment for the information and secondly, the messenger who was to deliver it has disappeared."

"He's dead after trying to pawn this crap on me." The Irishman took a sip of tea. "He paid a price for that error."

Faheem al-Vaziri's nostrils flared as he stared at McCaffrey with cold dark brown eyes. After several moments, the intensity of the stare softened and he took a sip of tea. "Then we are, as they say in chess, at check. Yes?"

"If you say so."

"Yes, we are. We possess the information you seek. Our messenger's motives in his attempt to cheat you were his, not ours. Therefore, we can move forward with the transaction."

"I'm not interested in meeting another one of your so-called messengers. I want it straight from the source, no middle-men."

"Are you willing to travel to Iran?"

A nod was his answer.

"They are overly sensitive about Westerners visiting their land right now."

"It won't be my first time there."

"No, I do not suppose it will

Chapter Ten

The White City area of Tel Aviv is a collection of approximately four-thousand buildings built, starting in the 1930s and on, using the concept of International Style which combines esthetics with function. Designed by immigrating Jewish architects from Germany, Tel Aviv has the highest number of buildings using this Bauhaus style of any city in the world.

Within this section of Tel Aviv, Nadia found a boutique hotel featuring a two-room suite within walking distance of Carmel Market. While Joseph and Ben-David conducted official business at the offices of Mossad, she and Wolfe checked into the apartment for an undetermined extended stay.

Nadia sang softly in French as she busied herself arranging the small quarters to her liking. Wolfe stared out the sliding glass door orienting himself to their location. She stopped singing, walked up behind him and put her arms around his waist. She said, "How long do you want to stay?"

He placed his hands on hers but did not turn around. "That's your decision. We'll stay as long as you like."

She took a deep breath and let it out slowly. "I was excited about the idea of coming here, but now…"

Twisting around in her embrace, he returned the hug and held her for a few silent moments. "What's wrong?"

Shaking her head, she did not answer immediately. Finally, she said, "I'm not sure. I have become accustomed to the openness of the land around our home in Missouri, I forgot how small and crowded everything is here."

Wolfe nodded, but did not interrupt.

She continued, "Plus, I know there are CCTV security cameras everywhere. That makes me nervous."

"Joseph is leaving tonight. If you don't want to stay, we can hitch a ride with him back to the States."

"No, I do not want to leave just yet. There are a few places I want to visit before we do."

"That's fine." He paused, enjoying the hug. "Why was Daniella Weiner staring at you this morning?"

Nadia broke from his embrace and silently walked to the kitchen area. She began to rearrange the items on the counter she had just arranged.

"Nadia?"

She turned and stared at Wolfe. "I do not know. It was unsettling."

"Did you know her from your time with Mossad?"

His answer was a shrug.

"You're hiding something. What is it?"

"Michael, I wish I knew. She looked familiar, but I am unable to determine why."

Wolfe folded his arms and frowned. "I thought it a bit strange. Do we need to talk to Ben-David about it?"

She stopped rearranging the kitchen, shook her head

and asked, "Talk to Joseph before he leaves? Maybe he'll know."

"I noticed it, too, Michael."

"Did Ben-David say anything about her?"

"Subject never came up. Why?"

"Nadia said her name sounded familiar but couldn't remember why."

Joseph did not respond right away. Wolfe glanced at his phone's screen to see if the call had ended. When he put it back to this ear, he heard, "Daniella Wiener has been with Mossad for about six years and is being groomed to take over the department after Uri retires. There's a chance she and Nadia crossed paths at some point.

"Nadia doesn't think that's the case."

"Do you want me to ask Uri?"

Wolfe grew quiet. Finally he said, "No."

"Okay. How long are you two staying?"

"Not sure. We had planned on staying a while, but now…"

"Because of Wiener?"

"No, I think Nadia has grown used to the openness of our home. She's feeling a little claustrophobic."

With a chuckle, Joseph continued, "I'm leaving around six tonight. You can come with me if you want."

"Thanks for the offer, but I have a few things I need to do here."

"Call me when you want to return. I'll make the arrangements."

"Thanks, Joseph."

The call ended and Wolfe stepped back into the small

apartment from the balcony. Nadia stood with her arms crossed. "Well?"

"He noticed her interest also but doesn't know why."

"Is he going to ask Uri?"

Wolfe smiled and tilted his head. "No, not unless you want him to."

She closed her eyes and took a deep breath. "I need to stop thinking about it." After opening them, she smiled. "I have other things planned."

"Good, so do I."

Wolfe felt silly on the rented motor scooter, but it was the easiest way to maneuver the narrow streets and alleyways of the ancient city of Jaffa. Years had passed since his last sojourn to the area and it took him a while to find the building he sought.

With the Mediterranean to his right and stone buildings to his left, he drove the scooter slowly down the brick pavement of the streets in the old seaport. He found the address he sought and parked the scooter in a spot near the street. The entrance appeared to have been modernized since his last visit. The arched entrance was now guarded by a heavy framed wood doorway. The sign next to the door proclaimed in Hebrew script the proprietor to be Wasserman Imports. Wolfe knew better.

The locked entrance clicked open after Wolfe pressed a button on the security pad next to the door. He entered and passed through the inner courtyard of the building. Once inside, he saw a tall man with a white full beard, open collar white shirt, black pants, black Kippah, round face, wire-rim glasses and a broad smile.

"*Shalom Aleichem*, Michael. It is good to see you again."

"*Aleichem Shalom*, Ben. It has been a while."

"Come in, come in." He gestured toward a door he now held open for Wolfe on the right wall of the courtyard. Ben Wasserman, an eighty-two-year-old retired Mossad agent who had taken a liking to Wolfe when he'd first arrived in Israel, never aged. He looked the same today as the day they first met.

Wolfe followed Wasserman into the interior of the building through a large warehouse full of pallets with shrink-wrapped stacks of cardboard cases. Through a door, located on the back wall of the warehouse, they entered a smaller sanctuary and office. The older man set behind a large oak desk, the surface of which was cluttered with a mountain of files and paper. He motioned Wolfe to a chair in front of the desk.

"It is so good to see you, my friend. As I suspected, the rumors of your death were greatly exaggerated."

Spreading his arms, Wolfe gave his friend a grim smile. "As you can see, I'm still among the living."

Wasserman noticed the slim gold band on his left hand. "I hope that ring indicates you are now married to Nadia Picard."

"It does."

"Good. You two are perfect for each other." He stood and went to a drip coffeemaker on his credenza. "Can I get you a cup of coffee?"

"No, thank you."

When the older man sat again, he frowned and leaned forward. "I assume you did not come by just to discuss your health. What can I do for you, Michael?"

"Danny McCaffrey."

With raised eyebrows, Wasserman sat back in his chair and sipped his coffee. "Last I knew he was dead."

Wolfe shook his head. "He was here. CCTV caught a glimpse of him near Carmel Market the other day. That's why I'm back in Israel."

Wasserman's eyes narrowed. "Are you working for the CIA again?"

"No, I work for Joseph Kincaid."

"I thought he was the National Security Adviser to the president."

"He is."

"Ah—Joseph is a good man."

Leaning forward in the wood captain's chair, Wolfe placed his elbows on his knees and clasped his hands together. "Ben, you used to know more about what was going on in Israel than the entire Mossad organization. Why was McCaffrey here?"

His answer was a smile and a shrug. "You give me too much credit. I am just a simple businessman now."

"Bullshit."

Wasserman laughed out loud. "Honestly, Michael. I do not know. But I will make some inquiries." He paused for a brief moment. "Why are you so interested?"

Sitting straighter, Wolfe said, "There are rumors he has something planned in the United States. Something we need to stop before it happens. That's why I'm trying to find him."

"What are the rumors telling you?"

"The details are unknown, but it has to do with terrorist activity against the US government."

Pushing his glasses up his aquiline nose, Wasserman smiled. "Come back tomorrow and bring that lovely wife of yours."

Nadia stepped off the back seat of the scooter as Michael set the kickstand. "I have not heard the name Ben Wasserman for years. Tell me again how you know him?"

"He's the uncle of someone I knew a long time ago."

As he stood next to Nadia, she placed her hand on his arm. "Does he know about me?"

"Yes, he wants to meet you."

She did not respond to her husband but followed him to the entrance of the courtyard.

Once they were buzzed in, they found Wasserman, once again, holding the door for his two guests. "Welcome. Please come, join me."

The chaotic state of Wasserman's office remained from the previous day. Only this time two wooden captain's chairs sat in front of the desk. Before he sat behind it, he turned to Nadia. "It is so nice to finally meet you, Nadia. Congratulations on your marriage. Michael is like a son to me. I still consider him family."

"Thank you, sir."

After sitting at his desk, Wasserman tilted his head. "When Michael started seeing you, I checked your file. Your work for the Mossad was impressive. It is unfortunate that circumstances changed and you both had to flee the country. Israel needs individuals like yourselves to protect it."

Not knowing what to say, Nadia remained quiet and glanced at her husband.

Wasserman turned to Michael. "I am glad you brought the sighting of Danny McCaffrey to my attention."

"What'd you find out?"

"Nothing good."

"Go on, Ben."

Taking a deep breath, the old man leaned forward. "How much do you know about him?"

Wolfe recited the facts he knew up to the point of the drone strike in 2010. "Beyond that, my sources believed him to be dead."

"As did the Mossad and numerous other intelligence agencies in Western Europe."

"But you found out where he was?"

"Sort of. There are no reliable sightings of the man until 2015 when he was spotted by a Kurdish asset for the Mossad. In May of 2015, ethnic Kurds rioted in Mahabad, Iran following the unexplained death of a twenty-five-year-old Kurdish hotel chambermaid. She supposedly fell to her death from a fourth-floor window of the hotel where she worked. When it was discovered that she fell trying to escape being raped by an Iranian military officer, the riots began. McCaffrey was photographed watching the events." Wasserman slid a picture across the desk to Wolfe.

He picked it up and examined it. The picture quality was poor, but the man's red hair and beard could clearly be seen. Handing the photo to Nadia, Wolfe said, "I take it the asset took the picture because of the red hair."

"That is what I was told."

"So, then what?"

"My source tells me they think he stayed in Iran until 2019. He was spotted in July of that year in Culiacan, Mexico. That's the home of the Sinaloa Cartel, considered one of the largest drug-trafficking organizations in the world. That is the cartel started in the 1980s by *El Chapo*. Why he was in Culiacan the same month Joaquín *El Chapo* Guzmán was sentenced to life in prison by the US is unknown."

"That corresponds with a theory circulating among the

various security agencies in Washington and one of the reasons I'm looking for him. The FBI has reason to believe he is working for the Sinaloa Cartel."

"Ah… That confirms something else my source told me."

"What?"

"They are funding his search for a weapon he can smuggle into the United States."

With a frown, Wolfe stared at his friend for several moments. "He's an accomplished bomb maker."

"Not a bomb."

"What then?"

"A bio-weapon."

Chapter Eleven

Uri Ben-David listened quietly as Wolfe laid out what he had heard from Ben Wasserman, although Ben's name never emerged in the conversation.

"Who was your source on this, Michael?"

"A little bird."

"How can I trust this revelation without knowing where you obtained it?"

Wolfe did not respond, keeping his focus on Ben-David.

"Very well." He turned to Nadia. "I suppose you will not tell me either?"

She shook her head.

"We have suspected that Iran was pursuing bio-weapons and WMDs for some time now, despite signing the Biological Weapons Convention, the Chemical Weapons Convention, and the Non-Proliferation Treaty."

"Uri, the one weapon McCaffrey could use to assassinate the President of the United States is a bio-weapon."

"How?"

"Multiple ways, all of them include massive civilian casualties along with the president."

"Your Secret Service has contingencies for those types of attacks."

"Yes, I am sure they have and I'm sure McCaffrey knows all about them. It's the unconventional approach we need to be concerned about."

"I would agree with you. I'll assume you've thought about it. How would you do it?"

Wolfe stared hard at the Israeli. "A stealthy guided missile launched by a small plane outside the no-fly zone surrounding the president and guided to the target by a hidden individual."

Ben-David remained quiet.

"You mentioned Israel was developing just such a missile."

A nod was his response.

"What if this small missile contains a bio-weapon and detonates in an air burst above a crowded-out door event being held by the president? Not only would the president be exposed, but hundreds, if not thousands would be as well."

"I'm sure the Secret Service has thought of that."

"I wouldn't know if they have or haven't. But even if they have, the missile could be programmed with a GPS system and would only need to target the area for an airburst."

"If that is what McCaffrey is doing, Michael, we have a totally different game concerning terrorism."

"Were you ever able to back-track him with CCTV footage?"

With a nod, Ben-David opened a laptop on his desk and touched the space bar. He turned it around so Michael and

Nadia could see the screen. He pointed to a satellite picture of Tel Aviv. "The first image we have of him is here, getting off a motor scooter. The driver hurries away and McCaffrey starts walking toward the market." The spot he pointed to was due south of the market area. "He walks past five CCTV cameras with his face obscured by a well-placed hat. The shot of him near Carmel Market with his face exposed apparently happened because someone bumped into him. You know the rest."

Wolfe nodded. "What about the motor scooter. Could you back-track it?"

"We can't find where it picked him up, but the first shot we have of it is in Jaffa with both men on the scooter."

"Near the port?"

"No, eastern side. Why?"

"Just curious. Where do you think he was traveling from?"

"Southern Israel."

Wolfe paused for a second. He already knew the answer to his next question, but he asked anyway. "What's in southern Israel?"

"You know that as well as anybody, Michael."

"The Gaza Strip."

"I'm afraid so."

Silence filled the office as Wolfe studied the laptop screen. Finally, he asked, "Why travel north through Israel when he could have taken a boat to Lebanon and avoided all the CCTV security cameras?"

"The blockade, for one. It would be safer for McCaffrey to travel by land rather than risk getting caught in a small boat in the Mediterranean."

"Where'd he go?"

"That, my friend, is something we do not know."

Taking his attention away from the computer screen, Wolfe looked at Ben-David. "I suggest you find out."

Wolfe parked the scooter in front of Ben Wasserman's building. Nadia sat behind him, her arms still around his waist. She asked, "Do you think Ben will have learned anything else by now?"

Taking his helmet off, Wolfe said, "Don't know, but we're running out of time. Let's see if he has."

When they approached the wooden framed entry door, Wolfe noticed the door was not completely closed. "Uh, oh." He leaned over and extracted the Walther PPK from his ankle holster.

Nadia removed her Glock 43 from a small purse attached to a long leather strap around her neck and shoulder.

After Wolfe pushed the door in a few inches, he listened. Silence prevailed within the courtyard as he and Nadia slipped in.

The shattered frame and open door leading to Wasserman's warehouse immediately drew Wolfe's attention. With both hands gripping his Walther, he peered into the interior space of warehouse. Four meters inside the large expanse lay a figure, facedown. The black pants, white hair and the black kippah contrasted against the white shirt with two blood-soaked holes in the center of the man's back. Wolfe turned to Nadia and motioned with his head to back out of the room.

Before exiting the courtyard, Wolfe untucked his shirt and placed the Walther at the small of his back. Nadia returned the Glock to her purse but did not withdraw her hand. Their walk back to the scooter seemed to take forever as they casually covered the distance.

Once on the scooter, their helmets in place, they left the scene and headed north out of Jaffa.

Wolfe concentrated on the road ahead and the two rearview mirrors on the handlebars as they sped toward central Tel Aviv. Five minutes into their journey, he touched Nadia's leg and clenched his fist. She tightened her grip around his waist just before he made a sharp right turn down a small alleyway. At the end of the passage, they came to a busy cross-street. Stopping the scooter, he concentrated on the rearview mirrors.

Nadia asked, "What did you see?"

"Two men in a white Kia have been following us since we left Ben's building. They were starting to get closer when I turned off. I don't think the Kia is small enough to navigate the alley."

She looked back in the direction they had come just as a motorcycle, similar to theirs, appeared around a corner. The driver held a pistol in his left hand. Nadia's hand emerged from her small purse, still clutching the Glock. She aimed the pistol at the oncoming motor scooter and fired twice just as the driver raised his gun.

With two fatal gunshots to the chest, the driver fell from the scooter and it slid out of control toward them. Wolfe revved the small engine and their motorbike shot forward, merging into the traffic of the busy cross street.

Wolfe parked the motor scooter next to a busy out-door market. After Nadia stepped off, he left the keys in the ignition and stood. They both held their helmets and walked away.

Nadia glanced back at it and said, "How long do you think it will take for it to be stolen?"

"Not long. If it's still there before our coffee is served, I'll be surprised."

They found a table in a café with outdoor seating within sight of the scooter. A waiter took their order as they settled in to watch. Two minutes later, two teenagers in baggy jeans and oversized T-shirts circled the bike. Wolfe displayed a slight smile as he watched. The waiter placed their coffees in front of them as the two young men's heads swiveled, searching for anyone paying undo attention to them. Satisfied nobody watched them, they grinned, climbed on the scooter, started the engine and drove away.

"I was wrong. It took a little longer."

With a chuckle, Nadia lifted her coffee and took a sip. "Now what?"

After taking his cell phone from his jeans pocket, he punched in a number. "We've been shopping since early this morning, Nadia. We returned to find the darn thing stolen." He gave her a mischievous grin. "And we have no idea when it was stolen."

She returned the grin. "Guess I should go buy something. It will look strange if we claim we were shopping and don't have any purchases.

Wolfe nodded as his call to the police went through.

The Mossad safe house sat in a quiet residential neighborhood in northern Tel Aviv at the end of a cul-de-sac. The only traffic on the street came from other people living in the area. As a result, only one vehicle was used to transport individuals to and from the house. A black low-slung Mercedes with dark tinted windows would pull into the garage and the door would shut before the passengers exited. Neighbors knew not to ask questions or knock.

Wolfe and Nadia studied the ten-inch Samsung tablet handed to them by Uri Ben-David. They sat at a small dining table in uncomfortable plastic chairs. Furnishings of the house were frugal and sparse.

Ben-David said, "The man on the motor scooter was a twenty-two-year-old Palestinian thug named Hazem al-Jalali. He is suspected of being involved in numerous terrorist attacks on Israeli citizens over the past five years. The Shin Bet is not shedding any tears about his demise."

Looking up from the tablet, Wolfe asked, "What about Ben Wasserman?"

"Ben had an abundance of security cameras in his warehouse. Keep scrolling—there is a good shot of his assassin pointing a gun at Ben. It was al-Jalali."

Nadia said, "I am glad I shot him."

"So are a lot of other people in Israel."

"What about the two men in the Kia I told you about?"

"Stolen. Police found it burned in an alley."

Finding the shot of the assassin pointing the gun at Wasserman, Wolfe studied al-Jalali's face. He looked up. "Why Ben? He was retired."

The Mossad Counter-Terrorism Director shook his head. "That's a good question. Was Ben the source of the bio-weapon information you told me about?"

Wolfe nodded.

"Then he apparently asked the wrong questions to the wrong individuals."

With narrowed eyes, Wolfe asked, "Can you get me all the information you have on this Hazem al-Jalali person?"

Ben-David gave Wolfe a knowing smile. "What did you have in mind?"

Still staring at the assassin's face on the tablet, Wolfe said, "McCaffrey's visit to the Gaza Strip and Wasserman's death are related. I need to know how."

Chapter Twelve

"Are you sure he is dead?"

Naseem al-Nouri nodded. "Yes, the body has already been disposed of."

"Did they identify him?" Hassan Abedi snuffed out his cigarette in an ash tray.

"I am sure they did. The fool failed to listen to his instructions about the American and the Israeli woman. He rushed in without thinking and now he is dead. When we inquired about the incident, the police acted like it never happened."

"Then we should too, my friend." Abedi lit another cigarette and blew smoke at the ceiling fan slowly turning above him. "I am told the Irishman is now in Tehran."

The Palestinian did not reply.

"If all goes as planned, he will acquire the materials needed to complete the project. But I am concerned about his ineptitude in being photographed."

With a shrug, al-Nouri answered, "I am not sure it

matters at this stage. We are far enough along someone else could complete the work. Remember—he is a tool, just like the Mexicans."

Abedi said, "I agree, the Mexicans can be replaced, there are many cartels with the money and desire to provide funding for our project. The Irishman is not so replaceable. He has a certain, uh—skill-set we need right now. He needs to be more careful."

"Then he must not return to Gaza. Have your brothers in Tehran keep him there until we have acquired the missiles."

"That will not be easy. He is a Christian, and they find him distasteful."

Narrowing his eyes, al-Nouri said, "We have had this discussion before, and I am quite tired of it. The Irishman, or someone like him, is essential to our plan. He has, if I might remind you, performed numerous services over the years, for your country's Ministry of Intelligence which they were either unwilling or incapable of doing."

The Iranian did not respond immediately as he took another drag on his cigarette. "My country is aware of his talents. I do not need to be lectured about it. All I am saying is it would be best for all of us if he finds another location, besides Tehran, to wait. What about Venezuela? You and your Hezbollah brothers have more influence there than we do."

"Maybe. For now, keep him in Tehran until we are ready."

Abedi shrugged. He turned and walked toward an open window in the upper floor apartment where they stood. After tossing the cigarette out the window, he stood with his hands behind his back and stared out. "We have more pressing issues needing our attention right now. What do we do about the American and the Israeli woman?"

"Why are you so worried about them?"

Turning to look at the Palestinian, Abedi frowned. "You do not find it strange they suddenly show up after being away from Israel for years right after the Irishman is caught on a CCTV camera?"

No response came from al-Nouri.

"I do. I also find it strange that the day after they show up, Wasserman starts asking questions he should not be asking."

"Wasserman was an old man who forgot he was old."

"Naseem, my brother, Wasserman and the American Wolfe worked together for years. I believe they met. A meeting we did not know about. Otherwise, why did the old man suddenly find an interest in our plans?"

"You may be correct. That is something I did not consider."

"Well, consider it. We need someone not so young and hotheaded as Hazem al-Jalali, may Allah have mercy on him, to rid us of these two interlopers."

Naseem al-Nouri gave a slight bow. "Consider it done."

Uri Ben-David sat behind his desk and read the memo Daniella handed to him. He read it twice before looking up at her as she stood in front of his desk. "So, Danny McCaffrey is in Tehran and meeting with a member of the Ministry of Intelligence. What did you say his name was?"

"Karim Qatari. He's a mid-level functionary we've had an interest in for several years."

Ben-David nodded. "Go on."

"He disappears for months at a time and then shows back up for a few weeks and then disappears again."

"Have our assets in Iran ever bothered to find out where he disappears to?" The scowl on Ben-David's face grew in intensity.

Daniella shook her head. "We do not have enough assets in-country to follow everyone at Qatari's level within the Ministry of Intelligence, Uri."

"I know, but it is frustrating not to know why he disappears." He drummed his fingers on his desk. "Do you think the Americans would know?"

She stood straighter and folded her arms. "I prefer not to get the Americans involved."

With a rare show of emotion, Ben-David bolted from his seat and leaned over his desk, his hands flat on the surface. In a low growl, he said, "Ms. Wiener, may I remind you that part of the job of Director of the Counter-Terrorist Division is to work with any foreign government willing to do so. We have few friends in the region, but the Americans have our same interests. I suggest you start cultivating relationships with them. Otherwise, your future with the Mossad might be in danger."

"I was merely…"

"I do not want excuses. Find out where Karim Qatari goes when he disappears, period. If the Americans can help, let them. If they cannot, ask the British or the French. I do not care who you use, just find out. McCaffrey was here in Israel less than a week ago and now he is meeting with a member of the Iranian Ministry of Intelligence. Does that not strike you as ominous?"

Her eyes remained wide from the unusually harsh rebuke. Daniella could only nod in response.

Ben-David continued, "Now, we both have work to do. Dismissed."

After she left, he sat and stared at the memo again before placing it in the shredder next to his desk. "Damn."

Joseph Kincaid recognized the country ID displayed on his government-issued iPhone. The screen also displayed the local time. Doing the quick math in his head, he realized it was midnight where the call originated. "This is Joseph."

"Good evening, my friend."

Joseph smiled when he recognized the voice of Uri Ben-David. "Isn't it a little late there, Uri?"

"Yes, but it comes with the territory."

"You sound weary."

"Worried is a better description. What type of assets does your government have in Iran?"

"I don't work for the CIA anymore."

"Yes, yes, we've had this discussion before. Tonight, I do not have the time or the patience for it. Please just tell me what you can."

"I'm sure we do, what do you need?"

"I need to know everything there is to know about a Ministry of Intelligence officer named Karim Qatari."

"Never heard of him. Why the interest?"

"He is having regular meetings with Danny McCaffrey. I believe that fact might increase *your* interest, or am I wrong?"

Before answering, Joseph stared at a picture on the opposite wall without seeing it. After a dozen seconds, he said, "Yes, it would. Where are they meeting?"

"In the mountains northeast of Tehran in a small village that does not appear on any map."

"How do you spell Qatari's name?"

Ben-David told him.

"Let me see what I can find out and I'll call you tomorrow."

Chapter Thirteen

The news of Danny McCaffrey's meetings with Karim Qatari lit numerous fires throughout the George Bush Center for Intelligence in the unincorporated community of Langley in Fairfax County, Virginia. Fingers were pointed and tempers flared as phone calls went unreturned and questions unanswered. The accuracy of any CIA assessments from inside Iran seemed to diminish.

During this firestorm, Jerry Griggs reached out to several of his old contacts still employed within the sacred halls of the CIA building. He quickly discovered a multitude of CYA programs already in full swing. After numerous failed attempts to discover anything concrete, he made a phone call.

"No one's talking, Joseph. What the heck did you do?"

"Huh." The NSA did not make another comment for several moments. "I just called Director King and asked what they knew about Qatari. That's all. Why?"

"The ass-chewing's are flowing down the command

chain as we speak. No one is being spared, from what I was told. Plus, nobody—and I mean nobody—is talking and everyone is blaming someone else for the problem."

"Guess I struck a nerve somewhere. I wonder…" Joseph grew quiet for several moments. "Thanks for checking, Jerry."

"No problem, boss."

Joseph searched his personal cell phone for a number with the cryptic label of 5+1. He smiled as he walked to his car after shutting down his office in the White House. Once behind the wheel and heading out into DC traffic, he pressed the send icon.

A cheery voice with an incredibly proper British accent said, "Kincaid, my good fellow. How nice of you to call."

"Good evening, Jonathan. I hope it is not too late for you?"

"Nonsense. Last I heard, you took a job within the Griffin administration."

"I did."

"National Security Advisor, I'm told."

"Correct."

"Is this an official call or an old-chum-reconnecting call?"

"I hope both."

"Charming. Official business first. What can I do for you?"

"Last I knew, you were third in line to the top spot at MI6."

"Second now."

84

"Congratulations. Are you on a secure line?"

"Always. Are you still friends with that marvelous computer hacker—what's his name—RJ, or something like that?"

"Yes."

"Good, then I know you're on a secure line as well. Ask away."

"I asked your cousins about an Iranian named Karim Qatari and the building in Langley suddenly went catatonic. What do you know about him?"

"Funny you should ask. The name meant absolutely nothing to us this morning—now he's been the subject of numerous inquiries and more than a few phone calls. We know more now than we did this morning. Why do you ask?"

"I'm curious. Care to share?"

"With you, absolutely. He's a virologist with a degree from the Swiss Federal Institute of Technology in Zurich. He spent a few years in Switzerland after getting his degree doing research and then returned to Iran in the late nineties. We originally thought of him as a mid-level functionary in the Iranian Ministry of Intelligence, and quite frankly, didn't pay too much attention to him. When we uncovered the information about his degree and that he had been put in charge of a new weapons project... Well, I must say, it made a few people around here a bit jittery."

"But you don't know what type of weapon, right?"

"With his degree, we believe it to be biological."

Joseph hesitated several moments to find his voice. "But you're not sure."

"No, we're not. While we've heard rumors of Iran dabbling with them, this is the first time we've determined that someone with the correct background was actually in charge of a program."

"Do you remember a chap named Danny McCaffrey?"

"Oh, bloody hell, yes."

"He's in Tehran and meeting with Qatari."

There was silence on the call. Finally, Joseph heard, "Oh, dear. That's not good, is it, old boy?"

"No. The problem I have going forward is I have to be judicious with my involvement because of my duties for the president. I can't be seen as coordinating anything for Langley."

"That's understandable."

"Yes, it is. However—"

"There's always a however, isn't there."

"In this case there is. I really don't have time for their CYA nonsense."

"CYA?"

"Yeah, cover your ass."

Jonathan Chapman chuckled.

Joseph chose his next words carefully. "I have to ask for a favor."

No response came from the MI6 Assistant Director for a beat. "Depends."

"There is a recording of an intercepted cell phone call where McCaffrey references attacking various world leaders. Your prime minister and my president were mentioned in the call. I have a man looking into it. He's not CIA but has all the skills."

"Will you share what your man finds out?"

"With you, yes."

"Then what's the favor?"

"How hard would it be for one of your SAS chaps to infiltrate someone into Iran?"

"What kind of linguistic skills does this someone possess?"

"Fluent in most of the middle eastern ones."

"What other skills does this person possess?"

"Ever hear of an American ex-pat named William Little who met with an unfortunate accident in Madagascar?"

"Yes, I understand he got in the way of a bullet fired from about a kilometer and a half away."

"My man made the shot. It was exactly 1600 meters, by the way."

"I'll get back to you when I have the arrangements made."

"Thank you, Jonathan."

Jerry Griggs sipped a beer as he watched Joseph pour three fingers of Glenfiddich twelve-year-old single malt scotch into a crystal tumbler. He said, "When you invite me to your house for these types of meetings, boss, you normally have something in mind that will, more than likely, get me in trouble."

"Nonsense, Jerry." Joseph raised the glass to his lips and took more than a sip. With a smile, he said, "Is your passport up-to-date?"

"Uh-oh."

Joseph nodded. "I need you to meet Michael in Israel. You two need to go sightseeing together."

"Am I to guess where?"

"I need you both in Iran."

Griggs frowned, "Last I checked, Iran wasn't too keen on having Americans wandering around their country on sightseeing tours."

"They aren't. That's why the two of you will not enter the country in the traditional manner."

Now it was Griggs' turn to smile. "Okay, you have my interest."

"I don't have all the details yet, but you two will be escorted by a SAS chap who knows his way around the mountains north of Tehran."

"And our purpose for this little excursion?"

"Karim Qatari."

"Ahhh…" Griggs took a sip of beer and then stared at the label for a few moments. "What exactly do you need accomplished with Qatari?"

"What does Michael do best?"

A knowing nod was Joseph's answer. Griggs asked, "Tell me about Qatari. What's he done?"

"Qatari is a trained virologist."

Griggs's eyes widened. He remained quiet as Joseph continued.

"The fact that Danny McCaffrey is meeting with him and that Qatari is in charge of some kind of weapons program, is starting to raise the hairs on the backs of MI6 and the Mossad's necks."

"What about the CIA?"

"They are currently too busy covering their backsides to understand the implications of these meetings."

"What about McCaffrey?"

"If possible, he needs to be in Michael's crosshairs, as well."

"Will Michael do it?"

"I haven't asked him."

"Before I go over there, don't you think it would be a good idea to do so?"

"My dear Jerry, why do you think I'm asking you to go to Israel?"

With a chuckle, Griggs took another sip of beer. "Because you need plausible deniability if this little sight-seeing tour you're suggesting goes south."

Joseph nodded.

Chapter Fourteen

Michael Wolfe sat quietly at the small breakfast table in Nadia and his apartment as Jerry Griggs went over the proposal for their mission in Iran. Nadia sat next to Wolfe with a frown on her face and one hand on his forearm.

When Griggs finished, Wolfe stared unblinking at him for several moments. Finally, he said, "Who's the dumbass that thinks this is even close to being a good idea?"

"The President of the United States."

"Why doesn't the CIA handle it?"

"They seem to have been caught with their pants down and are now too busy pointing fingers at each other."

With a slight shake of his head, Wolfe continued, "Who's the SAS guy?"

"Don't know yet."

"Find out."

Griggs nodded and made a note on the small pad in front of him.

Wolfe's tone was sharp. "I'm not going into Iran without a detailed plan. That's a good way to never leave the place.

I need to know the specifics before I even think about doing it. We'll need more information on Qatari. Plus, we need to know more about this village where McCaffrey and the Iranian meet."

"Agreed."

Wolfe walked to the coffee machine and poured himself a cup and then leaned against the kitchen cabinet. "Jerry, I don't like spur of the moment planning. It's a good way to get killed. But I do agree this Qatari fellow needs to be retired." He grew quiet as he sipped coffee and looked at Nadia. "I'll need you to coordinate communications."

She nodded.

He returned his attention to Griggs. "If this thing can't be planned so we are in-country no more than three days, I'm not agreeing to do it."

"Joseph thought it would take at least four days."

"Won't happen. Joseph's been out of the field too long. This needs to be a quick in-and-out operation, three days at max, preferably two. And, I might add, we don't even start planning until we know where Qatari is meeting McCaffrey."

"How do we determine that?"

Wolfe gave him a crooked smile. "How should I know? Follow him with a drone or a satellite."

Griggs pursed his lips. "Iranian air defenses are pretty sophisticated. I don't think a drone would survive. But a satellite…"

"Jerry, three guys wandering aimlessly around the mountains of Iran isn't going to work. We need to know where to go and when."

"I'll have Joseph get in touch with the National Reconnaissance Office and have them start working on it."

With a shake of his head, Wolfe said, "No, the request

should come from someone like Uri Ben-David. We need to keep Joseph out of it."

"True. Will Ben-David do it for you?"

"No. But he will if the request comes from Nadia."

She chuckled. "How do you figure that, Michael?"

"Because he feels guilty about what Asa Gerlis did to you."

"I did not get that feeling from Uri."

"Trust me, Nadia. He feels guilty." Wolfe returned his attention to Griggs. "Until we know where we can find Qatari, this project is on hold."

"Joseph won't like that."

"Joseph isn't the one going into Iran uninvited. He'll have to live with it." Wolfe paused for a second. "One more thing, Jerry. Not only do we need a plan for getting out of Iran, we need a contingency plan in case we all get separated."

"Who's going to do all this planning, Michael?"

"Me." Wolfe folded his arms. "Depending on who the SAS guy is, I'd prefer to do this by myself. It gives me more freedom to make split second decisions."

"Do you know your way around the Alborz Mountains?"

"No, that's why the SAS guy might be critical."

"I think you need me to go."

"Why?"

"I was considered a good spotter while I was a Ranger."

"You've never told me that."

Griggs shrugged. "It never seemed relevant."

Wolfe stared at the younger man. "I don't suppose you've been in the Alborz Mountains, have you?"

"No, I've tried to stay out of Iran."

"As have I." Wolfe took a deep breath and let it out

slowly. "Before we make too many decisions on this, find out who our guide will be."

After Griggs left, Wolfe grew quiet as he considered the prospects of getting in and out of Iran. Nadia watched him drink coffee at the small table and stare at a spot on the wall. She busied herself around the apartment and left him alone.

It was approaching dusk when he stood and found her in the small living area reading. "Let's go for a walk."

She smiled, put her book down and stood. "Where to?"

"That little café you told me about last night."

They walked in silence the first few minutes. Finally, he said, "Part of me wants to tell Jerry no and we go back to Missouri."

"Most of me wants that too, Michael."

He looked at her and smiled. "I really don't care about Danny McCaffrey and his delusional ambitions."

"Was it a mistake to come to Israel?"

"No."

She wrapped her arms around herself and shivered.

Glancing at her, Wolfe asked, "You cold?"

Shaking her head, she remained quiet for a few more seconds. "Worried."

"Don't be. I believe there is a seventy percent chance this little excursion into Iran will never happen."

"Why?"

"Because I don't think they have the ability to find out where Qatari goes when he's not in Tehran."

President of the United States Roy Griffin sat behind the Resolute desk and surveyed the three men sitting in a semi-circle in front of him. "You called this meeting, Dwight. Want to fill us in?"

CIA Director Dwight King sat directly in front of Griffin with National Security Agency Director Admiral Leland Berry to his right and Joseph Kincaid to his left.

King said, "We have reason to believe Iran is developing biological weapons, sir."

Griffin kept his expression neutral. "What do you mean by *reason to believe*?"

Taking a quick glance at Joseph, King continued, "There have been some, uh, developments, in the identity of an individual within their Ministry of Intelligence. The man's name is Karim Qatari and the last we knew he was a mid-level functionary and of no particular significance."

The president's expression did not change as he sat quietly listening.

"After it became known he had been put in charge of a new weapons system, we started looking at him more closely."

Joseph placed his hand over his mouth to cover his involuntary smile.

Griffin noticed.

The CIA Director continued, "It seems Qatari has a degree in virology from the Federal Institute of Technology in Switzerland."

"And you didn't know this before?"

"No, sir."

Drumming his fingers on the desk, the president frowned and looked at Admiral Berry. "Can you confirm any of this, Leland?"

"We've recently had some intercepts from within Iran

that suggest they have a new project in the works but nothing specific. With the revelation that Qatari is a virologist, we are going back into the archives to search for additional intercepts we might have missed."

Griffin smiled. "In other words, you guys blew it."

King nodded and Berry said, "Uh—yes, sir."

"So, we don't really know what this Qatari fellow is doing. Does that sum up the reality of this situation, gentlemen?"

Both King and Berry nodded in unison.

Looking over at Joseph, the president asked, "What are your thoughts on this?"

"I think we need a crash course on who Karim Qatari is. But more importantly, was he some rich Iranian's kid who bummed around Switzerland and barely made it through college, or is he a bona fide virologist with serious research in his background?"

King looked at the president. "It's the latter, sir."

Griffin's forehead wrinkled. "How did the CIA not know about this individual, gentlemen?"

"We, uh—we don't know, sir."

Taking off his glasses, Griffin closed his eyes and pinched the bridge of his nose. He remained quiet for what seemed like an eternity to the men sitting in front of him. Finally, he opened them and said, "Well, you know about him now. May I suggest finding out if this man poses a threat to this country or not?"

———

After King and Barry left, Griffin looked at Joseph and asked, "You know more about what's going on than you're telling me, don't you?"

"A little."

"Care to share?"

Taking a deep breath, Joseph said, "The Brits and the Israelis missed him too. MI6 has all-hands-on-deck finding as much about him as they can. The Mossad is also scrambling to find out what the heck this new weapons program might be. My concern, sir, is if they find it's a bio-weapon laboratory, they will take military action against the site."

"Would that be a bad thing?"

"Probably."

The president sat back in his chair. "Why?"

"With the current turmoil in the Middle East and the negative feelings the UN has against Israel at the moment, an air strike by Israel inside Iran could be the incident that sets off a war in the region. A war that would drag the United States into defending Israel."

"This country has been engaged in combat in the Middle East for over two decades. We don't need that right now."

"My point, sir."

"What do you suggest?"

"A joint mission with the Brits and behind-the-scenes assistance from the Israelis."

"Go on."

"We send in a team to eliminate Karim Qatari."

"Won't they just find another individual to take his place?"

"There is always that possibility. However, MI6 believes Qatari has been groomed for this opportunity for years. He's indispensable to the project."

"So, if Qatari is no longer running the program, it goes away?"

"It would be dealt a serious setback."

"For how long?"

"Best guess is at least another decade, maybe longer."

"A lot can change in a decade, Joseph."

"My thoughts exactly."

The president stared at his National Security Adviser for several long moments. He then nodded. "Make it happen."

"Thank you, sir."

Chapter Fifteen

Jonathan Chapman occupied a table at the back of the small café's courtyard sipping tea and waiting for his guest to arrive. Located between the café and an ivy-covered wall of a small hotel in the center of Rye, Sussex, the space contained eight umbrella covered tables. All were currently empty, except for where Chapman sat. His expected guest, while not late yet, would be making sure no uninvited individuals listened to their conversation.

Chapman's visitor appeared at the table and sat exactly at the appointed hour. "Kinda out of the way for a little get-together isn't it, Colonel?"

Smiling, the MI6 second in command said, "Yes, but the reason for our meeting needs to be kept out of the public eye, Sergeant Major."

"Ahh, got it. What's on your mind?" Ian McGill, a retired operative with the elite Special Air Service returned his old friend's smile. McGill's Scottish heritage had served him well during his time with the SAS. Rising to the rank of Sergeant Major, he had been involved with every hotspot the members of Parliament had committed the United Kingdom to during the past two and a half decades. Now in his mid-forties, he maintained the look of a man ten years his junior. His light brown hair, which he wore short, showed no signs of gray. A closely cropped beard adorned his oval face and his green eyes observed the world through rimless glasses supported by a long and narrow nose.

"How well do you know your way around the Alborz Mountains?"

"Like the back of me hand. Why?"

"I'll get to that. Have you ever heard of a man named Michael Wolfe?"

One of McGill's bushy eyebrows rose. "Aye."

"What do you know about him?"

"A damn fine shot, he was."

"What else do you know about him?"

"I heard that he died several years ago." McGill tilted his head. "Why are you asking about him?"

"Did you know him personally?"

"No, only his reputation."

"He's not dead, Ian."

"Good." McGill leaned closer. "Who's the Iranian that apparently pissed off Her Royal Majesty and the Americans?"

"You're a quick study, Sergeant Major."

"Been playing the game too long, sir. Now, what's his name?"

"Karim Qatari."

"Never heard of him. What's he done?"

"He's a virologist in charge of a bio-weapon project for the Iranians."

"Naughty boy."

Chapman nodded. "There's another person involved."

McGill remained quiet as a waitress approached their table. When he was asked what he wanted, he pointed at the cup of tea in front of Chapman and said, "Please."

She nodded and scurried away.

He watched her walk away and then turned his attention back to Chapman. "Go on."

"Danny McCaffrey."

"Bloody hell." He sat straighter and narrowed his eyes. "Thought he was dead, too."

Shaking his head, Chapman said, "No, he's very much alive. We have information he and Qatari meet on a regular basis in a remote village called Hir."

"That's close to the Lambsar fortress."

Chapman sipped his tea and then nodded.

McGill remained quiet as the waitress placed his tea in front him. He looked up and said, "Thanks, luv."

When she was gone, Chapman asked, "Since you know where Hir is, how hard would it be to get there?"

"Depends on your purpose. If you're on holiday, not too hard. If you have something stealthier in mind, a little more difficult. Remember the Iranians aren't too welcoming to a kafir like me."

"How would you go in?"

With a slight smile, McGill asked, "How many of us?"

"Three."

"Two would be better."

"Okay, how would you do it?"

"HAHO parachute jump."

Chapman remained quiet and sipped his tea again.

"That's why two would be better. Less likelihood of being spotted. Plus, it would have to be at night with night vision goggles in a moonless sky."

"How would you get out?"

"There's the rub, Colonel. Getting in is the easy part."

"But it could be done, right?"

"It could."

"Ian, we suspect Qatari and McCaffrey are working together to find a way to deliver this new weapon he's developing."

McGill kept his attention on Chapman as he brought his tea to his lips.

"There's chatter on the internet about a pending attack on the governments of Western Europe, Israel and America. Our conclusion is that the meetings between McCaffrey and Qatari are part of that chatter."

"Why?"

"Because McCaffrey has been in both America and Israel during the past month. Now he's meeting with Qatari."

"Not exactly conclusive evidence, Colonel."

Chapman shook his head. "No, it isn't, but it's all we have right now.

After a few moments of studying the liquid in his cup, McGill leveled his eyes on Chapman. "When do I meet Wolfe?"

"How fast can you get to Heathrow?"

"We know who the SAS guy will be, Michael."

Wolfe stared at Griggs with a neutral expression. "Who is it?"

"A retired SAS Sergeant Major by the name of Ian McGill."

A relaxed smiled crossed Wolfe's face.

"I take it you've heard of him?"

"Yes."

"Do you know him?"

"No, I've never met him."

"But you know of him?"

"You should too, Jerry."

Griggs frowned as he stared at Wolfe. "How so?"

"You were a Ranger?"

A nod was Griggs' answer.

"During your training, you had to make a number of night drops, correct?"

Another nod.

"McGill is the individual who helped standardize high-altitude-high-opening parachute jumps in the early 2000s."

"Thought that was Charles Bruce back in the 80s."

"Bruce was a key figure in developing the tactic, McGill helped perfect it. Now HAHO jumps are standard special forces insertion tactics."

"Oh, boy. That means we're going in with a HAHO drop, doesn't it?"

"That would be my guess. Probably the best way to do it. The plane can fly a normal airline route over the Caspian Sea—we do a HAHO jump and glide into Iran. As long as we don't have a lot of metal on us, radar will think we're a flock of birds or just a cloud."

Griggs pursed his lips.

Wolfe asked, "What's the matter, Jerry?"

"Nothing. I—uh—don't like jumping out of perfectly good airplanes."

"Relax, I was just speculating. McGill was stationed in the Middle East most of his career—he probably was chosen because he knows the mountains in northern Iran."

"Let's hope so."

Ben Gurion International airport is a busy airport, with flights arriving and departing twenty-four hours a day, seven days a week. The most active hours occur during the late evening and into the middle of the night. Into this hectic activity, Ian McGill arrived a few minutes after midnight. Before leaving Heathrow, he received a text message concerning his transportation from Ben Gurion. A driver would meet him with a sign reading *Yochanan Gill.* He smiled at the use of the Hebrew incarnation of his first name.

A man holding the sign stood close to the baggage carousel. He was of medium height, slender muscular frame, and a symmetrical face displaying a five-day old stubble. His dark brown hair was speckled with gray and he stared at McGill with intense hazel eyes. A slight smile came to the Scotsman's face as he recognized the individual holding the sign.

With an outstretched hand, McGill said, "Michael Wolfe, we finally meet."

As Wolfe shook his hand, he said, "The pleasure is mine, Sergeant Major." He paused and looked at the carousel. "Do you have any bags to retrieve?"

McGill smiled and held up his small carry-on duffel bag. "I travel light."

With a nod, Wolfe headed toward the exit and they left the terminal building.

The two seasoned military operatives exchanged few words until Wolfe drove his rental car toward the airport departure lane. He glanced at McGill. "You been briefed?"

A nod was his answer.

"What do you think?"

"Folly. Pure and simple, bloody folly."

Wolfe laughed out loud. "That's what I told them. But can we do it?"

A sly smile came to McGill's lips. "Aye, but only the two of us."

"Two days at the max."

"Agreed, no more. Timing will be critical."

"I am guessing here. Ingress will be a HAHO jump?"

A nod from McGill.

"I haven't figured out egress yet. Any ideas?"

"At the moment, no."

Chapter Sixteen

Wolfe and Nadia collected McGill from his hotel early the next morning for the drive to the meeting location. As Nadia opened the rental's back door for him, he said, "You're a lovely lass. Who might you be?"

She offered her hand. "Nadia Wolfe. I'm Michael's wife."

As McGill shook it, he said, "Michael seems to have gotten the better end of that deal. It's nice to meet you."

Smiling, she did not respond as he sat in the back seat. After closing the back-passenger door, she slipped into the front seat and Wolfe drove the car into Tel Aviv.

At this time of morning, rush hour traffic moved slowly. Watching Wolfe in the rearview mirror, McGill said, "I thought about our little dilemma last night."

Glancing at the same mirror, Wolfe said, "And?"

"How good is your Farsi?"

"Adequate."

"So's mine." He paused. "What about your German?"

Wolfe answered him in German, with a distinct Berlin

accent. "My mother was born near Potsdam. I spent several summers there with her."

McGill smiled and answered him in Scottish accented German. "Much better than mine. That seals it."

Returning to English, Wolfe asked, "Seals what?"

"My idea for getting out."

"Not following you, Sergeant Major."

"Our little task is going to cause a bit of a snit within Iranian Military Intelligence."

Wolfe did not reply. He kept his eyes on the road, glancing at McGill occasionally in the mirror.

"We need a diversion."

"Okay, then what?"

"The Iranians will think whoever did the deed will head north to the Caspian Sea for extraction. We need to make sure there is a reason they think that."

Stopping the car at a stoplight, Wolfe stared intently at McGill in the mirror. "I'm still not following you."

"I say, we do the opposite and head south. We commandeer a car, drive straight to Tehran and fly out commercially."

A cacophony of horns blared behind them as the light changed. Wolfe continued to study the ex-SAS man in the mirror, their eyes locked. A slight smile appeared as he returned his attention to the road and drove ahead.

The briefing took place in a Mossad safe house on the southern outskirts of Netanya. The unremarkable stucco structure appeared even more ordinary inside. The only furniture in the living room was an eight-foot folding table with six beige metal folding chairs positioned around it.

Uri Ben-David sat at one of the ends. He stared at Ian McGill with wide-eyes and an incredulous look on his face. "You can't be serious."

Both Wolfe and McGill nodded.

Turning to Nadia, Ben-David said, "I hope you do not approve of this hare-brained scheme?"

Without taking her eyes off her husband, she said, "Actually, it makes sense. More so than trying to be extracted from the shores of the Caspian Sea."

Turning to the two operatives, Ben-David folded his arms. "I will not authorize Israeli forces to assist you."

McGill smiled. "Did I mention that MI6 picked up chatter that Tel Aviv was to be ground zero for the first test of the weapon?"

The head of Mossad's counterterrorist department could only blink.

Continuing, McGill said, "Just before I left London, I received a text message from the Colonel. Care to see it?"

Ben-David reached for the phone offered to him. He stared at the image and the five words under it. The picture was a shot of the Carmel Market with the words, *Possible ground zero 1st test,* underneath.

Wolfe said, "Uri, how many people pass through there on a daily basis?"

"Thousands."

"We don't know what type of bio-weapon they're working on, but what if it's a highly contagious virus that has a long incubation period? How fast and how far would that virus spread?"

"It would spread to Europe and America. You would have a pandemic in a matter of months."

After nodding, Wolfe said, "Exactly. My bet is they won't test it until they have a vaccine ready."

A nod was his answer as Ben-David continued to stare at the phone. Finally, he looked up and said, "What do you need from us?"

Standing, McGill said, "A place to train in the Golan Heights and an out of the way location near Haifa for us to finalize the plans."

"Done."

———

With Nadia assigned to both communication and logistics, Wolfe and McGill started planning the insertion into Iran. A house on the outskirts of Haifa served as their headquarters and offered a small bedroom for the married couple. McGill stayed in a nearby hostel, commuting to the house via bicycle.

The first morning after settling into their new accommodations, Wolfe sat at the kitchen table, sipping coffee and reviewing something Nadia discovered on their laptop when McGill came through the back door.

Looking up, Wolfe pointed to the cabinet at a Mr. Coffee unit. "Grab some coffee and sit down. Nadia found something."

As McGill poured the liquid, he said, "Where is the lovely lass this morning?"

"Outdoor market. There wasn't anything here except coffee and the machine."

With his freshly poured cup, he sat next to Wolfe. "What've ya got?"

"A way into Iran."

"Aye, tell me."

"British Airways has a night flight out of Heathrow that flies to Mumbai, India."

"Not surprising. It used to be a colony."

Wolfe ignored the comment and pointed to a map displayed on the laptop monitor. "Look at the flight path."

"I'll be damned. Right over the southern Caspian Sea."

"Exactly."

McGill took a sip of coffee. "What altitude?"

"Around ninety-seven hundred meters."

"Hmmmm…" He paused. "A little high for a HAHO jump, but we could free fall for a while and then open the paragliders."

Wolfe nodded. "Chapman would need to arrange for the flight to be a private MI6 affair."

"I can take care of that."

"Ben-David told me last night, Mossad would provide us with German passports and identification paperwork. Know anything about farm tractors?"

"Only that I have no desire to drive one, why?"

With a smile, Wolfe explained, "Deutz-Fahr is one of the leading manufacturers of tractors and agricultural machines based in Germany. That country is still doing trade with the Iranians and they export all kinds of agricultural products to the country. We, my friend, will have paperwork identifying ourselves as two executives of Deutz-Fahr."

"Don't we need to know something about farming?"

"Not to worry, I've been posing as an international business consultant for decades. I can talk the talk."

"Okay, first problem solved. Where do we get a car?"

"Haven't gotten that far yet. What about the jump?"

"I'll handle that part. Once we're on the ground, you're in charge."

Wolfe nodded.

"Guess I should have asked you sooner, have you ever made a HAHO jump?"

"I was a sniper in the US Marines, Sergeant Major. What do you think?"

With a chuckle, McGill said, "In other words, you haven't."

"That would be a correct assessment."

"Have you ever made any kind of parachute jump?"

"A couple, but they were a long time ago."

"We'll start getting you trained tomorrow."

The small airplane cruised at 10,000 feet over the flat farmland south of Nazareth. With the jump door open, McGill shouted over the wind noise so Wolfe could hear. "Follow my lead. Count to fifteen and pull the cord. Do you remember how to steer the wing?"

Wolfe nodded as he stared out the door.

"I'll see you on the ground, Michael."

With that comment, the ex-SAS Sergeant exited the plane through the open door. With his heart pounding, Wolfe counted to ten and stepped out into the airplanes slipstream.

Once out of the plane, he counted to fifteen and pulled the ripcord. The colorful rectangular parachute deployed and slowed his descent. He could see McGill below him steering his chute to the left toward their drop-zone. After experimenting with the steering lines, he found the chute obeyed his tugs and flew the direction he needed to go. While his turns were not as graceful as the Sergeant Major's, he got the hang of it quickly and the tightness in his stomach eased.

The descent took longer than any of his jumps as a marine. After his initial nervousness, which he had not mentioned to the Sergeant Major, his confidence grew as he neared the landing zone marker. As instructed, he pulled both steering cords down just before landing and was able to walk as he touched down softly ten meters outside his target.

McGill clapped as he walked toward Wolfe. "Bloody excellent, Marine. You sure you haven't done this before?"

While proud of his accomplishment, Wolfe kept a neutral expression. "Positive."

"Hell, we'll make an SAS man of you yet."

During the following week, they jumped twice a day, making each jump more difficult than the previous one. Wolfe's confidence grew and he seldom missed the landing zone. During this period, Nadia worked with Mossad intelligence to determine where and when the next meeting of Qatari and McCaffrey would occur.

On the sixth day of their training, a cell phone call was intercepted by Unit 8200, which caused the internal planners within Mossad to quicken their preparation for the insertion. Uri Ben-David and Daniella Wiener met McGill, Wolfe, and Nadia at the safe house as the sun set over the Mediterranean later the same day.

"Are you two ready?" Ben-David paced as he addressed Wolfe and McGill.

Wolfe said, "Yes. Nadia told us you might have a place and time."

With a nod toward his assistant, the Director of Israeli Counter Terrorism said, "Dani will explain."

Wolfe stood next to his wife and could sense her stiffen as the young Assistant Director began her presentation. He glanced at Nadia and saw her folded arms, clenched jaw and narrowed eyes. A look he knew well. Nadia was seething. He would have to ask her about it when they were alone.

After going over the various details of the intercepted phone call, Daniella said, "It seems the bio-weapon is in the final stages of development. McCaffrey and Qatari will have their next meeting at a location near Tehran in the foothills of the Alborz a week from today. Our plans are to have everything in place for the insertion."

Ben-David stood off to the side with his arms folded and one hand on his chin, his gaze firmly centered on Daniella. Wolfe glanced at Nadia, who had closed her eyes and was slowly shaking her head.

"You disagree, Ms. Wolfe?" Wiener's tone dripped with sarcasm as she stared at Nadia.

Opening her eyes, Nadia said, "Yes, I disagree."

"This from someone who has no intelligence gathering experience."

Wolfe started to say something when Nadia shot him an angry glance. Keeping his mouth shut, he returned his attention to the assistant director.

Nadia said, "The evidence you offer, Ms. Wiener, suggests your conclusions, are at best, speculations. Not facts. I do not believe the contents of the phone call you have described warrants sending these two men into a situation that is still fluid and subject to change. Besides, current intel suggests McCaffrey and Qatari have never met in a location that close to Tehran."

McGill leaned over and whispered into Wolfe's ear. "Aye, I agree with your wife."

With a nod, Wolfe said, "You're basing your conclusion on one phone call with a vague reference to a meeting, is that correct, Ms. Wiener?"

A nod was his answer.

"Have you ever been in the field, Ms. Wiener?" Wolfe's tone remained calm.

The assistant director blinked rapidly. "Well, yes."

"Where?"

"London, Paris, and Munich."

The side of Wolfe's mouth twitched. "All safe places, Ms. Wiener." He paused and his tone grew cold. "Iran is not London, Paris, or Munich. It's the lion's den and the lions are hungry. Come back to us when you have collaborative intel based on more than one phone call."

McGill chuckled and Uri Ben-David tried to hide a smile.

Daniella Wiener tapped her foot. "The information is solid, Mr. Wolfe."

"Would you bet your life on it?"

She blinked rapidly for several moments. "I…"

"That's what I thought. The Sergeant Major and I will be risking ours. Get back to us when you have solid intel where we need to be and the exact time."

Chapter Seventeen

Wolfe lay in bed, his hands behind his head, waiting for Nadia to finish her shower. His thoughts centered on his pending insertion into Iran and the task of making a long-distance shot in a mountain range he knew nothing about. While he had confidence in the Scotsman's abilities, his natural inclination to rely on no one but himself and Nadia kept him from having complete trust in the man.

As these musings swirled in his head, he heard the water turn off and Nadia singing softly in French as she prepared for bed. After she slipped into bed beside him, she asked, "Are you still awake?"

"Yes."

She snuggled against him with her arm over his chest. "Why are we doing this, Michael?"

"Doing what?"

"Playing these silly games like we did years ago when we were younger. And please do not tell me for the betterment of mankind."

He remained quiet.

"So, you do not know either."

"I've been asking myself the same question and I don't have an answer."

"Don't have an answer or don't want to answer?"

"Don't have." He paused. "Probably a little of both."

She hugged him tighter and placed her head on his chest. "That is what I thought. We have a safe place in America that's ours. While I missed Israel, now that I am here, I miss our home even more. Why is that?"

With his arm around her shoulder, he tightened his embrace and took a deep breath. After letting it out slowly, he said, "Before you and I finally got together, the only individuals we could truly rely on were ourselves. We're both loners at heart."

"I know, but that does not mean I like being alone."

Wolfe kissed her forehead. "No, but it was how we had to survive. Our home back in the states is where we can relax, feel safe and enjoy being with each other. It's natural for us to want to be there."

She raised up on an elbow. "Then, let's go home tomorrow."

"Nadia, you know that's not possible. We came here to learn as much as we can about Danny McCaffrey. Now this business with the Iranians makes our quest even more complicated."

"Do you think Joseph knew about it when he sent us over here?"

"Don't know, but then Joseph is always three moves ahead of his opponents. I'd hate to play chess against him."

"I do not want you to go, Michael."

"I know. You're worried I won't come back from Iran."

She placed her head back on his chest and grew quiet.

Moments later, he felt a drop of moisture on his bare chest where her head lay.

He kissed her forehead again, "Don't worry, I will."

She rose again and gave him a hard stare in the dim light of the bedroom. "You don't know that."

"I have to know it, Nadia. Otherwise, my confidence disappears."

She laid her head back down and said softly, "I do not wish to lose what we have together."

"Neither do I."

In a soft voice, she said in French, "I do not want to cry. Please make love to me before I do."

Birds sang outside the small kitchen window the next morning as Wolfe made coffee and Nadia prepared a break-fast of yogurt and fresh fruit. As the water started dripping through the grinds, he turned around and leaned against the cabinet. "Have you figured out why you and Daniella Wiener don't like each other?"

She shook her head.

"The tension between you two yesterday was on full display."

Without turning around, Nadia said, "I did not care for her dismissive attitude about the dangers you and Ian will face going into Iran."

"When was she dismissive?"

Nadia shot him a fierce glance over her shoulder and then returned her attention to slicing the fruit. "She acted like the intercepted phone call was the final piece of the puzzle. You and I both know it was only the first of many pieces needed to see the complete picture."

"Ben-David must think she's good at her job."

"When did he say that?"

"He didn't, but she wouldn't be in her position if he thought otherwise."

She scooped the fruit off the cutting board and mixed it with the bowl of yogurt. Afterward, she spooned a portion of the mixture into a bowl and set it in front of Wolfe. She returned to the kitchen cabinet and stood there looking out the window.

"Are you going to join me?"

"I am not hungry."

Wolfe folded his arms and tilted his head. "What's the matter, Nadia? Something's eating at you."

She kept her gaze centered on a bird perched in a tree limb. She sighed and said, "She irritates me and I don't know why."

"That was exceedingly apparent yesterday. Did you two cross paths when you worked for Mossad?"

"No."

With a slight grin, Wolfe said, "Are you jealous of her position within Mossad?"

Closing her eyes for a moment, she chuckled and smiled. "No, I am not jealous of her position. I am thankful I don't work for Mossad anymore." After a slight pause, she continued, "To me, it seemed like she was trying to sabotage the mission." She looked at him. "I don't know, Michael. I just don't know."

Wolfe started to say something when McGill burst through the back door.

"Good morning, you two. Lots happening this morning. Time to get busy."

After consuming the omelet Nadia hurriedly made for him, McGill grinned. "The Americans confirmed where the lab is located. They also confirmed that Qatari is there."

After a sip of coffee, Wolfe asked, "How?"

"Satellite. Jerry Griggs called me just before I pedaled over here. He's putting the intelligence together for a briefing."

"Any sign of McCaffrey?"

After a shake of his head, McGill stood, took his plate to the sink, rinsed it off and then poured more coffee into his mug. "He didn't say. But they confirmed that Qatari is at the location and has been for at least a week."

"Go on."

The ex-SAS man sat down across from Wolfe. "We lucked out on this one, Michael. The lab is in a remote part of the mountains, northwest of Tehran about a hundred kilometers. It's in a relatively flat area between two mountain peaks."

"Why is that good?"

McGill held up three fingers. "One, I found a similar spot in the Golan Heights where we can train in similar terrain. Two, in that part of the mountains, the winds calm down around midnight until early morning. If we go in around three in the morning, we have a better chance of hitting our desired landing zone."

Wolfe sipped his coffee and let the Scotchman continue.

"And finally, we got a lucky break. Six days from today, we have a first quarter moon."

"And that means?"

"The bloody thing sets at midnight."

Wolfe stared at the liquid in his coffee mug. "How far are the mountain peaks from the laboratory?"

"Don't know."

"Can you show Nadia where this lab is on a map?"

"Sure."

Turning to his wife, Wolfe asked, "Let's look at this location on Google Earth. I might be able to determine several areas for us to land that would provide a good shooting solution."

Nodding, Nadia retrieved her laptop and turned it on. After McGill pointed out the location of the lab, Wolfe searched the surrounding terrain as best he could.

When he completed his survey, he looked up at McGill. "I'll need more detailed photos of the area."

"Griggs indicated he would have them for us at the briefing."

Wolfe looked at McGill and smiled.

Studying the detailed satellite photographs of the site, Wolfe used a magnifying glass and measuring calipers to examine various locations surrounding the laboratory. After two hours, he put the instruments down and said, "I've got four possible locations identified. But until we get there and use a laser, I can't determine exact distances."

McGill nodded and scratched his chin. "How close do you need to be?"

"Ben-David's secured a Barrett M107 for me. Effective range is around 1,800 meters, but in the mountains, I would prefer to keep it under that distance."

"How far under?"

"I would prefer 1,200 meters or a little less."

"What about wind? Won't that affect your shot?"

Wolfe gave McGill a slight smile. "Not after I show you how to read the wind."

"Aye."

Nadia watched the two men grow excited about their plan. She thought to herself. *Why did Daniella tell them the meeting would be near Tehran?* Her suspicions of the woman were growing stronger by the day. But without more facts, she chose not to express her concern.

Part II

Chapter Eighteen

After British Airways declined to assist the clandestine delivery of two individuals over the night sky of northern Iran and the Caspian Sea, Jonathan Chapman contacted an old friend. The old friend just happened to be the individual who had started Virgin Atlantic Airlines in 1984. While no longer active in the day-to-day management of the company, he still held sway over current decision makers.

Two days before the scheduled insertion of McGill and Wolfe, the flamboyant multibillionaire made arrangements for Virgin Atlantic Airline flight 354 from London Heathrow to Mumbai, India to have a crew supplied by British Special Air Service personnel and only four passengers. And two of those passengers would exit the plane north of Iran at a height of 32,000 feet.

An SAS Jumpmaster assisted Wolfe and McGill as they suited up for the jump. While they prepared, a slender figure with longish silver hair and a red goatee, watched the two operatives. He looked at McGill. "Chapman tells me you're quite experienced in these types of jumps."

With a smile, the Sergeant Major said, "I've made a few."

"How long will you be in the air?"

"Twenty minutes or so."

"That long?"

McGill nodded.

"How do you two intend to get out of Iran?"

With a slight smile, the Sergeant Major said, "We're going to fly out of Tehran as German businessmen."

The shorter man snorted. "Ballsy."

"That it is."

The former CEO of Virgin Airlines handed McGill a two-inch-thick envelope. McGill took it and tilted his head slightly. "What's this?"

"Your ticket out if the road to Tehran gets dicey."

With a simple nod, McGill secured the package in his backpack.

Jonathan Chapman appeared from the front of the plane and said, "We're two hundred kilometers out, which means, you've got less than thirteen minutes. The pilot will slow the plane down for exactly one minute to give you time to jump. Be ready."

"Aye, we're ready."

The SAS Jumpmaster placed his hands on both Wolfe and McGill's shoulders. "Let's head toward the back."

Both men nodded and followed him toward the rear of the Airbus A300. Certain modifications to the plane had occurred during the previous twenty-four hours, allowing the jumpmaster to depressurize a small area near the back door. These modifications also allowed him to open the door and extend a curved metal rod, which would force the jumpers under the planes rear wing.

When the three men stood next to the door, a red light

above the door blinked once. This was the signal for the jumpmaster to secure his restraining harness and open the door.

―――――――

Just before the door opened, Wolfe attached a strap with a snap hook on the end to the metal rod. He then closed his eyes to mentally go over his preparedness. His Barrett M107 was tightly strapped to the front of his body; his parachute straps were secured; his oxygen mask provided the life-giving gas he would need while falling from 32,000 feet and his night-vision-goggles were in place on his Kevlar helmet. Satisfied, he opened his eyes and turned his attention to the jumpmaster.

During his time as a Marine sniper, Wolfe always felt his stomach muscles constrict and his pulse quicken just before the start of a mission. Tonight, was no different. He felt his pulse quicken and a dryness in his mouth. Ignoring these sensations, he concentrated on what would happen in the next few minutes.

The roar of the plane's jet engines dominated all sound in the small compartment where the three men stood. Wind coming through the open door buffeted the three individuals as Wolfe felt the movement of the plane slow dramatically. The red light above the door flashed twice and the jumpmaster tapped McGill on the helmet. The retired SAS Sergeant Major dove out of the opening and disappeared into the night sky. Ten seconds later, Wolfe exited the plane in the same manner.

His training took over as the Airbus A300 disappeared behind him and the world grew suddenly silent. Through his NVGs, he observed McGill freefalling below him. He glanced at the altimeter on his wrist and watched his altitude decrease rapidly. At 25,000 feet, he pulled the ripcord and the chute deployed above him. Once this occurred, he glanced down and saw McGill's open chute. Now it was just a matter of following the Sargent Major to their landing site, forty miles to the south on the northern border of Iran.

With a moonless sky above him and the lights of the Iranian coast below, Wolfe concentrated on following McGill's parachute to the landing zone. They glided on a path leading to a relatively flat plateau four kilometers from the laboratory. Once on the ground, they would bury their unneeded gear and start the trek toward a spot Wolfe found in the satellite images he felt would make a good location for his shot. His final decision would depend on visually observing the position in the daylight.

Having left the confines of the Airbus 300 at 3:04 a.m., they were burying their chutes by 3:36. As they worked, McGill said, "I think we missed our landing spot by almost a kilometer."

Looking at the Sergeant Major, Wolfe asked, "Closer or farther away?"

McGill looked at his GPS unit on his wrist through his night vision goggles. "Farther."

"That's not too bad."

The Scotsman snorted. "Aye, but we would have been given a failing grade if it were a training jump."

Smiling to himself, Wolfe concentrated on getting his chute buried in the hard-rocky soil. When he was finished, he secured his backpack and rifle and then surveyed their surroundings in the green hue of the NVGs. He looked at the altimeter on his right wrist. "We're at an elevation of a thousand meters."

McGill nodded. "Aye, the lab's at twelve hundred meters; the spot you chose is eight hundred meters above it. Looks like we have a wee bit of a climb ahead of us."

"I thought I saw lights to the south a few minutes before we landed. Did you see them?"

"Yeah. It's a village about a klick from here."

"Village?" Wolfe kept his tone calmer than he felt.

Another nod from McGill. "I knew about it."

"When were you planning to tell me?"

"I just did." The ex-SAS Sergeant Major grinned, turned and started the trek up the mountain.

———

Lights from the small village could be seen as they neared. Hand signals were their mode of communication as they grew closer and skirted the sparsely populated community. Wolfe followed McGill, concentrating on his footing and keeping up with the man.

A raised clenched fist from McGill caused Wolfe to stop. Turning slightly, the sniper could see a slight grin on his partner's lips as McGill pointed to their right. Wolfe's gaze followed the gesture and observed two individuals about a hundred meters away entwined in a romantic encounter. From this distance, Wolfe could not make out too many details, but it appeared one of the individuals sat astride her partner, her hands on his chest and her head tilted up.

McGill signaled for them to keep moving and Wolfe followed.

With the village far behind them, the ex-SAS man turned and chuckled. "A couple of kids breaking the rules. I don't think they would have heard us even if we'd made a clatter."

"Probably not."

The climb continued until the eastern sky glowed with the coming dawn. McGill said, "According to the GPS, we're only half a klick from our destination. It'll be dawn soon—we need to hurry and get there before it gets too light."

Wolfe nodded and, like McGill, quickened his pace.

When they arrived, Wolfe could see the lights of the lab below them. With the sky growing brighter by the second, he flipped his NVGs up and surveyed the scene. The building remained in semi-darkness in the valley below them. Security lights burned brightly, casting shadows across the parking area and the main building.

Wolfe retrieved his Steiner rangefinder binoculars from his backpack and lay prone studying the scene. The building was a simple cinder-block construction with a flat roof. A small parking area lay to the south of the structure with stainless steel tanks located to the north. Tubing connected the tanks to the main building. A small area on the east side contained a few wooden chairs which appeared to be a break area for the workers. The west side of the building seemed to merge into the rock face next to it. Wolfe suspected a large part of the lab lay buried inside the mountain.

The location of the facility only allowed access from the south. From his vantage point, across the gully, he could target anyone in the parking lot, the break area or the location of the steel tanks. Satisfied he had chosen a strategic spot, he turned to McGill as he attached the suppressor to the Barrett M107. "We're good. Now we wait."

Chapter Nineteen

As dawn brightened, the sun peaked over the adjacent mountain, revealing additional details about the lab. Both Wolfe and McGill remained quiet as they waited in their lofty perch nine hundred meters above. Wolfe used his range-finding binoculars to determine exact distances to key locations around the facility. Where his best targeting solution would occur remained unknown. So, he mentally designated numerous spots and memorized the distances to those specific points.

Since their arrival, the outside of the facility remained quiet. There were three older cars already in the parking lot, but so far, no additional vehicles had joined them. At fifteen minutes after nine, a dusty, older model Peugeot arrived. McGill touched Wolfe's arm and pointed.

Training his binoculars, he watched as the car parked and the driver's door opened. A young woman with a scarf wrapped around her neck and covering her hair stepped out of the car. She strode purposely toward a door on the southern side of the lab. A long unbuttoned gray coat stretched well below her knees, covering most of her attire. After arriving at the entrance, she stood still and touched a badge on a lanyard around her neck to a keypad. She then opened the door and entered.

McGill whispered, "What do you think?"

"Morning shift." Wolfe trained his binoculars past the parking lot and observed several clouds of dust rising from the road leading to the lab. "More coming." He handed the spotter his binoculars and got behind his Barrett.

After aiming the Barrett at the door, he adjusted the scope for the distance he measured earlier.

"We've got two more cars entering the parking lot, Michael." McGill was quiet for a few seconds and continued. "Looks like three more behind them."

Wolfe trained the crosshairs of his scope on one of the cars as it stopped next to the car driven by the woman. "Can you tell who's in the cars that just arrived?"

"Negative."

Returning to silence, the two men watched as the lab's day shift arrived. McGill said, "I've got a tall slender male getting out of the third car. Looks to be in his twenties."

Concentrating his scope on the door, Wolfe remained silent as the newcomer touched his badge to the keypad and disappeared inside the building. Five minutes later, activity in the parking lot ceased.

McGill checked his watch, "It took an average of five seconds for each of them to open the door."

Wolfe did not respond.

"Will that work?"

"Yes."

"Think he's already here?"

"Hard to tell. My guess would be the three cars already here are either security guards or overnight workers."

The two men fell into silence again as Wolfe took his eye away from the scope and surveyed the scene below him. Time passed slowly as he kept his attention on the lab door.

At two minutes to eleven, another cloud of dust could be observed approaching their location. McGill trained the binoculars on the cloud and said, "I've got a Land Cruiser approaching. Looks like two figures in the front."

After taking a breath, Wolfe let it out slowly and trained the scope on the door again. The necessity of a person needing to place his badge against the keypad would give him an opportunity. "What's the wind doing down there?"

McGill put the binoculars down and got behind his spotters' scope. "Thermals are steady, with a slight breeze from the north. Less than ten kph."

"Got it." Wolfe made a slight adjustment to his scope.

"We might have something. Two men in suits with no ties just arrived in the Toyota."

Wolfe did not take the scope off the door. "Who?"

"Bingo." Using the spotters' scope, McGill trained the optical device on the older of the two men. "Positive ID, Qatari and McCaffrey, just arrived. They're just sitting in the Toyota."

"Doing what?"

"Talking."

"Let me know when they head toward the door."

A few more moments passed before McGill said, "On their way now."

Wolfe centered his concentration on the door and controlled his breathing. He remained silent, waiting for his targets to approach the door. When the older man reached into his open suit coat for his badge, Wolfe centered his scope on the target's chest and applied pressure to the trigger as Qatari moved his badge toward the keypad.

The drive to the mountain lab had taken over two hours from the outskirts of Tehran. Daniel McCaffrey's irritation increased by the second as the driver of the Toyota Land Cruiser talked incessantly about his prowess as a virologist. He listened silently and heard the same stories he had been told numerous times. If he had not needed this arrogant Iranian, he would have ended his existence a long time ago. But necessity demanded he stay on the man's good side.

With the Land Cruiser parked in what passed as a parking lot for the Iranian facility, the dust from the road settled around them.

"Ah, here we are, my Irish friend. It is time to conclude our agreement and then you will pay me the sizeable sum you have promised." Qatari's English had a slight German accent after spending two decades in the town of Zurich.

"Yes, Karim, I have your payment with me. You will get it after I've seen the finished product."

Qatari turned to McCaffrey and gave him a smile. "Shall we?" Both men opened their respective doors and the Iranian headed for the entrance with the Irishman five paces behind him.

McCaffrey watched the older man touch his name badge on the front door keypad and heard the unforgettable sound of a 45gram bullet striking a human body at 908 meters per second. Most individuals would freeze and stare in horror at the carnage invoked on the now-deceased Iranian's body as it was thrown violently sideways. His long history of fighting as an IRA terrorist gave him an edge most people did not possess. This experience allowed him to recognize what had just occurred. Without hesitation, he took measures to protect himself from the next bullet he knew was probably already on its way toward him.

When the trigger broke on the Barrett, Wolfe moved the scope toward the man behind the Iranian. The space was empty. "Shit, what happened, Ian?"

"He took off like he was on fire."

"Most people would have stood there wondering what happened. He knew immediately. I didn't think that part through."

"Aye, but as you say, it is what it is. He's heading toward the Land Cruiser."

Moving the rifle toward where Wolfe knew the vehicle was parked, he targeted the tires and pulled the trigger. One bullet in each of the visible tires caused them to explode. He then trained the .50 caliber weapon on the engine compartment and discharged three bullets into this section of the vehicle. When he was done, he looked up. "Where is he?"

McGill peered through the binoculars. "He disappeared behind the Cruiser. I can't tell if he got in or is cowering behind it."

Wolfe trained the Barrett on the rear of the Toyota and fired two bullets into the rear section and two into the front passenger area. He then ejected the ten-cartridge magazine and slammed another into place. Peering through scope again, he trained it on the driver's side door.

At this moment, the two men in the mountain above the secret Iranian lab heard emergency sirens sound below them.

"Uh-oh." McGill turned to Wolfe. "We've got to go, mate. We're out of time."

Wolfe looked up from the scope and cursed under his breath. "Shit." Targeting the engine compartment of the remaining vehicles in the parking lot, he fired one bullet into each of the remaining cars until he'd emptied the second magazine. He ejected this one and placed another in the Barrett.

McGill said, "What was that all about?"

"Ever see what a fifty caliber does to an engine block?"

With a smile, McGill said, "Aye, I have. There'll be no chasing us from those cars."

"Nope."

Both men gathered their gear and hurried off toward the south side of the mountain.

———

McCaffrey crouched on the ground, keeping the bulk of the Land Cruiser between him and where he suspected the shooter's position would be. The large vehicle shuttered with the impact of more high caliber bullets as he drew his body into a ball and covered his head in a vain attempt to protect himself. When the sirens sounded and he felt the concussion of more bullets hitting the surrounding cars, he opened the driver side door and slipped in behind the wheel. Keeping his head down, he turned the key Qatari left in the ignition and heard the ominous *click, click, click* of a starter trying to engage a non-responsive engine.

"Oh, bloody hell."

He stayed crouched inside the vehicle until the sirens stopped and the world around him grew eerily quiet. After ten minutes, he suspected the shooter was long gone and stepped out of the big SUV. Looking around, he saw engine coolant leaking onto the ground from each of the remaining vehicles. He smiled slightly with admiration for the attacker. He had made sure none of the cars in the parking lot would be giving chase and with the remoteness of the laboratory, it would be a long time before first responders arrived.

Looking up toward where he suspected the shooter had been, he realized his clandestine trip to Iran was more than likely over. His thoughts then turned to another recent experience in the mountains of northern Mexico.

Could this be the same sniper? If so, after twenty years, someone has finally tracked me down.

The thought sent a shiver down his spine.

Chapter Twenty

Scanning the morning CIA briefs, Joseph Kincaid stopped on one particular paragraph and read with additional care. He rose from his desk with the page in hand and walked down the hall to the Oval Office. He passed through the empty space and knocked on the door of the president's small private office.

"It's open."

Joseph entered and sat in one of the wing-back chairs next to the windows. President Roy Griffin turned around from the desk and took the offered page.

A small smile came to Griffin's face when he looked up and handed the sheet back. "Now, why would the Iranian military be brought to red alert status and the country placed in lock-down?"

"It's not a drill. Something must have happened."

"Have you heard from our friend in Israel?"

"No, sir."

Griffin leaned back in his chair, placed his elbows on the armrest and made a steeple with his hands and index fingers. He tapped his lips for a few moments and said, "Should we assume our friend was successful?"

"I don't like to assume anything, sir. But the facts point to that conclusion."

The president frowned. "This could make it more difficult for him to return safely."

"I've always admired his ability to adapt and overcome obstacles. Until I hear different, I will look forward to his return."

The president turned his attention back to his desk. "Keep me informed."

"Yes, sir."

McGill watched the check point on Road 59 from his vantage point at a higher elevation. "They're stopping everyone, Michael."

"They reacted faster than we anticipated."

"Seems to be the case." He took his eyes away from the binoculars. "What now?"

"I never did like the idea of flying out of Tehran airport."

"As I recall, it was your idea."

"Yeah, well, that doesn't mean it was a good idea. How far is Turkmenistan from here?"

"About four hundred kilometers. Why?"

"Azerbaijan?"

"About the same, give or take a few kilometers."

"So, by car about half a day either way."

"Yeah. What are you thinking?"

"Before I answer, how many checkpoints do you think there will be?"

"Going to Turkmenistan, a bunch. It's a major route with dozens of toll booths."

"To Azerbaijan?"

"Some. Probably not as many."

"Are there back roads?"

McGill caught on to what Wolfe was thinking. "Aye, and going toward Azerbaijan, we would probably find a few additional individuals trying not to be stopped as well."

"How much was in the envelope you were given."

"To be honest, I haven't taken the time to count it."

"Now would be a good time."

Retrieving the envelope from his backpack, McGill was quiet for a while. During this time, Wolfe observed the checkpoint to determine how thorough the inspections were. He noticed several incidents of truck drivers offering the men, conducting the search, an object and then immediately being waved through. A small smile came to Wolfe's lips.

"We've got forty-thousand euros, Michael."

Wolfe nodded and felt his two-week-old beard. "How long do you think they'll keep up this lockdown?"

"Day or two."

"How well do the Kurds and Azeris get along with the government in Tehran?"

"Depends. Most don't trust them."

"Exactly. Would you say some of them are even hostile to the Persian majority?"

"Aye, laddie, that they are."

"Then that, my friend, is how we are going to get out of here. We're going to find a disgruntled Kurd or Azeri who would be happy to make a few Euros and give Tehran the middle finger."

The trek north lasted three days. Staying close to Road 59 and with the aid of their NVGs, they traveled only at night. At four in the morning on the third day of their journey, they found an old abandoned ski lodge west of Chalus. Its location overlooked a major highway on the southern shores of the Caspian Sea. Known in Iran as a popular vacation spot due to the moderate weather and the nearby mountains, the town also sat on one of the main east-west routes for drug smugglers transporting their wares from Afghanistan to Europe, Road 22.

The ski lodge allowed the two men to rest, consume some of their rations, change into clothes more appropriate for their geographical location and determine their next steps. Early the next afternoon, McGill surveyed the scene below with his binoculars and said, "Iran has always had a problem with opium. In fact, earlier in the twentieth century, it was one of the country's chief exports."

Wolfe sat cleaning the Barrett as he listened. "Didn't know that."

"Aye, you never hear about it, because it would embarrass the Supreme Leader and the Guardian Council. But a lot of opium travels Road 22 from Afghanistan to Azerbaijan and then on to Europe."

"Not sure I want to get tied up with drug smugglers."

"Not gonna, laddie. But considering Iran's unemployment rate for minorities averages sixteen percent or higher, there are a lot of Kurds and Azeris looking for a way to make a living. So. smuggling's a common practice."

"Makes sense."

McGill nodded as he continued to use the binoculars on the scene below. "Chalus is a vacation spot for well-to-do

Iranians. Road 22 skirts the coastline for a little over two hundred kilometers and then turns into Road 49 for another two hundred to the town of Astara, Azerbaijan. Lots of secluded beaches for a good smuggler to pick up a load from the Caspian Sea and run it back to Chalus."

"So, we need to find one of those types?"

"That would be our best bet."

"How do we find them?"

"I think I see one right now."

Zendo Kesra's twenty-two years of life consisted of two key components, finding enough to eat and avoiding Iranian authorities. His ancient Suzuki Every cargo van displayed two-hundred thousand kilometers on the odometer. Zendo had no idea how many real kilometers the small vehicle had actually been driven. The reason—the speedometer had never worked since he'd bought it from an old Azeri smuggler two years ago. He maintained it himself and could fix anything on the vehicle. He chose not to fix the speedometer as it hid the miles driven on his smuggling route. Another reason he liked the van.

Staying out of the reach of the Iranian authorities occupied the majority of his waking hours as he drove the length of Road 22 and 49 on a continuous basis.

Pencil-thin and with the weathered face of a man twice his age, Kesra's daily ordeal consisted of finding back roads that circumvented Iranian check points. The existential aspect of his life would have driven the typical western European or their American counterpart insane with anxiety. To Zendo Kesra, it was the way it was and one had to deal with it.

On the last mile of his current journey, he started to relax as he guided the ancient Suzuki toward the rendezvous with his contact in Chalus. He pulled into the large covered warehouse and shut the engine down. After ten hours of driving, avoiding checkpoints and navigating the back roads of the Iranian mountains, he felt drained and exhausted. His schedule would allow five or six hours of sleep before he would need to take the newly reloaded van back north.

His contact waited outside the van and when Kesra stepped out, the older man said in his native Kurdish, "I am pleased your journey was successful."

With an exhausted nod, Kesra said, "The contents of the van are, of course, yours." He made a slight bow at the waist and continued. "All I ask is a few hours' sleep, my fee and a full van for my journey back north."

"Of course, my friend. You can sleep in the office. It has a cot and a hot plate for your tea." He gestured toward a small room at the back of the large warehouse.

Sleep came fitfully for Zendo Kesra. Despite his exhaustion, he woke frequently and struggled to get back to sleep. At three the next morning, he felt a hand clamp firmly over his mouth and another strong set of hands secure him to the cot. His eyes snapped open. What he saw caused a momentary spasm of panic.

A calm voice said in Persian, "Relax, we will not harm you."

The bearded face staring at him first appeared to be a Republican Guard and his panic heightened. He struggled against his captor, but the grip was too strong. After several minutes of resistance, he relaxed, opened his eyes once again and lay still.

"Good. Will you keep quiet and listen to me?"

Kesra nodded.

"What's your name?"

"Zendo."

"Are you Kurdish, Zendo?"

A dejected nod followed.

"Good. I'm not Iranian. I'm a Scotsman."

Zendo stared at the man above him and tensed. "A Scotsman, what is that?"

Another man, who stood off to the side, laughed. "Ian, he's never heard of a Scotsman. You'd better explain a little better."

"Aye." The bearded man released his grip on the younger man's shoulder and remained seated on the side of the cot. "I'm a Christian. Do you understand that?"

The young Kurd smiled. "So am I."

The man stood and reached into his pocket. He withdrew a one-hundred Euro note and waved it in the air. "Do you know what this is, my young Christian Kurd?"

Kesra quickly stood from his cot and stared at the money. "Yes, one-hundred Euros."

"As a show of good faith, I will let you have this. But you will need to hear our proposal if you take it."

The young man snatched the bill from McGill's hand before the Scotsman could finish his sentence.

"I will listen."

"My friend over there and I want to know something."

"What?"

"Are you a smuggler?"

The young Kurd narrowed his eyes. "Are you with the Iranian Military Intelligence?"

The man off to the side chuckled and the one in front of him said, "Do we look like we are?"

"Sometimes it is better to ask, Scotsman."

"No, we are not with the Iranian Military Intelligence. We are trying avoid talking to them."

"I do not consider myself a smuggler." He paused as he looked at the two strangers. "I consider myself as a man who pursues free enterprise."

The Scotsman folded his arms. "What could you do with three thousand additional one-hundred Euro notes?"

Zendo Kesra moistened his lips and stared wide-eyed at the man. "I could take my father and mother to Turkey and start a new life."

The bearded man explained to Kesra what they would need him to do.

Chapter Twenty-One

The sky above the Alborz Mountains lightened as the dusty Suzuki van trudged toward the city limits of Chalus heading west on Road 22. The cargo of American cigarettes originally loaded the previous day, now lay abandoned on the floor of the old warehouse. Instead the cargo consisted of two men, now dressed as Iranian day laborers, their equipment hidden under blankets and empty cigarette master cases.

As Kesra guided the vehicle toward the north, he silently rejoiced in his newfound fortune. He did not question the strange men who had suddenly appeared and offered him more money than he would make in his lifetime. Considering his current occupation, that lifetime promised to be short. The possibility of earning thirty thousand Euros kept his questions about these men unasked.

The individual who now sat in the van's front passenger seat had remained silent since the journey started. To Kesra's surprise, he spoke Persian with an accent. "Where's the first checkpoint?"

"Yesterday, it was forty kilometers west of Chalus."

"Would they have moved it?"

Kesra shook his head. "No, if anything, they might have taken it down. But I will bypass the location, just in case."

After this exchange, neither of his newfound benefactors spoke, which was fine with Kesra. He could concentrate on his driving and avoid the known checkpoints.

Wolfe, never comfortable relying on others, stared through the front windshield at the road ahead. At this time of morning, traffic was heavier than he would have liked. But a conversation with the Kurdish driver prior to leaving the confines of the warehouse had revealed how congested traffic on the road could be at all hours.

Stretched out in the cargo section of the van, McGill positioned himself behind Wolfe to keep a watchful eye on the driver. If Kesra displayed any signs of betraying the two men, the Scotsman would take appropriate action. This had been explained to the young Kurd as the doors to the warehouse were opened for their departure. The fact the young man simply shrugged when told gave Wolfe a little more confidence in him. Not much, but a little.

If driven completely on Road 22 and 49, their journey to Azerbaijan would be over by noon. Unfortunately, Wolfe knew the various detours they might have to make could add hours to the trip.

As the miles slipped past, checkpoints on Road 22 were non-existent. When they approached the largest city in Iran on the Caspian coast, the city of Rasht, Kesra told them he never drove through the town due to its size. The Rasht area was also the location of a turn off leading to Road 49.

East of Rasht, the young Kurd turned north on a small rural road which would lead them there near the town of Khomam.

As they approached the port city of Bandar Anzali on Road 49, they encountered their first unexpected checkpoint.

Time slipped by at a snail's pace as they sat in the long line of trucks and cars waiting to approach the checkpoint. McGill said, "How much to bribe our way through?"

Kesra remained silent as he stared ahead at the number of vehicles in front of him. Finally, he said, "It depends on how many individuals like me have driven through this morning. I have been counting the number of drivers who have handed money to the guards and they appear to be having a good morning, profit wise."

Wolfe asked, "What does that mean to us?"

"If we pay too much, they will suspect we are trying to hide something. If we pay them too little, they will not let us through."

From the back, McGill said, "There are three guards at the checkpoint. Is a hundred Euros each too much?"

Taking a quick glance at Wolfe and McGill, the young Kurd shook his head. "Not enough."

"Is two hundred each too much?"

Silence returned to the van as the driver stared ahead and blinked several times. After a minute, he said, "Maybe. I do not know. Start there."

Without hesitation, McGill handed the young man the money from his reserves.

When it became their turn to drive through, Kesra

rolled down his window, smiled and handed a stern looking guard his passport with the money inside. Wolfe watched the man's reaction and noted the slight smile when he found the money. In a practiced move, the cash disappeared into the man's right pants pocket. He handed the passport back to Kesra and bent over to look at Wolfe in the front passenger seat and McGill in the back. The small smile he had just displayed vanished.

In heavily Persian-accented English, the guard said, "Are you escaping Iran?"

Wolfe gave the man a quizzical look and said to Kesra in Persian, "What did he say?"

The young Kurd looked at Wolfe and shrugged. "I did not understand him. I think he wants more money."

The guard continued to stare at Wolfe and began to raise his ancient AK-47 toward the window.

In near fluent Persian, Wolfe asked, "How much? One hundred Euros each?"

The rifle barrel dipped and the guard's smile returned. A simple nod became his response.

Extracting three one-hundred Euro notes from his pocket, Wolfe handed them to Kesra, who offered them to the guard. Once the new money changed hands, the guard lowered the rifle and waved them through the checkpoint.

When the van was one hundred meters past the guard post, McGill let out a long breath and said loudly, "Bloody hell."

Turning around Wolfe chuckled and looked at his Scottish partner. "He didn't speak a word of English. Those were memorized words to be spoken at any vehicle containing more than one person in it."

McGill frowned. "How could you tell?"

"If I had responded in any other way, we would still be

back there with rifles in our faces." Turning his attention to Kesra, Wolfe asked in Persian, "Did you know what he said?"

A shake of the young Kurd's head was his answer.

"How many more checkpoints?"

"Only one, Astara. Very busy border crossing."

"Can we avoid it?"

"Only by crossing the border on foot in the mountains."

Wolfe looked back at McGill. "What do you think?"

"Aye, laddie, I think it would be best if we did."

Glancing at his wristwatch Wolfe noted the time. "It's just after two. The eastern side of the mountain will get dark quickly. Ian, have you ever been this far north in Iran?"

"No."

Kesra said, "This part of Iran has many people and many back roads. I can take you west on Road 16 to Kashfi. There you can walk across the border and avoid a lot of small villages."

"Will you pick us up on the other side?" This question from McGill.

"I have fulfilled my contract to get you to Azerbaijan."

McGill smiled slightly. "Not quite. Meet us on the other side of the border and there will be an additional thousand Euros for you."

Kesra smiled. "Do you have a map? We will meet in Alasa."

The Suzuki barely stopped rolling as Wolfe and McGill scrambled out on a seldom traveled section of Road 16. Without delay, they made their way into the wooded area adjacent to the asphalt road. After consulting the Scotsman's GPS unit, they determined the border was less than a kilometer to the north. The underbrush grew denser and more hostile as the two entered the tree-line. Once hidden by trees and the growing darkness, they turned to see if another vehicle might stop. None did.

Donning their night vision goggles, Wolfe and McGill made their way through the foothills of northern Iran.

With McGill in the lead, both men silently made their way toward Azerbaijan. When the two stopped to take a GPS reading, McGill turned to Wolfe and asked, "Think he'll keep his word and pick us up?"

"It depends. How much money did you hold back?"

"Half."

"What do you suppose the bounty is on us by now?"

"Probably a lot more than we owe him."

"And that, my friend, is why we need to be careful from here on out. Besides, before we left, Jerry and I discussed a contingency plan."

"I'm not surprised. What is it?"

"If he did not have confirmation we were out of Iran in three days, he would contact CIA assets in both Azerbaijan and Turkmenistan. I have the GPS coordinates we will need for either contact. If our Kurdish friend doesn't betray us, he can drive us to the location."

McGill chuckled softly, hitched his backpack tighter and returned to navigating his way toward the border.

Crossing the imaginary line separating the two countries consisted of noting it on the GPS—no other signs or markings existed.

Thirty minutes after entering the country north of Iran, Wolfe broke the silence the two men had maintained during their trek. "Ian, hold up."

Stopping, he turned. "What's up, laddie."

"Hasn't this been too easy?"

"What do you mean?"

"The lizard part of my brain keeps telling me escaping from Iran should have been more difficult."

McGill furrowed his brow. "Aye, I've been having the same thoughts, me-self."

"How far are we from where we're supposed to meet our ride?"

After a quick glance at his GPS, McGill pointed to the northeast. "About two klicks that way."

"The village of Alasa, right?"

"Aye."

"Alasa is practically in Iran. We just left the damn place. Why does he want us to double back?"

"Aye, laddie. Why indeed?"

"Because it would be easy for someone to hand us over to the Iranian for the reward being offered."

McGill looked to the northeast. "Do you think that's what he's up to?"

"I'd bet a steak dinner on it."

"You're on, mate. Let's find out."

Zendo Kesra stood between two large Iranian Republican Guards next to a black Peugeot sedan. The man standing in front of him leafed through Kesra's passport and took a deep breath. As he let it out slowly, he turned to stare at the young Kurd.

"So, you want to trade the location of the American assassins for your uncle's freedom and any reward being offered. Am I understanding you correctly, my young friend?"

Kesra nodded.

"Where will these two Americans meet you?"

"They did not identify themselves as Americans, Colonel Mahdavi. One said he was from Scotland and the other never said where he was from."

"I see. But you know they are the ones we are looking for?"

"Yes, Colonel Mahdavi. The one who did not identify himself carries a large gun."

"Very well. Where are they meeting you?"

"At a small café on the west side of Alasa."

"That is in Azerbaijan."

"Yes."

"When are they scheduled to meet you?"

"At dawn."

"I hope you are not lying to me, my young Kurdish friend."

A clear, cloudless sky morning revealed a black Peugeot sedan stationary in a dusty parking area fifty meters from the coffee shop. Pedestrian traffic at the small café remained nonstop during the time the passengers in the Peugeot observed local Azeris buying coffee and pastries for the start of their day.

Kesra sat between the two guards and nervously waited for the two men he had driven from Chalus to show up at the café. He said, "Maybe they are inside waiting for me?"

Colonel Mahdavi turned in the front passenger seat and glared at the young Kurd. "For your sake I hope so." He looked at the guard on Kesra's right. "Go with him. Make sure he does not wander out the back door."

One of the guards pushed Kesra out of the car and kept pace with him toward the building.

_____

Michael Wolfe observed the movement around the Peugeot through the scope on his Barrett M107 rifle. "What are you seeing, Ian?"

McGill observed through his spotters' scope. "Looks like our ride has brought a few uninvited guests to our rendezvous spot."

"Kind of what I thought. Shall I light it up?"

McGill didn't answer right away. Finally, he asked, "How far to this CIA rendezvous point you mentioned?"

"About ten klicks to the north."

McGill grinned as he watched the scene below through the scope. "Light it up."

_____

The Iranian-manufactured Peugeot 405 appeared large in the scope of Wolfe's suppressed Barrett. After placing the crosshairs in the middle of the rear portion of the car and the back axle, Wolfe applied pressure to the rifle's trigger. His pressure increased until it broke and sent a .50 caliber BMG round into the gas tank of the vehicle. The bullet passed through the metal lid and the subfloor of the trunk creating enough of a spark to ignite the gas fumes in the half-empty tank.

The resulting fiery explosion muffled the sound of the rifle shot. The back half of the Peugeot rose five feet off the ground as the trunk lid tore loose and flew through the air like a flipped pancake. All the remaining passengers inside were incinerated before they could attempt to escape the raging inferno.

Wolfe shifted his scope to see Kesra emerge from the pastry shop, followed by the guard acting like a shadow of the smaller man. Placing the crosshairs on the larger man's chest, he sent another .50 caliber round on its less than one second journey.

As the larger man collapsed, Kesra fell to his knees and began to pray.

Wolfe lifted the Barrett off target and said, "If the kid has any intelligence, he'll get as far away from there as possible."

"Think he's learned a lesson today?"

"Let's hope so. It's hard to fix stupid."

Chapter Twenty-Two

Nadia Picard-Wolfe busied herself in the basement of the Mossad's Collection division. Uri Ben-David had assigned her to monitor cell phone calls coming out of Iran. Now in her fifth day of listening, she could not help but have grave concerns for her husband. She knew Michael would communicate as quickly as possible, but according to the original plan, he and Ian McGill should have made contact two days earlier.

Ben-David walked up to her cubicle and cleared his throat. "Anything, yet?"

Nadia took off her headset and turned around. "No, but the amount of Iranian government cell phone traffic originating in the northern province of Gilan has tripled around the town of Astara."

"That's on northern border with Azerbaijan, is it not?"

"Yes."

"Is this a first for this level of communication?"

"Since I've been listening it is."

"Nadia, that is a good sign. If the option of going to the

Tehran airport didn't work, Azerbaijan would be their next best option."

A nod was her response.

He placed a gentle hand on her shoulder. "Try not to worry. I know it is hard, but Michael is a resourceful individual. When Iran went on lockdown five days ago, our sources told us he and McGill were successful. The fact they have not called off the lockdown means they have not found them. The longer the lockdown continues the likelihood of their escape increases."

She stared blankly at Ben-David. "I must get back to my duties."

He gave her a paternal smile, nodded and walked away. She turned back to the computer and secured the headset in a comfortable position over her ears.

Morning turned to afternoon as she continued to listen to intercepted calls from the northern providences of Iran. While she could understand many of the conversations in the various dialects, she did not hear the one voice she sought to hear.

At 3:20 p.m., she heard a voice speaking in Farsi that sounded vaguely familiar. The tone was right and the way the voice emphasized certain syllables teased her recognition. But the context was wrong and she finally dismissed it as a fluke.

By six p.m., she stood and stretched. A cup of coffee and a sandwich would renew her strength and allow her to listen awhile longer. As she picked up her personal cell phone, she felt it vibrate. Glancing at the caller ID, she saw UNKNOWN. With a single swipe she answered the call. "Hello."

"Is this Hope?"

It was the familiar voice she had spent the last five days

listening for and the code name to be used when he called. Excitement almost made her gush out Wolfe's first name. But she caught herself and replied in the way they had agreed to before his trip to Iran. "No, but I can get her."

"No need. Tell her my flight was cancelled due to storms. We had to go to an airport north where the planes are still flying."

"Any idea of when you will arrive?"

There was a pause on the call. "Two hours."

"Very good. I will tell her."

She ended the call and practically ran to Ben-David's office. When she stood in the doorframe of his office, she knocked four times. He looked up and saw the broad smile on her face.

"When?"

"Just now. He called my cell phone."

"Oh, dear."

"As you told me, don't worry. Michael and I hate cell phones. They're basically a radio, so anyone can hear what you say. We devised a code to utilize when he and Ian got out of Iran."

She saw her old mentor noticeably relax. "What did he say?"

"They're out of Iran and will be back in two days."

Ben-David smiled.

Wolfe turned off the cell phone he'd purchased in a duty-free shop in the Baku Heydar Aliyev International Airport and placed it in his pant pocket. McGill stood off to the side, watching for anyone paying too much attention to them. The journey from Astara, Azerbaijan to the capital of the small country had taken seven hours and covered two hundred and forty kilometers.

Walking to where McGill stood, Wolfe said, "Done."

McGill offered his hand. "This is where we part company."

Wolfe shook it and nodded.

"How are you going home, Michael?"

"I have to pick up an important package before I go."

"Aye, figure of speech. Where from here?"

"Frankfurt then Tel Aviv."

"Glasgow for me."

Nodding, Wolfe said, "It's been a pleasure working with you, Ian. Interested in staying after McCaffrey?"

The Scotsman raised an eyebrow. "Aye, laddie. I don't like his kind getting away."

"Do you stay in touch with Chapman?"

"Constantly."

"Expect to hear from him."

McGill picked up his backpack and slipped it over to his shoulder. "Looking forward to it."

Using his German passport supplied by the Mossad, Wolfe paid cash for his flight from Baku to Frankfurt. He had been wise to instruct the forger who made the document to have an entry stamp for Azerbaijan placed in the appropriate section. His departure did not raise any concerns as he passed through security. Since Azerbaijan was a product of the collapse of the Soviet Union, his German-accented Russian caused no one to raise an eyebrow as he moved through the airport toward his departure gate.

He passed one gate for Azerbaijani Airways and saw

McGill handing his boarding pass to an attendant. They both locked eyes, but neither man acknowledged the exchange.

Before departing the Astara area, McGill had divided the remaining Euros equally between them. Both would fly under their Mossad arranged cover of international businessmen. Prior to their flights, each man had secured a room at an airport hotel, taken a shower, and changed clothes purchased at a nearby department store.

Now seated in his first-row seat in the Lufthansa Airbus A300-800 business class section, Wolfe watched the plane speed down the runway and lift into the night sky. He leaned the reclining seat back and closed his eyes. Except for short catnaps, it was the first time in six days he had slept for any extended length of time.

The total trip from Baku to Frankfurt and then onto Tel Aviv took a total of thirty-one hours. The actual flying time was less than eleven but the long layover in Germany meant he needed to secure a hotel room near the airport and stay out of sight. He did not call Nadia during this period. He did send a text message to her with a four-digit number. This number would correspond to the time of his scheduled arrival in Tel Aviv. She would not meet him but let him rent a car and drive to their apartment.

When he finally arrived, it was past nine p.m. He slipped into the kitchen and noticed the place was illuminated only by nightlights in the open living room. He heard soft music coming from their bedroom. Putting the duffle bag on the kitchen floor, he smiled and walked softly toward the sound.

When he entered their candle-illuminated bedroom, he was greeted by Nadia, wearing only a see-through lace robe. No words were exchanged as they kissed and she unbuttoned his shirt.

Sunlight illuminated the room as Wolfe opened his eyes focusing on the window. He felt a presence next to him as Nadia stirred, placed her arm over his chest and snuggled against him.

She said, "Welcome back."

"Glad to be back. Oh, by the way, you can wear that robe anytime you like."

"I thought you might like it."

"Yeah, you thought correctly."

They were silent as he wrapped his arm around her bare shoulder. Finally, he lifted his head to look at the digital clock on the nightstand. "I haven't slept this late for a long time."

"Glad I can still wear you out."

He chuckled and put his head back on the pillow. After a deep breath and a long exhale, he said, "We need to get back to the States."

She raised her head to look at him. "Good, I am tired of Israel."

"McCaffrey survived."

"We heard."

"From?"

"Uri never said. He just told me that the virologist did not."

Wolfe was silent. "I screwed up, Nadia."

"I doubt it. But why do you think so?"

"I should have targeted McCaffrey first. The Iranian would have been transfixed with surprise. McCaffrey was not—he knew immediately what had happened and ran out of my scope MOA. Before I could get the reticle back on him, he was protecting himself behind a vehicle."

"I would not call that screwing up, Michael. You stopped Iran from finishing the bio-weapon."

"Did we? That's a question no one can answer right now."

They both fell back into silence as Wolfe stared at the blinds on the window.

"My fear is that McCaffrey has the weapon and is out there, somewhere, getting ready to use it."

Chapter Twenty-Three

The early morning flight from Tehran's Imam Khomeini International Airport to Charles de Gaulle International, northeast of Paris, arrived just after seven a.m. The terminal bustled with passengers as Danny McCaffrey passed through the arrival gate. Disguised with dark blocky glasses, a beard and hair dyed black, he no longer resembled the IRA terrorist featured in INTERPOL memos. Keeping his head down as he walked toward the Eurostar station for a train to Brussels, he stopped occasionally to browse at shops within the terminal to casually check for anyone paying too much attention to him. No one appeared to be.

The time approached noon when his train arrived at Brussels MIDI train depot. He found a table at a sidewalk café a few blocks from the station and ordered an espresso. Ten minutes later, as he sipped the hot beverage, a young man dressed in jeans, leather jacket and a colorful keffiyeh wrapped around his neck sat across from him.

The young man asked in French, "I understand the weather in Berlin is cold."

This was the proper question McCaffrey was waiting for. He replied, "I wouldn't know. I just came from London."

The thin young man relaxed and sat back in his chair. "I was told to offer whatever assistance you might need."

They both grew quiet as a waiter approached their table. The younger man ordered tea and the waiter left.

McCaffrey said, "I need someone to pick up a package at a DHL service point tomorrow at precisely ten a.m. It will be from Basrah, Iraq and addressed to this individual." He slipped a folded piece of paper across the table to the young Moroccan, who unfolded it, glanced and then placed it in a pocket inside his jacket. "The address of the depot is at the bottom of the page."

"Where shall we take it?"

"The Van Belle Hotel. Have them hold it for the name listed just above the address."

"Consider it done." He took a sip of his tea and stared at the black-haired man across from him. "Anything else I should know about this package?"

"Yes. You should send someone expendable."

With a knowing smile, the Moroccan stood, bowed slightly and walked away.

McCaffrey took a last sip of his now cold coffee, stood and walked in the opposite direction.

At nine the next morning, McCaffrey stood across the street from the DHL location. He remained in the shadows created by an alcove next to an ancient apartment building. He remained still as he watched the coming and goings of the pick-up point for packages. Fifty-five minutes later, a tall teenager walked nervously toward the entrance of the DHL facility.

Before entering, he stood facing the street and looked one way then the other. He wiped his mouth with the back of his hand and turned to stare at the door.

McCaffrey shook his head and mumbled, "Get it over with, you bloody fool."

After a minute of looking at the door and then the street, the kid walked in. Five minutes later, he emerged with the package tucked under his arm. Once again wiping his mouth with the back of his hand, he headed back the way he came.

McCaffrey waited thirty seconds. Not seeing anyone suddenly interested in the teenager, he pushed away from the wall he leaned against and followed. Keeping his distance allowed him to make sure no one followed. When he determined the lad was alone, he increased his pace and slowly caught up.

A busy intersection caused the younger man to stop and wait for a traffic signal. McCaffrey caught up and stood next to the kid as they waited. The Moroccan looked at him, but the Irishman kept his attention on the traffic. The package was under the arm closest to McCaffrey. As a large delivery truck approached the intersection at high speed, McCaffrey used a move he'd perfected over his long life as a terrorist.

The package was removed from under the arm of his victim and a shoulder shoved the unsuspecting kid into the path of the large truck. His body impacted with the flat front of the Mercedes diesel which caused it to fall under the wheels as the truck passed over him.

McCaffrey and the package disappeared before anyone realized an accident had occurred.

Jonathan Chapman read his morning summary of the previous day's events in Europe and frowned. He picked up his desk phone and punched in a number.

The call was answered on the second ring. "Yes, sir."

"There's mention of a young Moroccan teenager killed in a traffic accident in Brussels."

"Yes, sir, I put it in there for you."

"Why?"

"The young chap was a new recruit for one of the known terrorist organizations. Plus, the method of his death was familiar."

"How so?"

"Witnesses stated that a man standing next to him grabbed a package from under the lad's arm and shoved him with his shoulder into the path of a delivery truck."

"Messy."

"Yes, sir."

"Why was it familiar?"

"Danny McCaffrey has dispatched numerous individuals that way."

"Oh, dear. I remember now. Have our Chief of Station in Brussels check on it for us?"

"Yes, sir. I'll do so immediately."

MI6 Chief of Station Harrison Knight sat on a park bench across from the Brussels Police Station. He watched the front entrance with interest due to its proximity to the Brussels' Town Hall. The individual he needed to talk to made the two-minute walk between the two buildings twice a day. Once in the morning and again in the afternoon.

Patrick Bessette exited the police station, glanced in the direction of the bench and noticed the man sitting there with a newspaper in his left hand. With a nod he crossed the street and sat on the opposite side of the bench.

"Good morning, Harrison. Not surprised to see you today."

"Really. How so?"

"Because you British have a way of showing up at the most inappropriate times."

Knight chuckled. "Yes, we British are like that."

"What can I do for you?"

"A young Moroccan was killed in a traffic accident yesterday."

"Oh? Lots of Moroccans here in Belgium. What was his name?"

"Hakeem Fadel."

"Name's not familiar."

"He was the kid hit by a delivery van yesterday at Kroonlaan and R21."

"Ah, *that* Moroccan. What about him?"

"I need to see the CCTV video."

The Belgium prosecutor narrowed his eyes. "Why is her royal majesty's MI6 station chief interested in a traffic accident?"

"Morbid curiosity, Patrick."

Bessette laughed out loud and smiled at the Brit. When the smile was not returned, he grew serious. "I need to know a little bit more about why you want to see the video before I allow it."

Knight said, "Because we've seen this type of accident before. I need to see who was standing next to him."

"Tall fellow with black beard and hair."

"Let me guess, he took something from the lad and used his shoulder to push him into the path of the vehicle."

Now with narrowed eyes, Bessette scrutinized the MI6 operative. "How'd you know?"

"Let me see the video. If the man with the black beard and hair isn't who we think he is, I'll leave you alone. Otherwise, you have a more serious problem than just a traffic accident."

The Brussels prosecutor stood. "Be at my office in an hour."

"Thank you, Patrick."

"Let me see it again."

Bessette moved the mouse over an icon and left clicked the device. The short video replayed.

Knight leaned closer to the laptop and watched. "Let me see the mouse."

With the computer device in his hand, he played the video again and stopped on a particular frame. He then used the zoom function to enhance the face of the man with black hair. "Bloody hell."

"What is it, Harrison?"

"It's him."

"Who's him?"

"A rather nasty chap who used to be in the Irish Republican Army. He's now a freelancer and works for anyone willing to pay his fee."

Bessette's brow furrowed. "Was he after the package the kid held?"

"That would be my guess." Knight stroked his chin. "Where did the kid get the package?"

"We'd have to go back on other CCTV images to see if we can trace his steps."

"I would strongly suggest you do that, Patrick."

The phone on Jonathan Chapman's desk buzzed at exactly 6:09 p.m. He picked it up and said, "Chapman."

"Jonathan, this is Harrison Knight in Brussels."

"Harrison, old boy, how are you?"

"Don't have good news, sir."

Chapman frowned, "Oh, what did you find?"

"It's McCaffrey, sir. He's back."

"That's what we suspected."

"There's another problem."

"What?"

"The package he took from the Moroccan had just been picked up from a DHL facility. It originated in Basrah, Iraq."

"Oh, dear."

"There's more."

"Go ahead."

"DHL was kind enough to check with their facility in Basrah to see if they had a video of the individual who sent the package."

"And did they?"

"Yes, sir."

"Dammit, Harrison, spit it out."

"Uh…the person who dropped off the package was Reza Asadi, a known captain in the Iranian Military Intelligence."

"Oh, my."

Chapter Twenty-Four

The Beechcraft B55 Baron settled gently on the asphalt runway at the south end of the remote rural property. As it taxied toward the hangar, Nadia stared at their home northeast of the landing strip.

With her eyes glued to the house, she said, "I didn't realize how much I missed this place."

Wolfe smiled as he concentrated on steering the plane into position. He touched a button on the hangar door remote and let the plane idle as the large door opened.

"I've lived in a lot of different places, Michael, but they never felt like home or that I belonged there. This feels like home. Have you ever felt that way?"

He applied more power to the engines as he guided the plane into the now wide-open hangar. "I did about my place in Howell County. But then all the BS happened and it lost its allure. The fact that you and I designed this place makes it special to me."

He could not see it, but a tear slid down her cheek.

When the Baron was in its proper position, he shut down the engines and started his post-flight check list.

An hour later, the windows were open in the house, allowing fresh air to circulate, replacing the stale air left from being closed up for a month. With the plane secure in the hanger, Nadia unpacked while Wolfe prepared a grocery list of items they would need to replenish the empty refrigerator.

Halfway through this task, his cell phone vibrated. After checking the caller ID, he hesitated to accept the call. On the fourth ring, he took it, "Wolfe."

"I heard you were back."

"Yes, about an hour ago."

"Good, we need to talk."

"About what, Jerry?"

"McCaffrey."

Wolfe remained quiet, waiting for Griggs to say more.

"Aren't you curious to know what happened?"

"I know what happened. I was there."

"Yes, but you don't know what happened after that."

"I'm not comfortable discussing this on a cell phone."

"No worries, I'll be in town tomorrow. We can talk then."

"Fine." Wolfe ended the call and just shook his head.

Nadia stood off to the side, listening and watching her husband. "What was that all about?"

"Jerry will be here tomorrow to tell us what happened to McCaffrey."

She sighed. "Just before we left Israel, Uri told me a source in Iran informed them that McCaffrey was taken into custody by Iranian Military Intelligence."

"Did they tell him anything beyond that?"

She shook her head. "That was all they knew at the time."

"Well, I guess we'll find out more tomorrow when Griggs gets here."

Griggs sat across from him and Nadia at their small breakfast table. "While you two were returning from the east coast yesterday, a few interesting things developed."

Wolfe raised an eyebrow as he sipped coffee. "Are you going to tell us, Jerry, or are we to guess?"

"Joseph wants to know if you're still interested in tracking down McCaffrey."

Without answering, Wolfe stared at Griggs and sipped his coffee again.

"After your excursion into Iran, we didn't know if you'd still be interested. It's a fair question, Michael."

"The last time I saw him, he was cowering behind a Toyota Land Cruiser. What happened then?"

"Iranian Military Intelligence took him into custody. We don't know what happened afterward, but he showed up in Brussels a few days ago."

Nadia frowned. "Why Brussels?"

"Not sure. MI6 determined he picked up a package sent via DHL from Bashar, Iraq sent by an Iranian Military Intelligence captain."

Wolfe's attention centered on Griggs as he remained quiet.

"Did I mention, McCaffrey had some Moroccan teenager pick up the package and then killed the kid?"

"No, you didn't."

"Well, he did. That's the only reason we know anything of his whereabouts. When the Belgium State Security Service got involved, they were able to follow his tracks through CCTV. He got off a Eurostar train from France and met with a local well-known Moroccan dissident. We think that's where he arranged for someone to pick up the package. After he relieved the teenager of the package, he walked five blocks to a car parked on the street. He got in and drove away. They were able to trace the car as far as the city limits of Brussels heading northwest."

"Rental?"

Griggs nodded. "Auto Europe."

Nadia titled her head. "Where did they find it?"

"Calais."

Wolfe said, "Let me guess, he took a Eurostar train through the channel tunnel and is now in England."

"We don't know. They found the rental car in the train station parking lot, but after that, he hasn't been seen on CCTV since."

Nadia said, "He could have taken a ferry to England."

"He could have, but England has a lot of CCTV cameras. Plus, every police department in the country is on alert and actively looking for him."

Wolfe shook his head. "Leaving the car in Calais was a ruse. He wants people to think he went to England."

She nodded and added, "Calais is a major industrial seaport. It's easy to get a berth on a cargo ship. He could be anywhere by now."

Drumming his fingers on the table, Wolfe nodded. "I agree. If he has connections with a less than reputable sea captain, he could disappear and we won't see him until he makes another mistake."

Griggs stared at Wolfe and then at Nadia. "We didn't think of that."

Wolfe stood and walked to the coffee pot to refill his cup. He took the pot back to the table and filled Nadia's. He offered it to Griggs, who shook his head. Returning to the kitchen, he leaned against the breakfast bar and focused on his friend. "We probably need to make the assumption that's what he did."

Nadia asked, "What was in the package?"

"We don't know for sure. MI6 thinks Iran supplied him with a sample of the bio-weapon."

"A sample?"

Griggs nodded. "To test somewhere."

"Jerry, I hope everyone is more concerned about this than you seem to be."

"The CIA, Secret Service and the FBI are shitting themselves because of it."

Staring at a spot on the wall above Griggs' head, Wolfe absentmindedly sipped his coffee. After several moments of silence, he asked, "How many ports does Calais serve?"

Nadia typed something on her laptop and looked up. "The Straits of Dover is one of the busiest cargo ship channels in the world. He could be anywhere, Michael."

"My bet is he headed to a specific spot. He's headed to one of two places—Israel or the United States."

Griggs said, "Israel is relatively easy to monitor. They only have a few ports. The United States isn't so easy. There are multiple large seaports up and down both the east and west coast, Michael."

"You can discount the ones on the west coast. Ships from Europe generally travel to the east coast and ports in the Gulf."

"What about the Panama Canal?"

"Cheaper to offload in Houston and travel to the west coast by rail."

Griggs frowned. "That's still a lot of ports."

"Yes, but if he is trying to get to Washington, DC, there are really only two places he can go—New York and the Port of Virginia."

"Shit." Griggs stood, pulled his cell phone out of his jeans back pocket and stepped out of the kitchen onto the back deck to make a call.

Nadia looked at her husband. "Do you think that's where he went?"

Shaking his head, Wolfe said, "No, his style is to create a diversion. If—and I want to emphasize—*if* he did take a cargo ship, he probably went somewhere to shift attention away from the location of his real attack."

Chapter Twenty-Five

Danny McCaffrey hated traveling by sea. Despite this, it remained the safest and least scrutinized way for him to move between different countries. Since leaving Ireland two decades ago, he had spent more time on ships than on land. The fact this particular ship's captain was a fellow Irishman with the same political views, allowed his journey to be less distasteful.

The package retrieved in Brussels remained tucked away in its original steel container and stored in his backpack on the floor of his berth's small closet. Being a true paranoid had kept him alive for over twenty years in a business where short lifespans were common. He lay on his bunk with his hands behind his head and contemplated the steps he needed to take if the Iranians had double-crossed him. The one thing he'd already decided was that if they had, it would not go well for the individual who had assured him the weapon was ready.

As he lay there, an idea came to him. A way to test the bio-weapon without endangering his life at the same time.

A knock at his cabin door brought him out of his ruminative state. "Yes?"

"Danny, it's O'Shay."

McCaffrey stood and opened the door. The ship's captain, Patrick O'Shay, stood there with a smile and a bottle of Bushmills' Irish whiskey. "Thought you might want to get out of that room and tip a few."

"Where?"

"My cabin's bigger."

With a slight grin, McCaffrey nodded. "Lead the way."

With a half empty bottle of Bushmills' sitting on the table between them, O'Shay asked, "What kind of mischief are ya up to this time, Danny boy?"

Staring at his empty glass, McCaffrey reached for the bottle and poured two fingers. "I may be in over me head on this one, Paddy."

"You're always in over your head."

With a sad smile, McCaffrey raised his glass to his lips. "Not like now." He tipped the glass, leaned his head back and swallowed the amber liquid.

O'Shay frowned. "Want to tell me?"

"Don't want ta. It might not be good for your health."

"Nonsense, Danny. We go back too far. What can I do to help ya?"

"What's this ship's first port of call?"

"Caucedo, Dominican Republic. Why?"

Shaking his head, McCaffrey said, "No, the next one."

"Cartagena, Columbia."

"That's before you get to the Panama Canal, right?"

O'Shay nodded.

"How long before you return?"

"We go all the way to Santonio, Chile and back—about twenty-nine days."

"You can help by not mentioning or making note that I got off in Cartagena. When the ship returns, I'll rejoin you. No one will know I was in Columbia."

The captain frowned.

"Don't worry, Paddy. I've paid for the entire trip and I won't be asking for a refund."

The frown disappeared. "So, you need an alibi?"

A nod was his answer.

"What's in Cartagena?"

"I need to contact an old acquaintance and see if he needs my help."

O'Shay laughed. "Fine, don't tell me. It's probably best I don't know." He poured more whiskey into McCaffrey's glass.

"Probably."

"When we return, I must warn ya, we'll only be in port for a day. If you're not back, I have to leave whether you're on board or not."

"Understood, I'll be there."

"If you're not?"

"Cover the mirrors and tip a glass to me."

O'Shay raised his. "I'll see ya when we return."

McCaffrey stared at his now full tumbler. He smiled and the two old friends drained the whiskey in unison.

Jose Herrera shook the hand of the man with a black beard and hair. "You look different from the last time I saw you."

"Necessities of the times. Did they explain what I needed?"

Herrera looked at the disguised Irishman. "*Sí*, my business partner in Mexico asked me to give you my best cooperation. I have a—let's say—a competitor that needs to be discouraged."

McCaffrey folded his arms. "I need more than one individual involved."

"By all means, Señor Danny. Do you remember Pablo Escobar?"

"Yes."

"He was one of the founding members of our industry, but a man with an ego that got in his way and it eventually got him killed."

"How so?"

"Too lavish of a lifestyle. He thought of himself as a king and thus drew too much attention."

Remaining silent, McCaffrey let the man talk.

"Since then, we in the industry keep a lower profile and export the majority of our product. We make sure the proper politicians receive nice bonuses on a regular basis and we keep out of the limelight. My competitor is breaking these unspoken rules. He likes to hold extravagant parties for his family and political friends. He exploits his wealth and wants to return to the days of Escobar. We can't let that happen."

"When's his next party?"

"A week."

"Where?"

"At his estate in the mountains north of Medellin."

"What direction are the prevailing winds?"

"At this time of year, from the east."

"What's west of the property?"

Herrera smiled. "Trees and rocks for at least ten kilometers."

"Can you supply me with a small drone?"

"It would be my pleasure."

After a week of practice, Danny McCaffrey's ability to fly a drone improved daily. The one supplied by Herrera was small and relatively quiet. At an altitude of thirty meters, it sounded more like a large fly to unsuspecting individuals below.

From his vantage point east and above the oversized hacienda built on a small plateau northwest of El Peñón de Guatapé, McCaffrey watched the party unfold on the huge tiled veranda behind the structure as more visitors arrived. A mariachi band played under the roof of one of the numerous terraces and the guests sampled food and drinks from a long buffet line manned by white gloved servers.

As dusk turned to night, lights illuminated the attendees as they mingled and consumed aguardiente, rum, beer and an assortment of regional appetizers. The sound of the band and murmurs of multiple conversations reached McCaffrey as he surveyed the activities one hundred meters below him.

His binoculars magnified the images of each person well enough for him to recognize the individual Jose Herrera wished eliminated. With confirmation this individual was indeed attending his own party, McCaffrey put the binoculars down and activated the small drone sitting four meters to his right.

The small craft gained altitude quickly as he manipulated the controls and sent it to the west toward the festivities. He did not need to visually see the drone. A built-in camera allowed him a bird's eye view of the landscape underneath and a perfect way to maneuver the craft remotely.

With a gentle breeze from the east, he positioned the drone so that when the glass vial, attached to the underside, broke, the wind would scatter the contents toward the west. Positioning it at an altitude just above the hacienda's roof line and out of the party's illumination bubble, he pressed a small button on his remote control. He did not hear the glass vial break nor did he see the contents descend upon the unsuspecting crowd on the expansive veranda. After a minute of hovering, the small drone rose and McCaffrey sent it north. He kept it level as it flew away from the hacienda toward a group of taller mountain peaks. When the video picture blanked out, McCaffrey knew the device had crashed into a mountain side.

Once again, he trained his binoculars on the festivities below him and waited. Thirty minutes later, he saw a middle-aged woman bend over and start retching. She then clutched her throat and collapsed in front of a group of guests. As other individuals bent to help her, they too collapsed and toppled to the patio tile.

McCaffrey heard the first shouts of panic and cries for help as other members of the gathering realized something was terribly wrong. With his binoculars trained on the owner of the hacienda, he saw the man fall forty minutes after the drone deposited the bio-weapon onto the crowd. As chaos spread across the hacienda, he lowered the binoculars and watched the horrified crowd succumb to the ravages of a truly potent weapon.

The official death count for the incident at the mountain hacienda would eventually total fifty-one. The only survivors included the members of the mariachi band and servers who were protected by standing under the roof. That night, anyone with an open sky above them, received a fatal dose.

Columbian EMTs treated the incident as a massive food-poisoning accident until autopsies started coming back on the victims.

Retired Admiral Jorge Peris, the current director of the National Intelligence Directorate, the main intelligence agency of Colombia read the report given to him by his assistant. After reading the disturbing pages twice, he picked up the handset of a phone connected directly to the desk of the President of Colombia.

The call was answered immediately.

"Sir, I need to speak to you as soon as possible."

"About?"

"The incident in the mountains north of Medellin."

"How bad?"

"I believe this needs to be discussed in person."

"I will clear my schedule. Get here as quickly as you can."

"Yes, sir."

Chapter Twenty-Six

Jerry Griggs walked purposefully toward Joseph Kincaid's office located in the West Wing of the White House. His security badge, hanging from a lanyard, bounced against his chest in rhythm to his rapid stride.

When he entered the office, Joseph raised his gaze from his computer screen and said, "Close the door and take a seat."

As he lowered himself into the wingback chair in front of the desk, he asked, "What's the emergency, boss?"

Joseph looked over his glasses and offered a sheet of paper. Griggs stood, took the page and returned to the chair. As he scanned the document he muttered, "Oh, shit."

"I agree. Have you spoken to Michael recently?"

"We've talked daily since McCaffrey disappeared in Calais."

"He needs to know about the incident in Columbia."

Griggs read the memo again. He looked at Joseph. "Fifty-one casualties in a sixty-minute timeframe?"

A nod was his answer.

Griggs continued, "Unknown causes?"

Joseph nodded again. "I spoke to the director of their National Intelligence Directorate. His name is Jorge Peris, I've had the pleasure of meeting him several times."

"Is there anyone on this planet you don't know, Joseph?"

The National Security Advisor just smiled and continued. "At first the incident was considered a serious case of food poisoning. When autopsies showed something more complicated, they went into full hazmat protocol. His team found a crashed drone about a half-mile from the hacienda. On closer examination, they found a broken glass vile attached to the bottom of it. Chemical analysis indicated some type of residue on the glass. Their labs haven't been able to identify what it is, but the same compound was found on the bodies. They've agreed to send a sample to the CDC lab in Atlanta."

"Columbia officials agreeing to share with the United States?"

"When I explained as much as I could about McCaffrey, he agreed to send it as a favor to me."

"When will the sample be there?"

"The FBI is dispatching a plane to pick it up today." He glanced at his wristwatch. "In fact, it should have left five minutes ago. It should be in the lab by tonight."

"So, where does that leave us, boss?"

"McCaffrey and someone in Iran went to an awful lot of trouble trying to hide the fact he received a package from Iranian Military Intelligence. He arranges for an unsuspecting teenager to pick it up and then intercepts the parcel from the teenager. Who then immediately suffers a fatal accident. Then the Irishman disappears in one of the busiest ports on the English Channel. Three weeks later, a possible bio-weapon attack occurs in the mountains of Columbia."

"I take it you suspect McCaffrey is responsible. Do you think this was a test of the bio-weapon the Iranians were working on?"

"Food poisoning doesn't kill that many people that fast."

"Why Columbia?"

"Several reasons. First, McCaffrey is in tight with the Mexican drug cartels. Second, Columbian cartels still work closely with their northern neighbors. Plus, if you look at the terrain surrounding the hacienda, it's remote, isolated and easier to control."

Griggs stared at Joseph for multiple seconds without responding. Finally, he said, "Aren't you jumping to conclusions?"

Shaking his head, the presidential advisor continued, "Maybe, but I don't think so. The owner of the hacienda was a well-known leader of one of the minor drug cartels in Columbia. Peris believes the man finally pissed off the wrong person. We'll know more when the CDC conducts their tests."

"Let's say you're right. That means McCaffrey has the weapon and is more than willing to use it."

"Correct."

"Joseph, Interpol issued a Red Notice on McCaffrey. It would be almost impossible for him to use commercial airlines."

"I'm aware of that. But there are other ways."

"Such as?"

"Cargo ships."

"Beg your pardon?"

"Cargo ships. Some have berths for up to twelve passengers. Some as low as two."

Griggs took a deep breath and let it out slowly. "Didn't know that. Who's heading up the search for him?"

"The FBI, CIA, MI6 and the Mossad."

"So, what are you asking me to do if all these high-powered agencies are already searching for McCaffrey?"

"Those so-called high-powered agencies have spent the better part of a decade trying to catch him. And so far, they've failed."

"That didn't answer my question."

"Turn Michael Wolfe loose."

"What makes you think Nadia and I can find him? You said it yourself—the CIA, MI6 and Mossad are currently looking for him."

With a smile, Griggs said, "You have something they don't have."

"What's that, Jerry?"

"Geoffrey Canfield."

Wolfe did not respond.

Griggs continued, "Danny McCaffrey was all Canfield concentrated on at one time, correct?"

A nod was his answer.

"Canfield probably knows more about the Irishman than he does about himself."

"Possibly."

"And Canfield agreed to help, didn't he?"

Another nod.

"Michael, one of your strengths is finding people who don't want to be found. With Canfield's help, the two of you can't fail."

"You're being too optimistic, Jerry."

"Nonsense. You almost got him in Iran."

"Emphasis on the word *almost*."

With a smile, Griggs stood from his seat at the breakfast table in Nadia and Wolfe's kitchen and walked to the coffee pot. As he warmed the now-cold contents of his mug with fresh coffee, he turned. "To be honest, Joseph doesn't have a lot of confidence the CIA, Mossad or MI6 will be successful."

Nadia tilted her head. "Why Jerry?"

"McCaffrey's been on the run for a long time. He must have a method of traveling that eludes security checkpoints. Joseph has a theory about it."

"Want to enlighten us?"

Another smile appeared on Griggs lips. "He's traveling the world on cargo ships."

Nadia stood abruptly and left the room. She returned seconds later with her laptop, opened it and started typing.

Wolfe narrowed his eyes. "I didn't think of that." He turned to Nadia. "What are you checking?"

"There are only so many shipping lanes between Europe and Columbia, South America. I'm checking to see how many originate near the English Channel."

Griggs set his coffee mug down. "Determining how many of those ships carry passengers would narrow it down even further."

With a nod, Nadia stared at the computer screen. "There are about fifty thousand cargo ships currently registered in the world. The only statistic I can find is that a little over one percent carry passengers. There could be more now—that statistic is from 2014."

With a raised eyebrow, Wolfe said, "Even if it's two or three percent today, that would narrow our search down to fifteen hundred ships. How many of those travel from around the English Channel to Columbia?"

Griggs extracted his cell phone from his pocket and pressed a speed dial icon. When the call was answered, he said, "Do you know anyone in the US Merchant Marines?" He listened for a few seconds. "I'm shocked. You don't know anyone? Who would?" More silence. "Got it. Thanks."

He ended the call and looked at Wolfe and Nadia. "I can't believe it. Joseph doesn't know anyone in the Merchant Marines."

With a chuckle, Wolfe asked, "What did he say?"

"He told me to try calling them directly."

Both Wolfe and Nadia raised their eyebrows and glanced at each other. In unison, they said, "Chief."

"Who?"

Wolfe explained. "Rufus Carroll's an old friend of mine. He was a Chief of the Boat in the Navy and served on a number of different submarines. He currently runs a charter service in Key West. Let me give him a call."

***

"Traveling by cargo ship isn't like being on a cruise ship, Michael."

"I would assume not." Wolfe paused. "I wasn't even aware cargo ships were allowed to carry passengers."

"They are, up to a certain amount. After that number they have to meet strict standards, just like a regular cruise ship."

"So, the number of passengers would be limited."

"Yes."

"Who would want to travel that way?"

"Retirees with lots of time on their hands, the world traveler who hates crowds, business people being transferred to and from one country to another and want to stay with their possessions and those who don't like to fly."

"Or can't due to travel restrictions."

The phone call went silent for a few moments. "Security would be the same on a cargo ship as it is on a cruise ship, but there are ways around it."

"Explain."

"Just because you're traveling on a cargo ship, doesn't mean your passport won't be checked. Plus, the need of a visa to enter a port-of-call country is still required. But if you have a friendly ship's captain…"

"All those legal necessities go away."

Chief Carroll hesitated for a few seconds. "As a rule, yes."

Wolfe smiled. "How fast could you pick someone up in Grand Cayman?"

Chapter Twenty-Seven

Wolfe and Nadia watched as Chief Carroll eased *Escape* into its assigned slip located halfway to the end of the dock. Multiple feelings swirled inside Wolfe as he remembered the camaraderie with Geoffrey Canfield and then the man's ultimate betrayal. Even with this turmoil raging inside, he kept his expression neutral. Nadia felt him tense as she stood next to him, holding his arm. "What's wrong, Michael?"

"Nothing."

"Do not lie to me. Yes, there is."

"Even after our last trip to Grand Cayman, I'm still not sure how far to trust Geoffrey."

She squeezed his arm tighter. "Remember what Carla said. He and Marilyn are scared of you."

"I know, but…"

"Keep him at arm's-length until you decide."

He nodded as they stood outside Chief's office one hundred yards from the docks. Time passed slowly as they waited for Carroll to finalize the boat's arrival. When

Canfield and Marilyn Dawson stepped topside, Nadia felt Wolfe tense even more.

She patted his arm. "Just remember, they're probably just as nervous as you are. They don't really know what your true intentions might be."

He relaxed. "I didn't think of that."

She smiled. "That's what wives are for—to remind their husbands of the obvious."

He chuckled and patted the hand still clutching his arm.

Canfield and Marilyn Dawson walked in front of Chief Carroll as they made their way along on the dock. Halfway to his office building, the ex-Chief of the Boat turned his gaze to Wolfe and nodded once.

Wolfe said, "Apparently, they've agreed to help find McCaffrey."

"How do you know?"

"Chief just nodded."

"I didn't see that."

"That's what husbands are for—to notice things their wives don't."

She punched him playfully on the arm and then drew closer to him.

When the three individuals from the boat grew within speaking distance, Canfield offered his hand. "Damn glad to see you two again, Michael." He said to Nadia, "Thank you for the invitation."

"It's nice to see you, as well, Geoffrey." Nadia turned to Marilyn. "Is this your first time in the States?"

"Why, yes, it is. How did you know?"

"You had that look in your eye."

The older woman spread the fingers of her hand and placed it on her chest. "Oh, dear, I'm a tourist."

Nadia chuckled.

Wolfe remained silent as he studied Canfield and tilted his head. "McCaffrey has a new weapon."

Canfield's jovial smile disappeared. "Bloody hell. What now?"

"We think he has a bio-weapon developed in Iran."

"Dear gawd. Where is he?"

"Don't know." Wolfe nodded at Carroll. "Chief, can we use your office? I'd prefer not to discuss this in public."

Chief Carroll's office, while not large, contained a small conference room. Furnished with a round oak table, traditional oak Captain chairs and a coffee and tea service, it provided the spot for explaining to that day's clients, where they would be fishing. Today it became the setting to determine if Geoffrey Canfield knew enough about Danny McCaffrey to lend a hand in finding him.

Sitting across from the ex-MI6 operative and his lady doctor friend, Wolfe asked, "Were you ever able to determine how McCaffrey traveled from continent to continent without being detected?"

"Nothing definitive, but I have a theory."

"Let's hear it."

Canfield took a sip of his newly poured tea and said, "I think he travels by ship. When he left Ireland in 1998, a number of his mates left with him. We don't really know what happened to all of them. MI6 suspected a few changed their name and found legitimate jobs. Others died in the Middle East or returned to Ireland at some point years later. Those are the ones we knew about. The ones who changed their names, as far as we could tell, disappeared off the face of the planet."

"But you know the names of the men that disappeared, correct?"

"Yes, a few of them were women."

Nadia asked, "Could any of them have gotten jobs on cargo ships."

Raising his tea to his lips, Canfield nodded. "The men, yes, the women, not so sure. A good way for a man to hide is to join the Merchant Navy. In many countries, questions aren't asked about your background. As long as you're willing to work hard, few, if any inquiries are ever made."

After glancing at Wolfe, Nadia returned her attention to Canfield. "Would there be a way to track them down?"

Canfield grew quiet as he studied the liquid in his cup. They let him think as the room remained silent. After several minutes, Canfield said, "I'd need access to files buried deep within Vauxhall Cross. As you can quite imagine, I'm not exactly welcomed there right now."

"You're thinking old school, Geoffrey." Nadia pointed to the laptop in front of her. "Those files were digitalized years ago."

Wolfe said, "And I know someone who can get us access."

"Good of you to meet me here, sir."

Jonathan Chapman smiled as he sat next to Ian McGill at the bar of a small tavern near Vauxhall Cross. "Hard to turn down an invitation for a pint at my favorite pub." When the barkeeper appeared in front of him, Chapman pointed to the glass in front of McGill. "Same."

The man nodded and went to pour the Guinness.

McGill took a sip from his glass and stared at the mirror

behind all the bottles on the wall across from him. "I spoke to Wolfe this afternoon."

They both remained quiet as the newly poured stout appeared in front of Chapman. When the barman moved to help other customers, the MI6 assistant director asked, "Has he made any progress?"

"That's why you're getting a free Guinness."

Chapman smiled as he took a sip of the dark ale. "Tell me what you can."

"Can't say much because Wolfe didn't say much. You heard about the little incident in the mountains of Columbia, right?"

A nod was his answer.

The Scotchman continued, "Wolfe said they have evidence it was a rather nasty form of C. Botulinum."

The MI6 assistant director stopped in mid-sip and lowered his glass. "McCaffrey?"

"They think so."

"We knew about the incident, but the Columbian government is being tight lipped about it." He paused briefly and said almost to himself, "So that's what the Israelis were up to last night."

"Beg pardon, sir?"

"Israel fighter jets were supposedly on maneuvers last night over the Caspian Sea—at least that's what they're claiming. We thought it a bit strange, but they insisted." He took a sip of his beer. "It makes sense now. They made an air strike on the lab you and Wolfe visited. I'm sure the Americans have satellite photos of the attack."

"And the Iranians didn't protest the planes being over the Caspian Sea?"

With a shake of his head, Chapman took another sip. "I was wondering why. Now we know. Easier to pretend it didn't happen than to announce to the world what they were doing."

McGill nodded. "Which brings me to what Wolfe asked."

"Go on."

"They want access to the files on all the IRA men and women who followed McCaffrey out of Ireland."

"Did he say why?"

With a somber smile, McGill replied, "He said to ask you what happened to five individuals—Brian McHale, Patrick O'Shay, Rose Moran, Shamus O'Rourke and Kayla Doolan.

"Those names aren't familiar. Who are they?"

"The individuals who disappeared with McCaffrey around the turn of the century and have never been heard from again."

"If they were with McCaffrey, they're probably dead."

"Maybe, but they don't think so."

"Who's they?"

"Wolfe and a friend of yours."

"Answer the question, Ian."

"Geoffrey Canfield."

A smile came to Chapman's lips. "Wolfe finally got that old relic off that damn island, didn't he?"

"Apparently."

"What are they thinking?"

"McCaffrey seems to be able to travel anywhere in the world without being seen or caught. Why?"

"We've never figured it out."

"Exactly, Wolfe thinks he's being ferried about by some of his old mates who might be working as merchant seamen on cargo ships."

"Huh, that's an interesting idea." Chapman paused and

contemplated his beer. "Tell them they can have access, on one condition."

"What's that?"

"You're involved with the hunt."

With a grin, McGill said, "Wolfe already made the request."

Both men held their glass of beer up and lightly touched them together.

Chapter Twenty-Eight

"Sorry, Danny. I can't take ya there."

McCaffrey's nostrils flared as he folded his arms. "Why not?"

"I may be the captain of this ship, but I still have to follow a strict schedule. A detour to Port Progreso would raise flags I don't need."

"You owe me, Paddy."

"Aye, I do. But if I lose my job where does that leave you?"

Silence fell between the two men as McCaffrey realized O'Shay made sense. His demeanor changed and he relaxed. "Unable to travel anonymously. We don't want that."

"No, we don't."

Taking a deep breath, McCaffrey dry-rubbed his face. "I'll find another way."

"You'll have to."

Picking up his backpack, the ex-IRA bomb maker slung it over his shoulder and offered his hand to the ship captain. "Until next time, Paddy."

"Aye, Danny, 'til next time. Good luck to ya."

As he left the ship, McCaffrey's anger intensified. When he reached the bottom of the gangplank, he looked up to see if O'Shay was still visible. There was only a dark window marking the bridge's location.

While he knew O'Shay's refusal to take him to Mexico was the correct decision, never the less, the veins in his neck pulsed as the anger grew within him. He momentarily thought about returning to the bridge and permanently ending his relationship with Captain O'Shay, but the folly of doing so would not benefit himself or his task. Without wasting another thought on the matter, he walked rapidly away from the cargo ship and pulled out a cell phone from his jeans pocket. The phone had one number saved to memory and he pressed the send icon.

A computer-generated voice answered. *"Declare su negocio."*

McCaffrey answered in Spanish. "This is Red. Tell the Don I have a business proposition for him."

He ended the call and continued his trek away from the cargo ship toward an area where he could hire a taxi.

Jose Herrera tilted his head. "As a rule, I do not grant favors without expecting something in return." He paused and took a drag on his cigarette. As he blew the smoke out though his nostrils, he said, "But since you were instrumental in eliminating a competitor of mine, I will grant your request."

McCaffrey gave the Columbian drug-lord a hard smile. "Thank you."

"My competitor was planning to do the same thing to

me if I allowed him the opportunity. I seized the moment and now…" He paused and slapped McCaffrey on the back. "All thanks to you, I am still here and he is not. When do you wish to leave for the States?"

"As soon as possible."

"Three days. Is that soon enough?"

The ex-IRA insurgent's engrained paranoia caused him to hesitate. He stared at Herrera with cold eyes and said, "I would prefer to leave earlier. But if that's the best you can do, so be it."

Herrera raised an eyebrow. "Why such a hurry? There are many distractions I can offer."

"I have a task to accomplish."

"I see." He paused as he studied the Irishman's face. "A man of your talents would help me consolidate the various suppliers in my country. Abandon this task of yours and come work for me."

"How much would you pay me?"

Herrera told him.

"Most generous, Don Herrera. Let me think about it."

"Good. You will be my guest until you make a decision."

"Your hospitality is appreciated."

"Yes, appreciation is important. We will celebrate your achievement with a fine dinner and then, I will provide you with companionship during your stay."

"Not necessary."

Herrera gave McCaffrey a cold, menacing look. "Oh, but it is, my friend, it is the least I can do."

As the invitees gathered in the large dining hall, McCaffrey watched Herrera work the crowd. The strikingly beautiful young señorita with deep chocolate-colored eyes and long flowing black hair, who called herself Lia Vargas, held his arm. She explained who each of the attendees were.

"That is the mayor of Medellin and his wife."

"Really."

"Yes, they are frequent guests of Señor Herrera's dinner parties."

"I see. Who's that?" McCaffrey nodded in the direction of a man wearing a military uniform.

"That is Colonel Rivera. He is in charge of security for Señor Herrera's business."

With a frown, McCaffrey thought back to the conversation he'd had with Herrera when he mentioned that his competitor was too flashy and drew too much attention to himself. He looked at the woman. "Which business is that?"

"He is in the export business."

McCaffrey semi-smiled at the woman. "What does he export?"

"Coffee. Señor Herrera is the largest exporter of coffee beans in Columbia."

"I see." He patted the young woman's hand still clasping his arm. "What do you do for Señor Herrera?"

"I am his hospitality coordinator. I plan all of his social functions and make sure his new business partners enjoy their stay in Columbia."

"And for those responsibilities, I bet you make lots of money."

"*Sí, Señor*, I am generously compensated."

"What other duties do you perform for Señor Herrera?"

She looked up at him and smiled. "We can discuss that later." She touched his arm with her free hand and steered him toward one of the many bartenders preparing drinks for the crowd.

Watching Herrera move from guest to guest, McCaffrey made a decision. He would be on guard for the remaining time of his stay.

Herrera noticed McCaffrey leave the dining hall with the lovely Señorita Vargas. Once they were out of sight, he signaled for Rivera to join him in a secluded area away from the guests.

When the colonel stood next to him, he said, "The Irishman left with the woman."

"Yes, I noticed. What did you find in his room?"

"Only a backpack with a few clothes, money and a small hard case containing three vials cushioned by egg crate latex foam."

With a nod, Herrera remained quiet for a few moments. "I am afraid we may be consorting with the devil, Colonel."

"How so?"

"How many vials did you say this small case contain?"

"Three, there was an empty slot."

"Ahh…" Herrera grew silent. "I made him an offer to work for us. He will turn me down."

"How do you know?"

"I just know." He paused as he took a sip of his drink. "If Mr. McCaffrey is allowed to reach the United States and uses any of those remaining vials, fingers will be pointed at me. I cannot allow that to happen."

"That could be bad for your business, Señor."

"Sí, it could be devastating. We have a shipment leaving in two days for the Everglades. Make arrangements for our Irish friend to be onboard."

"Sí, Señor. I will make the arrangements."

"And Colonel, make sure Emilio is part of the crew and understands the importance of making sure Mr. McCaffrey is not onboard when they reach their destination."

The time was 2:18 a.m. when Lia Vargas slipped out of his bed and left the bedroom. He had not fallen asleep after their lovemaking, but remained still staring at the ceiling fan turning slowly above the bed. He anticipated she might leave early and send someone to his unlocked room. But by 3:02 a.m., no one had arrived.

He quietly dressed and then made his way to the large house's kitchen to start planning a surprise for the Don. It took less than thirty minutes to determine what he needed to do before he left the *hacienda* day after tomorrow. After finishing this task, he searched the Don's library and found the Taurus PT92 and two full magazines in the bottom right-hand drawer of a massive oak desk.

After returning to the bed in his guest room, McCaffrey fell asleep with his hand on the now loaded Taurus beneath his pillow.

Chapter Twenty-Nine

Canfield finished reading the files on Nadia's laptop. He pointed to a picture on the left side of the screen. "Paddy O'Shay."

Wolfe stood behind him with his arms folded. "What about him?"

"He comes from a long line of Irish Mercantile Marines. His grandfather was a cargo ship captain during World War II and died when a Nazi U-Boat sank his vessel."

"What about the father?"

"Same thing, captain of a cargo ship."

"Is the father still alive?"

With a shrug Canfield said, "He was in 2010, not sure about today."

"What's his name?"

"If I remember correctly, his name was John."

"Where did he live?"

"Belfast at that time. If he's still alive, the Irish Social Security Department might have an address for him."

Wolfe stepped out of office to stand on the front deck. As he looked over the docks in front of him, he took out his cell phone and dialed a number from memory. It was picked up on the third ring.

"I was about to call you."

"Where are you, Ian?"

"Heathrow. My flight's been delayed for Miami."

"Good. I need you to make a detour to Northern Ireland."

There was silence on the phone for several moments. "You got a lead on McCaffrey?"

"Maybe. We need you to find an Irish Mercantile sea captain named John O'Shay."

"Who's he?"

"He's the father of one of the men who left Ireland with McCaffrey. His name is Paddy O'Shay."

"Paddy is short for Patrick."

"Huh, didn't know that. Anyway, the grandfather was a Merchant Sea Captain as was John O'Shay. If the son followed in their footsteps, that could be our connection to how McCaffrey is traveling from country to country."

"What was the grandfather's name?"

"Shamus O'Shay."

"You realize this could be one of your American wild goose chases."

"Yeah, but right now it's the only goose chase we've got."

McGill chuckled. "I'll call you when I know something."

Tucked away off the A1 highway halfway between St. Johns and Douglas west of the village of Glen Vine lay a small cottage built in the early 1900's. Ian McGill parked his rented motorcycle in front of the house and took in the neat and well-manicured landscaping.

He placed his helmet on the seat and slowly approached the small gate in a waist-high stone fence surrounding the house. Once inside the confines of the yard, he took in more details of the structure. Made with white-washed bricks, the two chimneys, one at each end of the red-tiled roof, told McGill the home would be warm and cozy despite the northern oceanic climate of the island.

He knocked on the front door several times until he heard a distant voice. "In the back."

Walking around the bungalow, he reached the backyard and found a large garden. In the middle stood an elderly man staring at him.

McGill raised his hand and shouted, "Are you Captain O'Shay?"

With a thick Irish enunciation, the man said, "Who be askin'?"

In an enhanced Scottish inflection, McGill said, "Me. The name's McGill. Are you John O'Shay?"

"Aye. State your business." The man, who appeared to be in his late sixties or early seventies, leaned on the shovel he had been working with and stared coldly at McGill. His deeply lined and weathered face, the result of being at sea most of his adult life, displayed a frown.

"I'm looking for Patrick O'Shay."

The older man's eyebrows rose and his eyes widened. Just as quickly they returned to a scowl. "He's not here."

"I know. Where might I find him?"

With a raised arm, the man pointed to the southwest. "Out there somewhere. Haven't spoken to him in years. What's he done now?"

"Nothing. I just need to talk to him."

"Why?"

McGill stood at the edge of the garden and folded his arms. "That's between him and me."

To the ex-SAS operator's surprise, the old man smiled. "You and a lot of other people." He stopped leaning on the shovel and walked toward where McGill stood. When he was within a few feet, he said, "Paddy isn't around much these days. He's like his grandfather and his father—always gone. His poor sainted mother, God rest her soul, had to raise the boy by herself."

McGill kept quiet and let the senior O'Shay talk.

"Paddy's a ship captain, just like me. Only nowadays, he's at sea for longer periods than I ever was."

"Do you know the name of the shipping company he works for?"

A nod was his answer this time.

"Care to tell me?"

"Not until you tell me why you want to talk to him."

"He might know where Danny McCaffrey is."

Captain O'Shay narrowed his eyes and glared at McGill. "Paddy left that life behind."

"Are you sure?"

"Let's go in, it's cold out here."

McGill followed the old ship's captain into the rear entrance of the house.

With a displacement of 8,500 tons, Her Majesty's Ship *Defender,* became the fifth of six Type 45 or Daring-class air-defense destroyers built for the modern Royal Navy. Her keel had been laid down in 2006 and she'd launched in

2009. After completing her first sea trials in November 2011, she had been commissioned in March 2013. She was also the eighth ship in the history of the Royal Navy to bear the name *Defender*.

Ian McGill shook the hand of Michael Wolfe as they greeted each other on the HMS *Defender*'s helicopter deck after Wolfe stepped off a US Marine Corp MV-22B Osprey. Neither man spoke as the tilt-rotor aircraft spooled up its two engines for its return flight to the deck of the USN aircraft carrier John C. Stennis.

As the tilt-rotor aircraft rose and the sound diminished, Wolfe said, "Where's the ship?"

McGill pointed off to the west. "About a hundred nautical miles that way."

"Good to see you again, Ian."

"Bloody good to see you, too, Michael."

Wolfe asked, "Why did the father give up his son's location so easy?"

With a shrug, McGill shook his head. "Not sure. I can tell you he is not a fan of Danny McCaffrey. Called him an embarrassment to the Irish people."

"So, the father knew about McCaffrey?"

A nod was his answer.

Continuing, Wolfe said, "Did you explain why we need to find McCaffrey?"

"Didn't have to. As soon as I mentioned the name, Captain O'Shay took me into his home and poured us each a glass of Irish whiskey and did not stop talking for an hour."

"Huh."

"Chapman and most of MI5 and MI6 thought McCaffrey left Ireland because of the Belfast Agreement in 1998."

"That's what I was told."

"Captain O'Shay told me that was pure rubbish."

"So, what's the real reason?

"McCaffrey became an embarrassment to the leaders of the IRA. They turned on him and ordered his death."

Wolfe frowned as he listened.

"O'Shay told me the Good Friday Agreement would have been signed two years earlier except that McCaffrey set off a bomb in the Canary Wharf area of London on February 9th, 1996. Two people died and around thirty-nine others were injured. It also caused eighty-five million pounds worth of damage to the city's financial center. Sinn Féin tried to place the blame on the British Government to cover the fact McCaffrey had gone rogue. After the Belfast Agreement, things settled down for a while until Danny set off another bomb in August of 1998 in the North Ireland town of Omagh. That one killed twenty-nine people.

"That's when public support for the cause started to fade. McCaffrey became a pariah and targeted for elimination by the more moderate leadership of the IRA."

"So, he basically left to survive, not to keep the cause alive."

"That's what Captain O'Shay told me."

"How would he know?"

McGill smiled. "He did not admit it, but I think our Captain O'Shay was part of that moderate IRA leadership. He knew details about the bombings, MI5 and MI6 have never learned." After a brief pause, he continued, "According to the father, Paddy O'Shay was enamored with Danny McCaffrey at first. He followed the man out of Ireland, but suddenly returned six months later and asked his father to get him into the Merchant Marines. John

O'Shay didn't hesitate. He made a few calls and Paddy was inserted into an apprenticeship the next day. That's why MI5 never realized he returned. He was at sea almost immediately. Now he's an experienced cargo ship captain."

"If he's been helping Danny McCaffrey travel unnoticed for the past decade or so, it will end his career."

"Uh, maybe not."

Wolfe smiled at the Scotsman. "What did you agree to?"

"I didn't really agree to it, but after thinking about it, his proposal made sense."

"I'm listening, Ian."

"Now, granted, John O'Shay is trying to save his son, so I get that. But he suggested we use him as bait to capture McCaffrey."

"We don't know that's how McCaffrey's traveling around the world without being spotted."

"It is."

Wolfe folded his arms. "O'Shay told you?"

A nod from McGill. "The son is scared to death of McCaffrey. Apparently, something happened that he holds over Paddy's head. The father did not know what it was, but it must be pretty serious."

Wolfe concentrated through binoculars at the silhouette of the cargo ship *Shining Star*. "Where's it registered?" he asked without taking his eyes off the vessel.

Captain Arron Newman of the HMS *Defender* referred to a computer screen on the bridge and said, "Its flag of convenience is Panama, owned by an Italian shipping conglomerate and based out of the Port of Calais."

With a smile, Wolfe took his eyes away from the binoculars and chuckled. "You're kidding."

The skipper returned the smile. "Very common business practice of merchant ships. Forty percent of the world's cargo vessels are registered in Panama, Liberia and the Marshall Islands."

"Calais makes sense. That's where McCaffrey disappeared."

The captain folded his arms and turned to Ian McGill. "Do you two want back up when you board?"

"Aye, captain. A couple of your lads with SA80s would be wonderful. Also make sure we have a few mini-guns trained on the vessel."

"You expecting trouble?"

McGill shook his head. "Not unless McCaffrey's on board. We hope he is. Makes our job easier."

"What are the odds?"

Wolfe, still studying the ship through binoculars, said, "Best guess—not very good."

HMS *Defender* approached the *Shining Star* at thirty knots. The cargo ship maintained a constant twenty-four knot pace as the British destroyer drew alongside and matched the vessels speed. Over the ship's communication link, the conversation between the *Defender's* captain and the captain of the *Shining Star* grew tense during the first few minutes of the conversation. However, after the captain of the *Defender* explained the consequences of the *Shining Star* not adhering to the demands of Her Majesty's Royal Navy, the cargo ship slowed to a stop and agreed to allow a boarding party to come aboard.

———————

Captain Newman turned to McGill and smiled. "I believe it is now your show, Sergeant Major."

With a handshake, McGill said, "Aye, captain. Don't go away."

"Wouldn't think of it."

Since the HMS *Defender* had recently been on patrol in the Persian Gulf, the only battle dress uniforms on the ship were in desert camouflage. Wolfe and McGill wore these without any rank or unit insignia adorning the shoulders or chest area. Wolfe carried his Walther PPK in a concealed holster inside his waistband and a Springfield 1911 A-1 .45ACP in a hip holster. While familiar and proficient with the weapon, he preferred his PPK.

McGill placed a SIG Sauer P226 in his hip holster, adjusted his cap and glared at Wolfe. "You're not wearing a beret?"

Wolfe's eyes narrowed. "I was a US Marine. We don't wear them."

With a chuckle, McGill tossed Wolfe a beige beret. "You're on one of Her Majesty's Royal ships. Stop whining and put the bloody thing on." He turned and walked out of the ward room with Wolfe adjusting his beret as he followed.

The Wildcat HMA2 naval helicopter sat on the flight deck at the stern of the *Defender* with its rotor turning leisurely waiting for its two final passengers. As they climbed aboard the aircraft, Wolfe noticed four-stern faced young men bearing the rank of petty officers sitting ramrod straight holding their SA80-A2s tightly. He also noted a helicopter crewman manning a Browning M3M heavy machine gun pointed out the left side of the aircraft.

McGill placed a headset over his ears and motioned Wolfe to follow suit. When Wolfe had his in place and the microphone positioned properly, the Scotsman said, "These lads were handpicked by the captain." He turned his attention to the four young men. "Heads up, lads, this could get interesting."

The rotors of the helicopter spooled up and the pilot turned to look at McGill, who gave him a thumbs up. The craft lifted from the helo deck and nosed over toward the *Shining Star*, a hundred meters to the west.

With a steady twenty knot wind out of the north, the pilot expertly flew the craft and hovered over the cargo ship's stern. Four ropes were released and the four petty officers rappelled down to the deck below as the machine gunner trained the M3M on anybody attempting to ambush the descending men.

Wolfe and McGill followed down the ropes to join the men standing guard. Once they were safely on the ship, the helicopter rose and hovered menacingly off the stern with the M3M pointed at the ship's conning tower.

Captain Patrick O'Shay refused to shake the hands of the two men standing in front of him on the ship's bridge. His arms were folded and he displayed an intense scowl. "So, what's this intrusion by Her Majesty's Royal Navy about? My company will be lodging a protest about this illegal stoppage."

McGill smiled. "Ya might want to rethink that protest, Paddy."

The captain's eyes widened with the use of his nickname. But he quickly returned to a harsh frown.

The Scotsman continued. "We want to know where Danny McCaffrey is hiding."

"Who?"

"Don't play games with me, laddie. We know more than you think we do."

"I don't know anyone named Danny McCaffrey."

"Not according to your father." McGill's penetrating stare did not waver from the younger captain's face.

Wolfe stood next to McGill and studied O'Shay's reaction. The ramrod straight posture and jutting chin seemed to wilt at the mention of elder ship captain. He recovered slightly and placed his hands on his hips. "My father is an old man whose grasp of reality is slipping."

"He seemed pretty sharp when I spoke to him the other day."

There was silence on the bridge as the two men stared each other down. Finally, Captain O'Shay relaxed and turned away from McGill toward the front of the bridge. "Danny McCaffrey died a long time ago. My father's fantasies are exactly that—fantasies."

Wolfe handed McGill a piece of paper with an image printed on it. With a glance at the picture, the ex-SAS operative offered it to the captain. "Doesn't look dead to me."

O'Shay turned back and accepted the piece of paper.

The picture was a security camera image of Danny McCaffrey stepping off the gangplank of a ship. Clearly visible was the word *Star* in the upper left corner of the image. McGill said, "Care to comment?"

The captain considered the picture and maintained his scornful scowl. He handed it back to McGill. "So." He paused briefly. "There are hundreds of ships whose name ends in *Star*."

Wolfe said, "That picture was taken by a security

camera at the Port of Cartagena five weeks ago. Two weeks later, fifty-one people died in a mountain hacienda from unknown causes. The unknown cause turned out to be a biological weapon developed by the Iranians in a lab near the Caspian Sea. Your buddy McCaffrey was at the Iranian lab and in Columbia." He paused for a reaction as he studied O'Shay. When the captain displayed a neutral expression, Wolfe continued, "We also know that McCaffrey is in possession of additional quantities of the bio-weapon. Since that picture proves he came to Columbia via your ship..."

McGill added, "That makes you an accomplice to the deaths of fifty-one souls, Paddy, me boy."

The only response was the captain's eyes switching back-and-forth between Wolfe and McGill. With beads of sweat now forming on his upper lip, O'Shay took a deep breath and let it out slowly. "I didn't know..."

"Where is he, Paddy? And don't lie to me again." McGill's hand was on the butt of his Sig Sauer still in its holster.

O'Shay studied his shoes as a drop of nervous perspiration dripped off his nose. He looked up at McGill and Wolfe. After taking a deep breath, he blew it out slowly. "I'll tell ya what I do know."

On the helicopter ride back to the HMS *Defender*, McGill turned to Wolfe, adjusted the microphone on his headset and said, "Where'd you get the picture of McCaffrey getting off the boat in Cartagena?"

Wolfe pulled the picture out and looked at it. He pointed to the figure of McCaffrey. "That's a picture of him from a security camera captured in Tel Aviv." He smiled and handed it to McGill. "The picture of the ship is from an actual security camera shot in Cartagena. Nadia is becoming quite adept with Photoshop."

McGill laughed.

Chapter Thirty

The explosion occurred at twelve minutes past two in the morning. The resulting fireball could be seen from Cartagena ten kilometers to the west. Later, it would be determined the blast was caused by a ruptured propane supply line leading into the rural hacienda. The conflagration consumed the structure rapidly due to additional propane supplied by the tank and the amount of wood used to build the home. The only survivors were the guards who kept unwanted visitors from surprising Don Jose Herrera while he slept. Those guards helplessly watched the hacienda burn. Unable, or unwilling, to assist those inside, they silently melted into the surrounding countryside before first responders could arrive.

At almost the exact same moment the explosion destroyed the Herrera hacienda, the first body of the cigar boat's crew slipped into the water. The second one followed immediately. Danny McCaffrey surveyed the ocean-going craft in the moonlight. Capable of speeds approaching eighty knots, it could outrun most of the ships the Coast Guard might utilize to pursue it. It was also invisible to land-based radar. Only a helicopter or the chance meeting with a Coast Guard cutter would allow his presence to be known.

After the last body of the three-man crew slipped under the surface, McCaffrey addressed the cargo. With a sharp knife, he made a slit in each bundle before easing it off boat's stern. When this task was completed, he eased the idling boat away from the area and headed north toward Key West. With luck he might make it unnoticed, but if he did, there was no longer any illegal drugs onboard. While being stopped by the Coast Guard would complicate his arrival in the United States, it would not be catastrophic.

The only problem would be if stopped, the searchers might find the small vial of Iranian bio-weapon he had hidden within the engine compartment. He possessed an American passport proclaiming him to be Bryan McNeal, a nationalized Irish American from Boston. He also possessed over twenty thousand dollars in his backpack.

Navigating with the boat's GPS system, he kept the running lights off, pushed the boat to its maximum speed and headed toward the docks at Key West two hundred nautical miles to the northeast. With a waning crescent moon a quarter of the way up the eastern sky, he settled in for the two-and-a-half-hour voyage.

Colombian National Police Capitán Mario Artigas picked through the smoldering ashes of the now-leveled home of Don Jose Herrera. His assistant, Carlos Romero, followed him, taking pictures as they searched what little remained of the structure.

Romero pointed east of where they stood. "Capitán, the bodies were found over there."

Artigas looked in the indicated direction of the younger man. "I understand not much of them remained."

"No, sir. Larger bones and teeth were all that were found. They used the teeth to determine the identity of the victims."

"Has it been determined where the fire started?"

After a nod, Romero said, "The fire marshal told me a rupture in the propane supply line in the kitchen appeared to have been caused by a small explosive device."

A small smile appeared on the Capitán's face. "So, someone finally got to the Teflon Don."

"It would appear that way, sir."

"The first explosion occurred in the kitchen, yes?"

"*Sí*, the fireball caused the second floor to collapse immediately. The Don's bedroom was directly above the kitchen."

Artigas winced. "He and his wife probably never knew what happened."

"No one will ever know."

"Any other bodies?"

"One, sir. The remains of what is thought to have been a guard were buried under charred timbers near the staircase on the first floor. An AR-15 style rifle was found close by."

"Just one guard?"

"Only one body."

"Jose Herrera always had five or six guards protecting him." He looked at his assistant. "Maybe they are the ones responsible for this unfortunate accident."

"Is that what we will call this?"

With a smile, Artigas nodded. "*Sí*, I believe so. If we proclaim it to be an accident, hopefully the turf war that follows might be less severe. If we announce that Don Herrera was killed in a deliberate attack, the country will be plunged into a bloody battle. We don't need that right now. We will officially call this an unfortunate tragedy."

Ex-Chief of the Boat Rufus Carroll began readying his vessel for the fishing-charter scheduled for two vacationing couples from Kansas City, Missouri just before dawn. A sliver of sun peeked over the horizon as he made final preparations for the day's outing, scheduled to begin at eight later that morning. During his efforts, he noticed a sleek long cigar boat approach the dock. He stopped and stood to watch it maneuver into the dock area. Familiar with every boat stationed at this dock, he did not recognize this particular one.

With a frown and an enhanced sense of curiosity, he stepped off his boat and walked toward a slot designated for guest boats. As the boat entered the slip, Carroll waved and shouted, "Need a hand?"

The driver of the long boat nodded and lowered two inflatable fenders over the side of the cigar boat. He then tossed Carroll the stern line, which Chief secured to a cleat. The man then shut off the engine and walked to the front of the boat and offered Carroll the bow line. When the boat was secure, the driver hopped off the bow and said, "Thanks. Where's the dockmaster?"

Carroll pointed toward a building at the end of the long

wooden pier. "There. Should be someone at the desk. Where ya from?"

"Miami."

With a nod, Carroll looked at the long vessel. "Nice boat. Are you here for some fishing?"

The boat driver did not answer right away and glanced around uneasily. "Uh, yeah, fishing."

Before Chief could say another word, the man turned and walked rapidly toward the dockmaster's building.

With a smile, Carroll shook his head. "Fishing, my ass. You've got something else planned."

He studied the boat and determined his first impression was correct. With a slight shrug, he returned to his boat to finish getting it ready for his clients.

As Carroll guided his craft into his assigned dock, he noticed the cigar boat still in the slip where it had docked earlier in the day. After bidding his guests goodbye and securing the boat, he walked to the dockmaster office and stepped in.

He waved at the receptionist, a middle-aged woman with sun-bleached hair and a deep tan, "Hi, Sheryl."

"Chief Carroll, how was the fishing today?"

"They got their money's worth."

"Good. What can I do for you?"

"The cigar boat in slot fifty-two."

"What about it?"

"I helped the guy dock this morning. He indicated he was here for some fishing. Thought I'd try to drum up some business."

"I wasn't here this morning when he registered. Let me see what I can find out for you. Fifty-two, right?"

Carroll nodded.

She started typing on her computer, paused, frowned and typed again. "Huh."

"What's wrong?"

"Nothing. It says here he brought the boat down for a potential buyer. Paid for a week with cash, told Harvey he was staying at the Marriott." She looked up. "Doesn't sound like he's planning on fishing."

"Guess I heard wrong. Thanks." He turned and walked out of the building and stared at the long boat tied securely in its slip. He mumbled to himself, "Like I said this morning, fishing, my ass."

He pulled out a cell phone from a pocket on his cargo shorts and searched for a number. He found it and pressed the send icon.

The call was answered on the fourth ring. "Wolfe."

"Michael, what would you say if I told you a guy with an Irish accent arrived in Key West this morning in an expensive cigar boat outfitted like a drug runner's boat?"

Chapter Thirty-One

By sunset, Florida's Bureau of Criminal Investigations and Intelligence, plus the Coast Guard were swarming over the cigarette boat, and under sections 932.701-932.706, F.S. of the Florida Contraband Forfeiture Act, seized it. Preliminary tests of several storage areas were off the charts with trace elements of cocaine and various other illegal drugs. Once the boat could be taken to a more secure location, further tests would find further evidence concerning the boat's utilization.

The local Marriott had no record of anyone checking in matching the description of the boat's owner, nor did any of the other hotels on the island.

Into this chaotic situation, Michael Wolfe quietly slipped into town around midnight and met with Carroll.

"Is this the guy?"

The ex-Chief of the boat studied the security camera shot of McCaffrey taken in Tel Aviv earlier in the year. "Yeah, that's him."

Taking a deep breath, Wolfe let it out slowly. "Shit." He

looked out the front window of Carroll's office and stared at all the halogen lights illuminating the slip still containing the cigarette boat. "McCaffrey finally made it here."

He handed Wolfe a piece of paper. "At least you know what name he's using."

After studying the page and looking up, Wolfe frowned. "Bryan McNeil."

"Yeah, Sheryl Kirby is the receptionist in the dockmaster's office. She gave me a copy of the rental agreement for the slip just before the cops arrived. That's the name on his passport. He paid cash for a week telling her boss he was waiting for a potential buyer."

"In other words, he's not coming back."

"Probably not."

They both stood at the window, watching the long craft being pulled out of the slip and tied to a Coast Guard tugboat. After the two vessels disappeared into the dark, the halogen lights were switched off and the area returned to the normal nighttime illumination by incandescent dock lights.

"What do you think, Chief?"

"I've seen this before, Michael. Those types of boats are fast. Some of the ones built for Formula One racing can go 140 miles per hour. The one they just took away was an older model, so I would say at minimum it had a top speed of at least 100 miles per hour. It was also stripped down for smuggling. McCaffrey either stole it or hitched a ride on it. If he hitched a ride, no telling what happened to the crew and the original cargo."

"Those were my thoughts. Will there be any way the Coast Guard can determine who owns the boat and where it came from?"

"Not if it's been used for smuggling. The serial numbers

on the engines might tell them who built the boat. But beyond that, probably not."

Wolfe nodded thoughtfully. "I was afraid you'd say that."

"Where do you think he'll go?"

"Only way he can go—north. I need to make a phone call."

Jerry Griggs sat in front of his boss' desk listening to a phone conversation the National Security Adviser had placed on speakerphone. Joseph tapped his finger on the desk as he listened. During the conversation his frown deepened and the tapping increased in tempo.

"So, you're telling me there is no way to know who owns the boat, Commander?"

"No, sir." Vice Admiral of the Atlantic Fleet, Mike Armstrong, continued, "The serial numbers on the twin Mercury's indicate it was built by the Cigarette Boat Racing company in 2008. The original owner and the boat disappeared off the coast of Florida in March of 2013. Now that the boat has been recovered, we can surmise it was ambushed by drug runners, the owner killed, and the vessel turned into a smuggling boat. There are traces of illegal drugs all over it."

"Any fingerprints?"

"Four distinct sets."

"Any IDs from those?"

"Only one. A known Columbian thug and smuggler—his name is Emilio Salazar—we've detained him a number of times. The others are not in our database."

"Commander, if you would be so kind as to send me

those fingerprints, I can have an agency check them against a more extensive database."

"Yes, sir. Where shall I send them?"

"To me, via email. Here is the address." Joseph recited his email and said, "Commander, this is a matter where I need your utmost discretion."

"I will need to inform the admiral."

"Yes, you will. Please have him call me after you speak to him."

"Yes, sir."

The conversation ended and Joseph turned his attention to the man sitting across from him.

Griggs said, "You suspect something?"

"My guess is one of those sets of prints will belong to Danny McCaffrey."

A nod was the response from Griggs.

"I'll send them to Chapman. I would think MI6 would have a sample of his fingerprints on file, somewhere."

"One would think so."

"Where's Michael?"

"Waiting to hear from us."

"Is he still in Key West?"

"Yes."

"Where's Nadia?"

"Babysitting Canfield and the Dawson woman in Missouri."

"Get them to Key West as fast as possible. They can start their search there."

"Yes, sir."

As Griggs stood to leave, Joseph said, "Jerry."

"Yes?"

"The president is leaving this afternoon for a two week stay at his home in California. When he gets back, there are a number of outdoor events he is scheduled to attend."

Remaining quiet, Griggs kept his gaze on his boss.

Joseph continued, "I have attempted to convince him that canceling them would be in his best interest."

"Let me guess—he refused."

As he nodded, Joseph inhaled deeply. After a long sigh, he said, "You've got two weeks to find McCaffrey and make him disappear, forever."

Griggs gave his boss a half smile, turned and walked out of the office.

Two hours later, after receiving the fingerprints from the Vice Admiral in a digital file, Joseph checked the time and realized it was mid-afternoon in London. He picked up his secure line and dialed.

The call was answered immediately. "Joseph, good to hear from you."

"I hope you still think that way in a few minutes."

"Nonsense. What can I do for you?"

"Do you have Danny McCaffrey's fingerprints on file anywhere?"

"Yes, have you found him?"

"We think he's in the States."

"Oh, dear. But you're not sure."

"No. We think he arrived in a drug smuggler's boat in Key West early yesterday morning. A witness told us the man was alone in the boat when it docked, but the Coast Guard found four sets of prints after the boat was confiscated."

"Go on."

"We need positive proof it was him."

"Send them. I'll have someone compare them immediately."

"Thanks, Jonathan."

"Smuggler's boat, huh?"

"Yes."

"Know where it's from?"

"Don't know yet."

There was silence on the line for several seconds. "Joseph, an old friend of McCaffrey is spilling his guts about him. He told us he let him off in Columbia and now that country has lost two major cartel leaders."

Joseph frowned. "Two? We knew about the bio attack. What else happened?"

"It appears McCaffrey's benefactor, Jose Herrera and his wife died in a tragic accident at their home West of Cartagena."

Joseph paused briefly. "When?"

"Four days ago. The bodies were identified only yesterday."

"Jonathan, I need the fingerprints checked immediately."

"They just showed up in my email. I'll get someone on it right now."

"Thanks."

The call ended and Joseph leaned back in his chair as he stared at the phone.

An hour and a half slipped by while Joseph concentrated on other duties besides the pursuit of Danny McCaffrey. When the phone buzzed, he glanced at the caller ID and grabbed the handset. "What did you find?"

"Joseph, I strongly suggest you curtail the activities of your president."

"You matched the fingerprints?"

"Yes, Danny McCaffrey was on that boat. Your president is in danger."

"Have you met President Griffin?"

"No, can't say that I have."

"There will be no curtailing. We'll just have to find him."

"Let me know if I can help."

"Where's McGill?"

"Port of Calais."

"Get him to the States to help Michael."

"Good idea."

Jerry Griggs arrived in Key West a little after sunset. Wolfe pulled to the curb in the passenger pick-up area after which Griggs threw his duffel bag in the back seat. As soon as he sat in the front passenger seat, Wolfe pulled away from the curb.

With a quick glance at the driver, Griggs said, "Fingerprints from the boat confirmed McCaffrey was on it."

Keeping his eyes on the traffic ahead, Wolfe nodded. "I could have told you that, but it's good to know for sure."

"McGill will be here in the morning."

"Good."

"How quick can you get Canfield and Nadia here?"

After a slow shake of his head, Wolfe glanced at Griggs. "We're wasting precious time here. McCaffrey disappeared two days ago and could be anywhere by now. Why are we meeting in Key West when we should be headed north?"

"Where do you propose we go?"

"Jacksonville. Canfield refuses to fly commercial and it would take me almost a day to fly there and back. Nadia rented an SUV and left five hours ago. She's driving them to Jacksonville. The trip is about sixteen hours, so I can have us there before they arrive."

"What about McGill?"

"He's a resourceful chap. He'll figure it out."

Chapter Thirty-Two

After leaving the dock, McCaffrey laid low in Key West. He spent a few hours in a small diner sipping coffee, eating breakfast and searching the internet on a cell phone. The phone was a throwaway taken from the body of one of the dead crewmen he dumped into the Gulf waters.

At a local discount store, he purchased a change of clothing and toiletries before checking into a small bed and breakfast establishment five blocks from the Earnest Hemmingway Home and Museum. There, after a shower, he slept for the next seventeen hours.

During breakfast the next morning, he overheard an elderly couple at the table next to him discussing their plans to leave by mid-morning. They would be driving back to Miami to catch a plane scheduled for departure in the after-noon. Both the man and woman spoke with a distinct British accent. As he listened, he realized an opportunity to travel north without leaving a trail had presented itself. He stood, went to his room and prepared to meet the couple at their car.

The couple's white Chevy Malibu, with the Dollar Rental sticker on the window, sat in the B and B's parking area. It had been easy to identify after McCaffrey observed the man load luggage a few minutes earlier. McCaffrey stood next to the driver's door when the couple approached their car. As they grew near, he bent over and placed his hand inside his backpack.

"Excuse me sir, I need to get into the car."

Looking up, McCaffrey smiled and the man returned the smile. "Sure, mate." He withdrew his hand from the backpack and held the Taurus 92 pointed at the man's chest. With a harsh Northern Belfast accent, he said, "Get in the car, both of you. I'm in the back. Don't yell and you won't get hurt."

The old man stared at McCaffrey with wide eyes and the woman, standing behind him, frowned. "Chester, tell this ruffian to let us be."

In a calm tone, the man said, "He has a gun, Mary."

"Oh, dear." She stamped her foot and whined. "I told you I didn't want to come to America."

McCaffrey motioned for the man to get in the car. "Hurry."

The trip north proceeded without incident as Chester drove stoically and Mary whimpered. It was somewhere on the Seven Mile Bridge when McCaffrey noticed no cars approaching or following. He said, "Stop the car. I'm letting you two out. You'll be able to catch a ride soon."

Pleased to be close to ridding he and his wife of the Irishman, Chester obediently stopped the car. After a moment's hesitation, he and Mary got out and huddled close to the side of the bridge. As McCaffrey approached the open door on the driver's side, he pulled the Taurus from behind his back and shot Chester and Mary with two shots each to the head. The force of the bullets pushed the man's head back so hard, he toppled over the waist-high concrete barrier on the side of bridge. Mary was pushed back, but being of shorter stature, she did not follow her husband over the wall. McCaffrey hurried to the dead woman and lifted the body over. He glanced down at the water and saw the woman slip beneath the surface.

McCaffrey said, "Serves you right for being damn British unionists." Without another thought, the last IRA insurgent got behind the wheel and continued his trek northeast to the mainland.

Parking the stolen car in the Allapattah Metrorail Station, he left the keys in the ignition with the expectation the car would be stolen within the hour. The ride on the Metrorail to the Brickell Station put him in the middle of the financial center of the city. From the station, it was a short walk to a private bank based in Geneva, Switzerland.

After presenting his letter of introduction to an assistant manager, he was escorted to an office in the center of the building and a meeting with Senior Vice President, Catalina Cazalla.

Introductions were made and after the shaking of hands, they both sat. She behind her desk and he in an expensive leather chair positioned in front of the desk.

"What can we do for you today, Mr. McNeil?"

"I will be in the States for the foreseeable future working on a project for my employer. The firm has deposited funds into this bank and my letter of introduction grants me access to those funds. They will be my operating capital for this venture."

The woman sat ramrod straight, her hands clasped and forearms on the desk. She just nodded.

"I need to add a name to the account. She is my assistant for our project and will need access to the account."

"Mr. McNeil, as a private bank, our goal is investment and wealth management, not transactional banking."

"I understand. One of the reasons the money is here is due to a long relationship between my employer and your home office in Geneva. However, if I am to do my job successfully, I will, at times, need access to those funds, as will my assistant."

"I see. We can set up protocols for quick access if that is what you require."

"It is."

"Very good. Can I have the account number please?"

McCaffrey recited it as she typed on a keyboard in front of a flatscreen monitor on the side of her desk. After studying the screen, a small smile appeared on her lips. She scribbled something on a legal pad and said, "Do you know what the average size your withdrawals will be?"

He shook his head.

"We can do it several ways. If you know when you will need funds and in what town, we can transfer money with an ACH Transfer. It takes about three business days, but there is a smaller fee for this type of service. On the other hand, if you need money the same day, we can do a wire transfer to the institution of your choosing. However, the fees for this service are much higher."

"Who should I contact for these services, Ms. Cazalla?"

She handed him a business card. "I would be happy to take your call."

He nodded. "Thank you."

A taxicab, paid for in cash, deposited him at Miami's largest car dealership at 3:35 p.m. By six, he'd taken possession of a newly leased Toyota RAV-4. The lease payments would be automatically withdrawn from the account at the Swiss private bank. The fictional company set up by an anonymous Iranian would be the lessee of the vehicle. McCaffrey's alias of Bryan McNeil appeared nowhere on the paperwork.

A stop at a Men's Warehouse location in North Miami provided a new wardrobe allowing the ex-IRA terrorist a more sophisticated appearance. It also gave him the opportunity to dispose of the clothes purchased in Key West. An additional stop at a local Walmart provided personal grooming supplies and a suitcase.

By ten that evening, he'd paid cash for a room in a small beach front motel near the town of Port St. Lucie and was on the road again by six the next morning.

His northward trek would take him through Jacksonville, Florida and beyond.

Chapter Thirty-Three

About the time Danny McCaffrey passed through Jacksonville heading north on Interstate 95, Michael Wolfe assisted Nadia with unloading the rented SUV. Jerry Griggs escorted Canfield and Marilyn Dawson to their rooms at a Spring Hill Suites motel north of the town.

Wolfe asked Nadia, "How was the drive?"

"Never ask me to do that again."

He chuckled. "Geoffrey can be difficult."

"I'm not talking about Geoffrey. Marilyn talked incessantly about the cities we passed through. She told me every little detail about Memphis, Birmingham, Atlanta and a few other towns I had never heard of. Apparently we passed through them."

"She was nervous around you."

"For fifteen hours?"

"Maybe she likes history?"

Nadia just shook her head.

"Did Geoffrey have any thoughts about where McCaffrey might go now that he's in the States?"

"No, he barely spoke during the drive."

"That's unusual. He normally has a lot to say."

"He probably couldn't because Marilyn was constantly talking."

With a smile, Wolfe closed the rear hatch of the vehicle and headed for the back entrance of the hotel with the luggage.

When they arrived at Canfield's and Marilyn's room, Wolfe noticed an agitated British ex-pat.

"What's wrong, Geoffrey?"

"Your Mister Griggs has informed me that McCaffrey hasn't been seen in three days."

"That's correct."

The two-room suite was large enough for Canfield to pace. He stopped long enough to ask Wolfe the question. After hearing the answer, he started pacing again. "Not good. Bloody not good."

"What are you talking about?"

"When Danny McCaffrey goes to ground, he becomes extremely dangerous."

Jerry Griggs stood off to the side, his arms folded. "How?"

Canfield stopped pacing again and stared at Griggs. "When McCaffrey goes anywhere, he will not do so until he has finances in place, contacts he can use and a way to travel that is hard or impossible to trace. In other words, he disappears." He paused for a moment. "And he doesn't care who he harms if they get in his way."

Wolfe said, "Apparently, you've seen this before."

A nod was his answer.

"Does he set it up, or do others?"

"Depends on who he's working for. When he was with

the IRA, he did. When he started working abroad, his bene-factors took over those arrangements."

With a tilt of his head, Wolfe asked, "Give us some examples?"

"When he was in spotted in Gaza City in 2001 for the first time, a source told me that McCaffrey traveled in and out of the Gaza Strip with ease. He always had access to large sums of money and underground contacts helped him infiltrate Israel.

"Same thing occurred when he went to Afghanistan in 2003. According to sources, he always had access to money and moved throughout the country without being harassed by the Taliban. Not easy for a Westerner in that country." He fell silent as he went to a window in the room. Staring out, his hands clasped behind his back, he took a deep breath and let it out slowly. "My fear is that the Iranians will be providing the necessary funds and contacts for him here in the United States. There are thousands of ex-pat Iranians here. Who knows if they are loyal to the current Persian government or not?"

Griggs pulled out his cell phone and walked to the suite's door. "I'll be in my room making phone calls." He left, leaving Wolfe and Canfield alone with the two women.

Wolfe asked, "Geoffrey, the United States has financial sanctions on Iran. How would they be able to provide McCaffrey with cash?"

After a backward glance and a sardonic smile, Canfield answered, "The sanctions your country placed on Iran are mostly symbolic. Imposed to placate the public, critics and the news media. In reality, those regulations have no teeth. The Iranian Ministry of Intelligence knows how to circum-vent any obstacle the US government levies. Trust me,

McCaffrey will have access to money. Money he can use to travel extensively without leaving a paper trail."

Nadia pursed her lips. "How would he travel? You can only rent a car with a credit card."

"True, but there are other ways."

"Such as?"

"Steal a car."

Wolfe chuckled. "Not a long-term plan."

"No, but it is a way."

"Agreed, but he will need to be in this country for an extended period if he waits for an opportunity to attack the president in an open-air event. Jerry told me the president is in California for two weeks."

"Planned or unplanned?"

"I'm told planned, but who knows?"

With a nod, Canfield turned his attention back to the window and the scenery outside the hotel. He was quiet for several minutes. "I would say we have two weeks to figure it out, Michael."

Griggs returned to the room with a grim expression. "Coast Guard recovered two bodies around the Seven Mile Bridge on Highway A1A. They were two British tourists from London who had been staying in Key West. Both had been shot in the head twice. Their rental car was found stripped and abandoned in a rough part of Miami yesterday."

Canfield grimaced. "Where in the head?"

"Forehead."

"Oh, dear."

Nadia asked, "What's wrong, Geoffrey?"

"McCaffrey likes to look his victims in the eye as he dispatches them."

Wolfe met Ian McGill at the Jacksonville airport and brought him up-to-speed as they drove to the hotel.

"So, we know he made his way to Miami."

Wolfe nodded.

"Anything since then?"

"Nothing."

"Basically, we're sitting on our arse while the lad makes his way willy-nilly around the country?"

"That's a good way of putting it."

The ex-SAS operative snorted. "We're wasting time."

"I agree. Got any ideas?"

"Thought you had an airplane."

"I do."

"Where is it?"

"Airport, here in Jacksonville."

"How many passengers does it hold?"

"Six—myself and five others."

"Then we need to find out where this guy is and get ready to move."

Catalina Cazalla reviewed the submitted paperwork from Topaz Consulting, LLC. The amount of assets deposited by the company into her bank was substantial. Plus, the initial appearance of those funds was recent. The visit by Brian McNeil a week after the sudden deposit and the equally sudden leasing of a car by the company seemed normal. Until this morning.

She reviewed the cash transfers from the account into various banks up and down the east coast. Three transfers, one to a bank in Savannah, Georgia, the next one to a Bank of America facility in Charleston and another one scheduled for a small bank in Myrtle Beach. All of the transfers were under ten thousand dollars. This fact gave her pause.

Being a Swiss bank, the rules of banking privacy were well stated in the banks charter. But she was an American first. She was not sure why the man calling himself Brian McNeil bothered her. Was it the poorly dyed black hair with red roots, the slight Irish accent, or the fact his clothes didn't match his demeanor or his level of sophistication? Something was wrong with the entire affair.

She picked up the handset on her desk phone and punched in the extension for the young man who kept the bank's computers running smoothly.

He answered immediately. "Paul Tyler."

"Paul, this is Cat."

"Hello, Ms. Cazalla."

"We received a deposit of thirty million dollars on the third of the month into an account owned by Topaz Consulting LLC."

"Yes, ma'am."

"Do you remember it?"

"No, ma'am, but I can look it up."

"Please."

She heard loud clicking as the young computer geek typed on his keyboard.

"Ah, here it is. What did you need to know?"

"Can you tell me where the deposit originated?"

"Uhhh…" He was quiet for a few seconds. "That's weird."

"What's weird, Paul?"

"The money came from a clearing house in Geneva, but

the original funds were from two banks in the Middle East and one out of Monterrey, Mexico."

"Can you trace the funds beyond those banks?"

"That's what's weird, I can't. Normally, I don't have any trouble doing that, but not with this transaction. I can see where they were deposited into the clearing house account and from which bank, but not beyond there."

"Do you see that often?"

"No, ma'am. Normally all of the transactions are visible."

"Could it be on purpose?"

"Maybe, but I would have to do more digging. Do you want me to?"

"Not at the moment. Thanks, Paul."

"Anytime, Ms. Cazalla."

The call ended and Catalina Cazalla tapped her finger on her lips as she studied the top of her desk. She picked up the handset again and dialed the number for a friend of hers who worked at the Federal Reserve Bank in Atlanta.

Chapter Thirty-Four

Evening had long since passed when Wolfe and Nadia retreated to their own room at the Springhill Suites. After a fifteen-hour drive and four hours conferring with Canfield, Dawson and McGill, Nadia went straight into the bathroom and took a long shower. When she emerged, she wore a Nike T-shirt, Under Armour running shorts and her long black hair wrapped in a towel.

As she made herself a cup of tea from the in-room coffee service, she said, "If McCaffrey is so dangerous, why isn't the FBI heading up his capture?"

"Because he's threatening the president, it's actually the Secret Service in charge."

While hot water dripped into a paper cup with the teabag, she turned. "We don't work for the Secret Service. Why us?"

He shook his head slightly. "Technically, you and I work for Joseph, which means we work for the president in a roundabout sort of way. Jerry explained it to me one night over a beer. We're kind of like a scalpel. While all the alphabet agencies have their hands tied by Congress and the Media, we don't. We can go in, do the dirty work and get out. No one knows we've been involved and we don't create additional problems. Besides, the Secret Service doesn't want the public to know a crazy ex-IRA terrorist is running around the country with a bio-weapon aimed at the president."

"What about the FBI?"

"Supporting role."

She took a deep breath, let it out with a sigh and crossed her arms. "In other words, we're expendable."

He walked over to where she stood and took her into an embrace. She hesitated to return the gesture at first, but then succumbed and held him tight. She whispered into his ear, "Go take a shower and then come to bed."

Two hours later, they lay in each other's arms as Wolfe caressed Nadia's hair. With the room illuminated by the parking lot lights from a small opening in the curtains, he could see a worried look on her face. He said, "No, we are not expendable."

"It feels that way."

"Nadia, you and I both know we work better by ourselves. That's how we were trained. The first time we have to answer to someone besides Joseph or Jerry, we're done. We'll head back to our place and do something different."

"Let's do that now."

He smiled as he kissed her forehead. "Not yet, maybe tomorrow."

She glanced at the digital clock on the nightstand. "It is tomorrow."

"Figure of speech."

She snuggled tighter against him but remained quiet.

"Are you worried about something?"

"I didn't tell you when you arrived back in Israel, but during the time you and Ian were trying to get out of Iran, I was monitoring communications in the northern part of the country. I did not sleep, barely ate and realized I did not know what I would do if you never came back." After a brief pause, she broke from his embrace and rose up on one elbow to look at him. "I was terrified, Michael. I do not wish to feel that way again."

"We've had this conversation before, Nadia. We can quit anytime you want."

"I know."

"And?"

"I am French, Michael, I like to complain."

"And I love that about you. But…"

"I do not wish to quit right now. But I want you to be careful."

"I—we, will both be careful."

"Something else happened during the time I listened to phone calls."

"If I remember correctly, there was a lot happening."

She ignored the sarcasm. "It was the day you called. About three hours before we spoke, I thought I heard a familiar voice talking in Farsi."

"Whose voice?"

"That was what was weird about it. I thought it sounded like Daniella Weiner."

With a frown, Wolfe sat up and studied her dimly lit face. "Are you sure? Why didn't you say something earlier?"

"Because I wasn't sure. I dismissed it as being my imagination. The situation was wrong and the context of the conversation did not make sense."

His frown disappeared and he chuckled slightly. "Just because you don't trust her doesn't mean she's a spy, Nadia."

"That is why I didn't mention the conversation until now. But now that we know McCaffrey's in the States, the words I heard make sense."

"What did they say?"

"The voice I thought was Daniella kept talking about money being sent to a bank in Miami."

Jerry Griggs joined Wolfe and Nadia in the breakfast area of the hotel the next morning. He sat a cup of coffee on the table before taking a chair. "We had a development last night."

Wolfe raised an eyebrow. "What?"

After taking a sip of the coffee, Griggs smiled, "Guess."

Nadia chuckled. "Jerry?"

Setting his coffee cup down, he leaned forward. "I got a call from Tom Stanton, who is the Assistant to the Special Agent in Charge of the presidential detail early this morning. The Secret Service Field Office in Atlanta received a call from the Federal Reserve Bank about a possible link to McCaffrey."

With a frown, Wolfe took a sip of coffee. "I thought they were keeping a lid on who knows about McCaffrey."

Nodding his head slightly, Griggs continued, "They are, but because of his position, Stanton is one of the individuals who knows about him."

"Okay, got it. Go on."

Griggs took another sip of coffee. "Apparently, a Geneva based private bank in Miami received a substantial deposit about two weeks ago. A man showed up at the bank four days ago with the appropriate paperwork to claim the deposit. He set up arrangements to transfer funds from the private bank to other financial institutions."

"Jerry, skip the history lesson, why did the Secret Service call you about this?"

"Because the guy had black hair with red roots, spoke with an Irish accent and is depositing less than ten thousand dollars in numerous banks up and down the east coast."

Wolfe blinked several times as he stared at Griggs. "Shit."

Nadia said, "What's so special about under ten thousand dollars?"

Turning his attention to his wife, Wolfe said, "Any cash transaction over that amount requires Form 8300 to be filled out. That's the rule under the Currency and Foreign Transactions Reporting Act, started in 1970, that states all banks must report any deposits or withdrawals over ten thousand dollars to the Internal Revenue Service. The law was enacted to help identify illegal drug transactions."

Griggs chuckled. "And we've seen how well that's worked."

"There are ways around everything, Jerry. Go on."

"There were four deposits arranged, two have been collected and another one for today."

After taking a sip of coffee, Wolfe asked, "Where?"

"Myrtle Beach, South Carolina."

"He's collecting funds on his way to Washington."

"That would be my guess."

Wolfe glanced at his watch. "At this point, it isn't

possible for us to get to Myrtle Beach in time to intercept him."

"I'm aware of that."

"We only have the one picture from Tel Aviv to go on. I'm not sure I would recognize him."

Nadia asked, "What about security camera images at the banks he's visited?"

Griggs dry rubbed his face. "He knew where the cameras were. His face is obscured at the two locations he's already been too."

"What about the location scheduled for today?"

"Joseph has requested we be involved to make sure we identify the right person."

Wolfe tapped the tabletop with his index finger. "Jerry, Canfield would be able to identify him. Where's the fourth deposit scheduled?"

Griggs placed a piece of paper on the table and slid it to Wolfe. "Greensboro, North Carolina day after tomorrow."

After staring at the paper with the bank name and address, a small smile appeared on Wolfe's face. "Get everyone packed and checked out. As soon as I can determine the best airport to use, we can be there by afternoon."

The Universal Bank location in west-central Greensboro sat on the northeast corner of a busy intersection. Across from the site, a Panera Bread served the local business and residential areas of the surrounding community. As a spot known for its coffee and healthy casual dining, it also served as a go-to spot for busy individuals who need a Wi-Fi connection for work or a meeting with coworkers.

Danny McCaffrey sat next to a window, his back against

a wall, with a full view of Universal Bank. A laptop sat in front of him, but he paid it little heed. He was making sure nothing out of the ordinary took place at the bank, which held $9,678.00 in US dollars for him to retrieve.

The tables around him filled, emptied, and filled again as he sipped coffee and occasionally took a bite of a turkey-bacon-avocado sandwich. So far, he saw nothing out of the ordinary at the bank.

The time approached eleven-thirty when two young women in their early twenties, each with name badges identifying them as employees of Universal Bank, sat at a table next to him. Their conversation gained his attention immediately.

"How long have they been there?" The tall one with long blonde hair placed her drink and her order sign on the table as the shorter dark-haired woman followed suit.

"I got to work at nine and they were huddled in the branch manager's office."

"Who do you think they are?"

The dark-haired girl shook her head. "Don't know. One has a British accent."

McCaffrey's attention increased when he heard about the accent.

The blonde took a sip of her soda. "My grandmother is from Scotland and the mean-looking guy talks just like her. I bet he's from there."

"Probably. The other one is the mystery guy. I haven't heard him speak, yet."

"He's cute though."

"Ew—he's old enough to be your father, Linda."

"Yes, but he's still cute."

"Whatever."

McCaffrey stopped listening, stared at the bank across

the intersection and frowned. He had close to thirty thousand dollars cash in his possession. He would have to figure out how to get more soon, but avoiding any possible trap was more important.

He closed the laptop, placed it in his leather satchel, stood and walked out of the restaurant, the thought of collecting his money from this location abandoned. As he approached his car, he took a recently purchased cell phone from his bag. Once inside the SUV, he dialed an international number.

After the phone call, he parked in an obscure location across from the bank to observe the individuals leaving. After the bank closed, he recognized one of the individuals who walked out. The man with the British accent, the two girls mentioned, was indeed from England. McCaffrey recognized him immediately even though it had been over fifteen years since he had last seen the man.

Geoffrey Canfield stood outside a large Ford SUV, talking to two other men for several minutes before they all entered the vehicle and drove away.

The Toyota RAV 4 followed.

Chapter Thirty-Five

After observing passengers depart from the Greensboro Station for several hours, McCaffrey studied a woman in her mid-fifties wearing a stylish navy-blue pant suit, silk blouse and large leather bag hanging from her shoulder on a long strap. He made his decision after a quick glance revealed she did not wear a wedding ring on her left hand.

He laid the newspaper he was pretending to read on the bench next to him and stood. She walked with a confident stride toward the station exit and the parking lot beyond.

Quickening his pace, he caught up with her as she arrived at a car, he suspected was hers—a dark gray BMW M4. He approached just as she opened the driver's side door and prepared to enter. With a swift move, he shoved her into the car hard enough to cause her head to hit the opposite door.

Slipping into the driver's seat, he shoved her legs upward, causing her head to be forced onto the floorboard under the glove box. He located the keys she dropped on the middle console. Before starting the BMW, he retrieved a device resembling a remote garage door opener from his front pants pocket. Backing the BMW out of its parking space, he drove past the RAV4 and pressed the button on the remote. A small flash could be seen in the SUV. He then tossed it into the back seat. Where it landed, he did not care.

A few blocks from the train station, the woman started to moan. He pointed the Taurus 92 at her and said, "Stay quiet."

Another moan.

"Stay quiet and you won't get hurt."

Greensboro Police Department Patrolman Bob Johnson could see a flickering glow in the sky as he accelerated his Ford Police Interceptor toward the location. With red lights flashing and siren at full volume, he approached the J. Douglas Galyon Depot known as Greensboro Station. It contained the Amtrak depot in downtown Greensboro and also served as the city's main hub for regional and city buses.

As he slowed, he cut the sirens, but kept the light bar on replacing the rotating red lights for blue. Stopping a safe distance from the burning Toyota RAV4, he stepped out of the patrol vehicle, keeping it between him and the fire.

He spoke into his shoulder mic, "ETA of GFD this location."

The dispatcher replied, "ETA GFD, two minutes."

"Roger. Request an ambulance."

"Body?"

"Not sure yet, but you never know."

"Roger."

Five minutes later after the Greensboro Fire Department arrived and doused the remaining flames, Johnson peeked inside the vehicle and sighed with relief at seeing no evidence of a burned body.

A fireman walked up to Johnson. "Hey, Bob."

"A little excitement tonight, huh, Mike?"

With a nod, the fireman said, "Did you look inside yet?"

"I glanced, didn't see a body. What'd you see?"

"Flashpoint."

"A flashpoint?"

Mike Cannon, a ten-year veteran of the Greensboro Fire Department, nodded. "Yeah, it wasn't an electric fire and didn't originate in the engine compartment like most vehicle fires. It started on the driver's seat. I'll show you."

———

Jerry Griggs studied the inside of the burned Toyota RAV4. He bent over and sniffed several times. He straightened and glanced at the VIN number on the dashboard. He then stepped away from the vehicle.

As the sky lightened in the east with the approach of dawn, multiple police units, two firetrucks and a growing contingent of ATF officers milled around the burned-out SUV.

Griggs approached the policeman identified as the first responder and asked, "When did you get here?" He glanced at the officer's name patch. "Officer Johnson."

"Little after two a.m."

"Were there any other cars around it when you arrived?"

"No, it was isolated by itself, like you see here."

"Did you smell anything out of the ordinary when you arrived?"

The police officer pursed his lips and stared at the burned SUV. "No, I don't recall smelling anything out of the ordinary. Why?"

"Just curious. Thanks." Griggs walked toward three men standing off to the side away from the commotion surrounding the vehicle.

Ian McGill said, "What do you think?"

"VIN number matches the vehicle identified by the private bank in Miami. I also smelled something that reminded me of my time in Afghanistan."

One of Canfield's eyebrows rose. "Can you get me close enough to smell it?"

With a nod, Griggs escorted the ex-MI6 operative toward the car. When they returned, Canfield looked agitated. "It was McCaffrey. Diethyl ether is his trademark accelerant. Low ignition point and it leaves a sweet smell which is all over the inside of the SUV."

Wolfe stared at Canfield for a few moments. He extracted his cell phone from his jeans pocket, turned from the group and dialed as he walked away. When the call was answered, he said, "Nadia, check to see if the money is still at the private bank in Miami."

"Okay, give me a minute."

"I'll wait."

He heard clicking on a keyboard as she used their access to the account given to them by the bank. As she typed, he stared at the Toyota, waiting for the answer he expected.

"It's gone, Michael. Balance in the account is zero."

"Kind of what I thought. McCaffrey knows we're on to him."

"What do I need to do?"

"See if you can trace it."

"Not sure I remember how."

"If you need it, you know who to call."

"Okay, if I need to, I'll use it. But..." The call went silent as Wolfe displayed a slight grin. "Michael, I think I remember how. I'll call you back."

Ian McGill watched as Wolfe returned the cell phone to his jeans pocket. "What're ya thinking, laddie?"

"He knows about us."

"Agreed. But how?"

"Don't know. Nadia just checked the bank account in Miami and it's been emptied."

"Which way do you think he went? North or south?"

Looking McGill straight in the eye, Wolfe said, "Neither. I have a feeling this was another diversion. He didn't take the train. He just wants us to think he did."

With a slight tilt of his head, McGill grinned. "Aye, what makes you think that?"

"He hasn't been predictable so far and we need to stop thinking he will be."

"Michael, we can't sit around waiting for him to make a mistake."

"No, I agree."

"So how do we find someone who seems to be one step ahead of us all the time?"

Wolfe's eyes narrowed. "Why's McCaffrey here in Greensboro?"

"Not following ya, mate."

"Why here?"

"He had money to pick up."

"Yes, I know, but why burn your own car? Why here?"

"Haven't a clue."

"You're right, we don't know, but North Carolina has a very high concentration of individuals with Irish descent. What if one of the individuals who left with McCaffrey is in the area?"

"You're speculating."

"Yes, but what else do we have to go on? He's here for a reason."

With a hard stare, McGill finally nodded. "I'd have to agree."

"Let's have Jerry check with the local police to see if someone failed to return from a train ride."

Ashley Snow felt disoriented. Being upside down with her head in the BMW's foot-well did not help. She heard a male voice telling her to be quiet with an accent she did not immediately recognize. Her body remained contorted with her facing away from the driver. "Who are you?"

"Shut up."

She tried to turn to get a look at her assailant.

"It would be wise for you to not turn, lady. The less you see of me the healthier it will be for you."

She stopped trying to move and kept her face away from the driver. With as calm a voice as possible, she asked, "Are you going to rape me?"

"If you don't shut up I will. *Now be quiet.*"

As tears welled in her eyes, Ashley Snow wondered if she would ever see her sons and grandchildren again.

Wolfe stood gazing out the Embassy Suite's window in their room as a plane took off from Piedmont Triad International Airport. His eyes tracked the path of the Boeing 737 as it climbed and disappeared into a cloud.

Turning slightly, he watched Nadia sitting at the small desk in the room working on a laptop computer. "What are we missing, Nadia?"

Raising her head, she stopped typing. "Concerning?"

"McCaffrey."

"Lots of things. But you know that. Why do you ask?"

He smiled ever so slightly and returned his attention to the window. "Yes, I'm aware we don't know a lot. It's been two days since his car was found burned out and he hasn't surfaced. Why is that?"

"I don't know."

"Neither do I, but I can guess."

She stood and walked up beside him. He immediately placed his arm around her shoulders.

He continued, "He hasn't surfaced yet because he's holed up somewhere and just waiting."

"What if he isn't here? What if he's stolen a car and hundreds of miles away?"

"I don't think he did."

"How do you know?"

"I don't know for sure, but I do know he's smart. If he steals a car, he runs the risk of being stopped by the police. There's a nationwide BOLO out under his real name and the name he leased the car under. He can't board a train, rent a car or fly commercially without using an ID. Police are looking for him up and down the east coast. If he stole a car, he would have been spotted by now. Therefore, I don't believe he stole a car."

Nadia put her arm around his waist. "That makes sense. How do we find him?"

"I think it's time Ian and I have another discussion with McCaffrey's friend the ship captain."

Chapter Thirty-Six

THE NEXT DAY

Standing in the shadows within an alleyway across from the small bar near Belfast's Harbor, Michael Wolfe watched the front door of the establishment and waited. The time approached midnight and the streets were deserted except for the occasional pub patron leaving or arriving.

Wolfe waited for one specific customer to leave—Patrick O'Shay, former ship's captain and now regular customer of this particular establishment. With a neutral expression, steady breathing and zero movement, he waited patiently, just like his days as a sniper. Twelve hours earlier he had boarded a Learjet at Joint Base Andrews for the fast trip to Ireland.

At fourteen minutes past midnight, the door of the pub opened and Patrick O'Shay stepped out. He looked up and down the street, paused, placed a cigarette between his lips and flicked a lighter. O'Shay inhaled deeply and exhaled the smoke through his nose. Turning to his left he stuck his free hand in his jacket pocket and set off toward his apartment.

After counting to ten, Wolfe left the darkness of the alley shadows and followed.

Two blocks later, as O'Shay tossed the cigarette in the street and placed that hand in his jacket pocket, Ian McGill stepped out from an alcove and stood in the path of the ex-captain.

"Little late to be walkin' by yourself, Paddy. You might get tossed."

O'Shay recognized McGill and removed his hands from the jacket. "You! You're the reason I lost me job."

"No, you're the one who made the decision to help McCaffrey."

As O'Shay lurched forward to attack McGill, Wolfe came from behind, slipped a black hood over the man's head and kicked O'Shay behind his right knee. The Irishman collapsed as McGill rushed in to secure his arms.

A van screeched to a halt next to the three men. Wolfe opened the sliding side door and they threw O'Shay onto the cargo area floor. Both men scrambled in after the now-bound and blind Irishman.

Jerry Griggs sped away from the area before Wolfe could close the sliding door.

As they headed away from the harbor, O'Shay sat with his back against the van wall, his feet spread out in front and hands tied behind his back. The black hood remained where Wolfe had placed it earlier.

"Where you takin' me?"

McGill said, "We're going to a quiet little place where we can talk without being interrupted, Paddy."

"I don't know where he is."

"I don't remember asking a question."

"But that's what you want to know."

"Like I said, I didn't ask you anything. Now, shut up."

"Danny warned me about you guys in MI5. You're going to kill me, aren't you?"

"We're not MI5. And no, we aren't going to kill you. Although at some point you might wish we would."

O'Shay fell silent for several minutes. Finally, he asked, "Who are you, then?"

"Let's just say we are an international group of concerned citizens."

"Somehow I doubt that."

They arrived at the isolated farmhouse owned by British Intelligence a little after three in the morning. The only illumination came from the Fiat van's front headlights as Jerry Griggs stopped the vehicle close to the back door. Wolfe and McGill escorted their captive into the house while Griggs parked behind a neglected barn.

When Griggs entered the large room off the kitchen, O'Shay sat in a straight back wooden chair, his hands bound behind him and his feet secured to its legs. The black hood remained and his head slumped forward.

The room contained only one source of light and it separated O'Shay from the other three men in the room. Wolfe stood behind Griggs and McGill, his arms folded, staring intently at the bound man.

With his chin still resting on his chest, O'Shay said, "Do what you will. I'll not be talkin' to ya."

McGill displayed a slight grin as he stepped around the light and yanked the black hood off. "I told you, Paddy, we're not with MI5. We have other resources at our disposal to help persuade you that cooperating is in your best interest."

Squinting at the bright light, O'Shay remained quiet.

Wolfe stepped around the light and leaned over. With a menacing glare, he asked in a voice on the verge of a growl. "I want a phone number."

O'Shay snorted. "What makes you think I have one?"

Taking his cell phone out, Wolfe tapped an icon and O'Shay's voice could be heard. The background noise indicated he was in a raucous bar. "He's in the States." A muffled voice could be heard but not understood. "Aye, he needs money. His original plan fell apart."

With a touch of an icon on the phone, O'Shay's voice fell silent. Wolfe leaned closer. "Want to hear the rest of it?"

Staring at the phone, O'Shay looked up at Wolfe. "How?"

"You need to be more careful who you sit next to in a pub, Patrick."

There was a slight nod from the bound Irishman.

"Do you call him?"

"No, he calls me."

"What's the number?"

"Different burner each time. That's why I can't call him."

"What number does he call?"

A sly smile came to O'Shay's lips. "I forget."

Wolfe's mouth twitched as he stared down at the man in the chair. "You know, Patrick, I know a lot of ways to hurt a man. But, in your case, you probably wouldn't care because you've been through it before."

The smile did not leave the Irishman's face.

"My friend with the Scottish accent tells me you have several old colleagues looking for you. But since you've been at sea for at least a decade or more, they've stopped looking.

What if a little bird told them where to find you? Would that be of concern?"

The smile disappeared.

"Kind of what I thought. Care to tell me how McCaffrey makes contact with you?"

Nadia Picard Wolfe woke in the hotel room and reached over for Michael. His side of the bed was empty. With a heavy sigh, she remembered their parting embrace before he'd left for his flight to Ireland. The room felt empty and cold as she shuffled to the window to look out. Gray overcast skies and a steady rain greeted her, increasing the melancholy she felt.

After dressing and making a cup of coffee using the in-room machine, she sat at the computer and checked emails. Nothing from Michael.

Determined to get out of her funk, she Googled the name Daniella Weiner. After numerous attempts failed to find anything, her fourth attempt produced an interesting bit of information. Using a customized search engine, given to her by Alexia Gibbs, she found an obscure reference to a young Daniella Weiner who, along with her mother and father, had been killed in a Palestinian suicide attack in the mid-nineties.

On a hunch, she used a technique taught to her by Alexia over a year ago, to make a secure call to the head of Mossad's Counter Terrorist Division. When the call was answered, a cautious voice said, "Hello?"

She spoke in Hebrew. "Uri, it is Nadia Picard."

Her response was a hearty chuckle and a familiar voice

in the same language say, "Hello, Nadia. I will assume you are not in Tibet."

"No, a friend of Joseph's has been working with me on my computer skills."

"Good. I hope you are well?"

"Yes, as I hope you are as well."

"And Michael?"

"Off saving the world."

Another chuckle. "What can I do for you?"

"Sorry for the call, but I need a question answered."

"I will see if I can."

"Before I ask, it might offend you. If it does, I apologize, but there is a serious reason for my question."

A long silence ensued. "Go ahead."

"Where was Daniella Weiner born?"

"Neve Dekalim, a part of the Gush Katif settlement bloc in the Gaza Strip. Why?"

"So, she was born in a place that no longer exists, correct?"

"It was evacuated in August 2005 during our unilateral disengagement agreement with the Palestinians. Again, why do you ask?"

"How well do you know her?"

"Nadia, before I answer any more of your questions, you have to answer mine. Why do you ask?"

"Please, Uri, one last question. Then I will answer yours. What were her parents' names?"

"Josef and Noy Weiner. According to her personnel file, after they left Nev Dekalim, they immigrated to Florida in the United States. They were killed in 2010 by a drunk driver near Miami."

"Uri, Josef, Noy and five-year-old Daniella Weiner were killed in a Palestinian suicide attack in 1995."

There was an extended silence on the call. Finally, she heard, "Where does this information come from?"

"There is a digital copy of a newspaper in the archives of a group dedicated to the historic preservation of those that lived in the Gaza Strip settlements. A story about the attack was in their newspaper. I can send you a copy of the file if you wish."

"Send it."

Chapter Thirty-Seven

The fact she had not been assaulted by the man with the Irish accent gave Ashley Snow little comfort. The threat of being raped and killed hung in the air every time she had contact with him. Sequestered in the basement of the house she owned in Greensboro without being tied up or gagged caused her to be even more nervous. The closest neighbor lived at least a half mile away. The basement did not possess a window or exit except the one staircase leading to the ground floor. Banging on the door and screaming did little to change her situation so she'd stopped. Now in her third day of captivity, she wondered if anyone realized she was missing.

She and her late husband had purchased the house fifteen years earlier. Afterward they discovered anyone in the basement could hear every step someone took upstairs. This had always annoyed her. Now this flaw in the floor construction allowed her to monitor her captor's location at any given moment. She could tell when he was heading toward the staircase to the basement; she knew when he was in the kitchen and she could distinguish when he left the house.

Ashley stood at the top of the staircase and stared at the door, her frustration growing with each passing second. Her husband had replaced the simple six-panel door a decade ago with a soundproof metal door to keep the sound of their then-teenage son's video games from invading the upstairs. Instead of a door she could easily punch through, she faced an insulated steel barrier. Knowing her captor was currently away from the house increased her despair.

With a loud sigh and tears leaking down her cheeks, she descended the staircase.

Rural Country Side – Southwest of Belfast, Ireland

"He seldom uses the same cell phone twice and he's not told me how he obtains them. I never know when he is going to call either, so I keep my phone with me all the time. Once he's called, I delete the phone number."

Wolfe held O'Shay's phone in his hand and scrolled through the recent call register. He tossed it to McGill and said, "See if any of your buddies at MI6 can check the numbers that called it and see which ones are missing. The missing ones will be McCaffrey."

McGill grabbed the phone out of the air, nodded and walked out the back door of the farmhouse.

Turning to the still-bound Irishman, Wolfe continued, "Why's he calling you?"

"So, you are with MI6?"

"He is. I'm not. Now, why is he calling you?"

"CIA?"

"You're avoiding the question."

"He needs money."

"And?"

"I made a few calls."

"How much did you get him?"

"Couple of thousand. Danny still has friends in the community, not many but a few."

"A couple of thousand is a drop in the bucket compared to what he needs."

A nod was his answer.

Folding his arms, Wolfe said, "You're lying to us. Want to try again?"

"It's the truth, I swear."

Leaning over to be at eye level with the ex-terrorist, Wolfe glared. "I'm a patient man, Patrick, but your constant lying is getting old. Why is he calling you?"

"I told you."

Straightening, Wolfe glanced at Griggs and nodded toward the back door. "Let's go. This is getting us nowhere. We'll have our Scottish friend call Mr. O'Shay's ex-pals and tell them where he is."

Griggs headed toward the back door and Wolfe followed. Just as he was exiting the house, he heard, "Wait."

With a raised eyebrow, he looked at Griggs. "Check on Ian's progress with the phone. I'll see if our guest has reconsidered."

Standing in front of the bound man with arms folded, Wolfe waited, saying nothing.

"I need my job back. Then I'll tell you everything."

Wolfe gave him a sly smile, but only shook his head.

"I can't stay around here. I have to get back to sea."

"I don't think you appreciate your situation here, Patrick. We are not in negotiations."

"But I have information you need if you want to find Danny."

Wolfe shook his head slightly again, turned and walked toward the back door.

"McCaffrey isn't in the United States for the reason you think he is."

Stopping, the ex-sniper turned. "I don't recall telling you what I thought."

"He's not there to just kill the president. It's bigger."

Returning to the spot he'd occupied before, Wolfe said, "Go on."

"Will you get my old job back?"

"I'll think about it. Now what's bigger than killing the president?"

"He's planning to release his bio-weapon during a joint session of your Congress and kill everyone in the room. That's what's bigger."

McGill looked at the small house where O'Shay remained tied to a chair. "Do you believe him?"

"Not sure we have the option." Wolfe also stared at the structure. "What did you find out about the phone numbers?"

"They're working on it, but Chapman was told if McCaffrey is using burners, they'll be able to find the numbers, but that's about it."

"Will they be able to find out where the phones were purchased?"

"Yes—not that it will do us any good."

"You never know."

Several yards away, Griggs ended a call on his cell

phone and walked back to the two men. "According to Joseph, the only joint session of Congress slated in the near future is the State of the Union Address. It isn't supposed to occur until early February next year. That's over four months away."

"I doubt McCaffrey believes he can wait four months," said McGill.

Wolfe's attention had not wavered from the house. "Jerry, does the president have any meetings with foreign leaders in the next few weeks?"

"The President of Mexico is scheduled to be in Washington next week after the president returns from California. Why?"

"Is there a chance he'll ask for a joint meeting of Congress?"

Griggs stared at Wolfe for a few moments. "Shit." He took his phone out and walked away from the other two men. After talking on his cell phone for several minutes, he ended the call and returned. "All they are waiting on is for the Speaker of the House to set the date. It's not finalized yet. He wants to plead his case for starting a new joint effort with the US to curtail the drug traffic between the two countries."

With a frown, Wolfe said, "That plays in perfectly into the wishes of the cartels and Iran. Eliminate the US government and the Mexican President in one event." He paused for a few heartbeats. "Gentlemen, I believe we have to believe what O'Shay is telling us. Let's go see if we can get him to tell us what else he knows."

***

"Not until I have my old job as a ship's captain back."

McGill chuckled. "Paddy me, boy. If I remember correctly, you're the one that screwed the pooch on that one."

"Those are my terms. Take 'em or leave 'em."

Wolfe said, "Why do you want to get back to the sea so bad? Are you hiding from someone or multiple someones?"

"I liked my job."

"Not buying it. When I mentioned our Scottish friend was going to call some of your ex-pals, you freaked out and suddenly wanted to talk. Why is that?"

"I did not."

"Then you won't mind if we call them to give you a ride home?"

The look of terror lasted only a microsecond on O'Shay's face. He recovered and said, "Go ahead. You'll never know where McCaffrey is hiding if you do."

"And you know?" This from McGill.

"Aye, I do."

Taking a deep breath, Wolfe closed his eyes for a brief second. "I don't think you know. So, I'm not inclined to grant your wishes." He looked at McGill. "Call them. We'll take off as soon as they know how to get here."

With a nod, McGill walked out of the house to make his call.

O'Shay's eyes followed him until he was out of sight. He wet his lips and looked up at Wolfe. "You can't do that."

"Already did. Sorry, Patrick. We'll be miles away when the fun begins."

"Her name is Kayla Doolan."

"Where does she live?"

"Not sure. Danny never told me. She's part of a group that went to the States to raise money for the cause and never came back."

"So, she's been in the States for twenty years?"

"More than that—she left a few years before the Belfast Accords in 1998. They were married at one time."

Wolfe displayed a sly smile. "Married?"

A nod was his answer. "Word was she was pregnant. The child was born in Paris and given up for adoption."

"But you don't believe that."

A shrug. "They didn't get married in the church, so I'm not even sure it was legal. Danny McCaffrey is a lot of things, but he's a Catholic first. So, I doubt she was."

Silence fell over the room as Wolfe stared at O'Shay and shook his head slowly. When McGill stepped back in, he noticed the silence and remained quiet.

With an exasperated sigh, Wolfe said, "Patrick, I'm going to do you a favor. We're going to leave you now. Some of our friends will be here shortly to take you back. I'm sure they will have questions for you as well."

"I thought—"

"You thought wrong." Wolfe leaned over to be at eye level with the ex-sea captain. "These chaps are with MI5. They will have lots of questions for you, which will include a trip to a courthouse."

O'Shay's chin hit his chest as he slumped over. "Bloody American."

Chapter Thirty-Eight

Cruising at 35,000 feet, the Gulfstream G450 cut through the night sky on its flight path toward Joint Base Andrews at 475 knots. Michael Wolfe sat in the front starboard seat and stared out into the darkness. Although he could not see the full moon above the aircraft, he could see the vast ocean below him illuminated from its glow.

Jerry Griggs sat across from him, seat back and eyes closed. McGill remained in Ireland to oversee the official interrogation of Patrick O'Shay. Wolfe returned his attention to the scene outside his cabin window. His thoughts alternated from how to find Kayla Doolan to packing his Beechcraft and flying Nadia and himself back home.

As the internal debate leaned toward going home, his cell phone vibrated. He immediately accepted the call after seeing the caller ID. "I was just thinking about you."

"When will you land?" Nadia's voice did not have its normal playfulness.

"Not for another three hours."

"I'll pick you up."

"That would be great." He paused for a moment. "I was also thinking about us packing our bags and going home."

"I wish we could, but not yet."

"What's wrong?"

"We can discuss it when I pick you up."

As the rented SUV exited the grounds of Joint Base Andrews with Nadia behind the steering wheel, Wolfe turned to her. "You look tired. Want me to drive?"

She looked at him briefly and shook her head. "You're tired, too."

"It's five hours back to Greensboro. We can stop somewhere for the night."

"Kind of silly paying for two hotel rooms at the same time."

"True. Let me know if you want me to drive."

"I will. Jerry staying here?"

A nod was her answer.

"Are we on our own now?"

"No, he wanted to see his family for a few days. While he's doing that, we'll see if Canfield can finally make himself useful."

Nadia remained quiet for a few moments and then said, "I discovered some information about Daniella Wiener while you were gone."

He stared at her. The lights from the SUV's dashboard illuminated her profile. A profile he never grew tired of seeing. "Is that what you didn't want to discuss on the phone?"

She nodded.

"What'd you find?"

After a deep breath, she answered, "I finally remembered her."

"From where?"

"She worked for Asa Gerlis."

"Uh-oh."

A nod. "She was going to be my control, but then the incident in Barcelona occurred. I've never talked to her or had contact with her. She was just a name that I apparently forgot."

"Do you think that is why she acted so odd at our first meeting?"

Nadia nodded slightly. "There's more. While you were gone, my curiosity got the better of me and I started searching the internet for anything I could find on her."

Wolfe leaned back in the seat with his head against the headrest. "I'm not going to like this, am I?"

"I didn't. In 1995, a Palestinian suicide bomber blew himself up on a bus in the then Israeli settlement of Neve Dekalim, Gaza Strip. Among those killed was a family of three. Josef and Noy Wiener and their young daughter."

Closing his eyes, Wolfe knew what was coming next.

"The young daughter's name was Daniella."

"Does Uri know about this?"

"He does now." The conversation grew silent for a while as Nadia drove south. "I'm now positive the voice I heard talking to someone in Iran was Daniella."

"Did you tell Uri about the conversation?"

"No and I don't intend to until he determines her real identity."

"Probably best." He hesitated to say what he needed to ask her. But went ahead. "We have another mystery woman to find."

"Who?"

"Her name was Kayla Doolan when she left Ireland. There was a rumor she was pregnant with Danny's child about the time she went to Paris for six months. Apparently, she returned to Ireland for a brief period before she left for the US. After a few years, she disappeared and has never been heard from again."

"Could she be dead?"

"Possibly. If she's still alive, McCaffrey will try to find her."

Conversation in the SUV changed to a comfortable silence. Around four in the morning, just north of Lynchburg, Virginia, Nadia's eyes started involuntarily closing. Wolfe took over the driving duties and let her doze off and on for the next two hours.

When they arrived at their hotel in Greensboro, the scene they witnessed jarred both of them into full alertness. Multiple police cars, two ambulances and a GFD EMT Unit crowded the portico in front of the Embassy Suites.

With a growing sense of dread, Wolfe drove the Ford SUV around to the parking area behind the hotel. After parking the vehicle, they hurried into the first-floor entrance, where they were immediately stopped by a police officer. "Sorry folks, we have a medical emergency on this floor. You'll have to wait."

Wolfe glanced down the hall and determined the medical emergency the officer referred to was in Geoffrey Canfield's room. He extracted his US Marshal ID. "Officer, I am US Marshal Patrick Ryan and this is my partner US

Marshal Holly Harper. If the medical emergency is in Room 166, we're already involved."

The police officer stared at the IDs and then at Wolfe and Nadia. He then nodded for them to follow him. When they got to the room, the policeman spoke in a low whisper to a plain clothed individual who stared at Wolfe and Nadia for a long time. He approached them.

"US Marshals, huh?"

Wolfe nodded.

"You know the occupants of Room 166?"

"Yes."

"Fugitives?"

Wolfe shook his head. "They were assisting us in tracking one."

"What're their names?"

"Are they alive or not?"

"Just answer my question."

"Geoffrey Canfield and Marilyn Dawson, residents of Grand Cayman Island in the US on a visa as consultants."

"Let me see your IDs."

Both Wolfe and Nadia obliged.

The plain clothed officer relaxed and said, "You can view the crime scene from the door. We haven't finished processing the room yet."

Wolfe stood in the entrance and saw the foot of the bed and a body on the floor at the end of it. Geoffrey Canfield lay on the floor like a ragdoll tossed to the ground. His eyes were open and a small dark hole appeared above the right one. "How many shots?"

"The man, only one. The female, two, one in the chest and the other to the side of the head. She apparently was already in bed when the intruder entered the room. We believe someone knocked on the door. The man opened it and was shot. Then the suspect entered the room and executed the woman. No one heard any shots—the only reason we were called is someone complained about hearing a woman scream."

"What caliber?"

"From the size, I would say a twenty-two."

With a nod, Wolfe said, "I need to make a phone call."

Chapter Thirty-Nine

Guilford County Sheriff Deputy Susan Milford pressed the doorbell button next to the front door of the rural home and waited. No answer. She tried it again with the same response. After the third time, she stepped back from the door and walked down the wrap-around deck toward a large picture window. As she peered in, she heard a muffled female voice beneath where she stood. She stopped moving and listened closer. Then she heard it—a woman's voice below the deck screaming for help.

She spoke into her shoulder microphone and said, "Car seventy-two, need assistance and possible ambulance this location. Wellness check discovered possible victim."

An hour later, Ashley Snow, hands shaking as she sipped tea, summarized her ordeal to two Guilford County detectives as she sat at her kitchen table. The two detectives sat across from her taking notes. A tall, slender African-American stood off to the side, his arms folded as he listened to the woman describe her captor.

"He had black hair. You could tell it was a store-bought hair dye. You know, too black. Plus, you could see the red roots. I'm not an expert, but I believe his accent was Irish."

One of the detectives asked, "Did he assault you?"

She shook her head. "He threatened to, but he never did."

The female detective asked, "How long has he been gone?"

"He left just before noon yesterday. He hasn't been back."

The female deputy looked at the tall man standing off to the side. "Do you have any questions for Ms. Snow, Agent Griggs?"

"Yes, I do."

Ashley looked up at the man as she took another sip of tea.

Griggs asked, "Tell me again where he abducted you?"

"Train station in Greensboro."

"Why were you there?"

"I work in Washington, DC three days a week and from my home the other two. I was returning when he grabbed me."

"So that's why no one missed you for five days?"

She nodded.

"Thank you, Ms. Snow."

Griggs walked out of the house and glanced at the helicopter parked in an open field behind the large home. He took his cell phone and punched in a number. The call was answered immediately.

"What'd you find out, Jerry?"

"He's driving a dark gray BMW M4." He recited the license plate.

"I assume the police have this information?"

"You would assume correctly. National BOLO has already been issued. What's going on at your end?"

"No one saw the intruder. But you just confirmed something we saw on the hotel's security camera."

"What's that?"

"A dark gray BMW M4 was recorded driving past the hotel around one a.m., exactly twenty minutes before several first-floor guests reported hearing a woman scream. Five minutes prior to that, two men are seen entering the lobby. One goes to the elevator, the other heads down the first-floor hall. Security cameras do not record him leaving that way. But the ones in back catch him leaving out the back entrance."

"What about the man going to the elevator?"

"Just got back from staying with his mother in the hospital. He told police he passed a man smoking a cigarette in the smoking area. They think the intruder was standing there waiting to follow someone inside."

"Did the cameras get a good picture of the guy?"

"What do you think, Jerry?"

"He knew where the cameras were."

"Not a clear shot from any angle."

"What about the front desk. Did they see anything unusual?"

"At that time of night, a college student was the only one there. He was studying for a mid-term and wasn't watching the front desk too closely."

"So, nothing to identify McCaffrey at the hotel."

"Nothing, except the way Canfield and Marilyn were executed."

Griggs remained quiet for a few moments. "Where are you and Nadia?"

"We checked out. We're in a café called Anton's Coffee Shop, a couple of blocks from the Embassy Suite."

"I know where it is. I'll join you in about forty minutes."

The shabby office, located near the seaward cargo door of the warehouse, contained furniture from the 1950s, and smelled of human sweat, corroded steel and diesel fuel. The overweight man behind the military surplus metal desk in the cluttered office smiled at McCaffrey as he counted out hundred-dollar bills.

"Always a pleasure doing business with you, Danny. You always bring us the best cars."

McCaffrey remained quiet as he watched the counting process.

The fat man continued, "Per our agreement, the BMW's already in a container with a few others and will be loaded by midnight."

A nod was his response.

"Also, as we agreed,"—the man handed the stack of bills to McCaffrey "—five thousand cash."

"Considering you'll probably sell the damn thing to some Arab in Abu Dhabi for fifty-thousand, I'm getting screwed."

With a shrug, the car smuggler said, "I have expenses."

"Right. Where's the car you promised me?"

"It's an SUV, parked outside." He tossed a set of keys to the Irishman. "A black Kia Sportage, clean registration and a legit Virginia license plate."

"How'd you manage that?"

With a sly grin, the man said, "Trade secret."

McCaffrey smiled for the first time. "I'll be going."

"Always a pleasure, Danny. Like I said, the cars you bring us are always top notch."

Without another word, McCaffrey slung his backpack over his shoulder, exited the office and traversed the warehouse expanse to the parking lot outside. True to the smuggler's word, a black Kia Sportage sat waiting for him.

Back on Highway 58, he headed west toward south Interstate 95 and Raleigh, North Carolina.

Jerry Griggs sat next to Nadia in the booth and pointed at the menu. "Anything good?"

Wolfe sipped his coffee. "Best coffee I've had since we left Missouri. Burgers are good and Nadia liked the chef's salad."

The waitress, a fifty-something woman who would need two-inch heels to be five-foot tall, appeared by their booth and smiled. With a gravelly voice, she asked, "What can I get ya, hon?"

Griggs pointed at the menu. "Haven't looked. What's your special?"

"Everything."

He chuckled. "Okay, cheeseburger and a garden salad."

"Drink?"

"Coffee and ice water."

She left and Griggs leaned over the table. "We have a lead on Kayla Doolan."

With his coffee cup almost to his lips, Wolfe paused and raised an eyebrow. "Where?"

"Raleigh, North Carolina."

Nadia took her cell phone and thumbed something on the keyboard. She looked up. "It's a little over an hour east of here on I-40."

Wolfe asked, "How solid is your intel?"

"Immigration data from 1996. A Kayla Doolan came in on a student visa from Belfast and applied for citizenship in 1998. She became a naturalized citizen in June of 2001 under the name Kayla Callaghan." Griggs paused as the miniscule waitress set plates in front of him.

"Anything else, hon?"

He shook his head, "No, thank you." When she left, he continued, "I did one of those internet searches on her and found she's the owner of O'Dooley's Kitchen and Pub in Raleigh and has been since 2010. She's lived in the same house for the past twenty years and still has a mortgage on it. No convictions or even a traffic ticket. Apparently, she married someone by the name of Shamus Callaghan in 2000, but he is now listed as deceased. I couldn't find anything on him. For some reason, he's a black hole on the internet."

Nadia asked, "Did he even exist?"

"Good question. On the report I generated, his birth date was in 1980, but did not list the state. Couldn't find a death certificate either. My suspicions are he never existed and she used it to change her name."

"How would you do that?" This from Wolfe.

"Not sure. I did a similar report on myself to see how much I could trust the report. Employment info was accurate. Some of the other stuff, not so much. I think we can assume she owns the restaurant and where she lives."

With a frown, Wolfe asked, "Why not just have the FBI run a background check on her?"

"Joseph wants this kept within the family, so to speak." He paused. "For now."

"Got it. At least we know where she works and where she lives."

Griggs nodded. "So now what?"

"I think Nadia and I need to spend some time at an Irish pub in Raleigh."

Chapter Forty

O'Dooley's Kitchen and Pub occupied a standalone building in front of a busy strip mall on the east side of Raleigh. Even though the time approached five in the afternoon, there were few tables available at the popular spot. Wolfe and Nadia entered and were escorted to an out-of-the-way table in a corner of the dining room. To Wolfe's surprise, it possessed a clear view of the bar and half of the tables in the establishment.

Nadia looked at the menu with a scrunched-up face. "What are bangers and mash?"

Chuckling, Wolfe said, "Sausage served with mashed potatoes. Fixed properly, it's not bad."

"I am French, Michael. Sausage and mashed potatoes do not belong in the same sentence, let alone on a plate. I don't think I will try it."

"Probably best."

"My gawd, do the Irish not know how to fix anything without mashed potatoes?"

"Corn beef and cabbage is good."

Her nose scrunched again. "Other than that, what looks good to you?"

He did not answer as he stared at a woman in her late forties or early fifties talking to two men sitting at the bar. Slender and tall, her long reddish hair fell chaotically around her shoulders. All Wolfe could see was her profile. Her appearance depicted a note of elegance but at the same time suggested a hard life.

"Nadia, look at the woman standing behind the two men at the bar."

Taking her eyes off the menu, Nadia located the woman and said, "Do you think?"

"I'd bet on it."

He took a picture of her with his cell phone and sent it to McGill with the question: *May have found Kayla, can you confirm?*

It took McGill over an hour to respond. By that time, Wolfe and Nadia had finished their meal. She had ordered a salad, which she'd complained about and Wolfe had requested fish and chips, which he'd picked at and finally pushed away. As he read the text message, he looked up to see if the woman was still in the dining area. She was not.

"McGill showed the picture to Patrick O'Shay; he confirmed it's her. What other details are in the report Jerry sent you?"

"Not too much other than what he already told us. I Googled the business and found a newspaper article calling it one of the best Irish pubs in North Carolina."

"I'd hate to eat at the worst one."

Nadia glanced at Wolfe as he stared at the woman now standing behind the bar pouring a beer from the tap for a customer. "I take it you have a plan?"

"Not really. We need to know if she's still in contact with McCaffrey."

"How do we do that?"

"Have a private chat with her at her house."

The last employee left right at 10:23 p.m. after which Kayla Callaghan set the alarm system and locked the back door to O'Dooley's Kitchen and Pub. Being the first person at the restaurant in the morning allowed her to park her five-year-old Jeep Grand Cherokee next to the rear door.

Wolfe and Nadia watched from a safe distance parked among the strip mall employees' cars. When the lights on the Jeep came on, Wolfe started the engine and followed Kayla as she drove east from the area.

The journey lasted five minutes and concluded when the Jeep pulled into the garage of a ranch-style home in a neighborhood not far from the strip mall. After parking two doors down, they watched as the garage door closed and lights appeared in the house.

"Should we go talk to her now, Michael?"

Wolfe folded his arms on top of the steering wheel and rested his chin on top. "Maybe, but I also don't want to spook her. She might have a way to let McCaffrey know someone's looking for him. Then he disappears again."

Silence fell over the two for several moments. Nadia grinned. "What does someone who works in a restaurant all day do when they come home?"

With a slight smile, Wolfe looked at her. "Throw your clothes in the washing machine and take a shower. Let's go."

With the front storm door unlocked, Wolfe retrieved an object from his jean pocket resembling a pocketknife. He chose one of the slim blades within the tool and had the front dead-bolt and door lock open in less than twenty seconds. Once inside, they found a modestly furnished front room illuminated through the front picture window by a streetlight. Off to their right, they could hear the muffled sound of a shower running.

They silently searched the house without finding anyone else. When the shower stopped, they made their way back to the kitchen and turned on the lights. Nadia positioned herself in the shadows of the front living room while Wolfe sat at the kitchen table, his Walther PPK resting next to his left hand.

They did not have to wait long.

Kayla Callaghan emerged from the darkened hall, mumbling about having not turned off the kitchen lights. Wearing a robe and a towel wrapped around her hair, she emerged into the kitchen, stopped and stared at Wolfe sitting at the table.

"Who the hell are you?" Her voice did not display surprise or fear, only a distinct Irish accent. She acted like someone who had found herself in the same situation before.

"Where's your husband, Kayla?"

"Who are you?"

"Where's your husband?"

She folded her arms. "I'm not married. Now get out of my house."

"Twenty plus years ago, you married a man I'm looking for. Where is he?"

The defiant attitude disappeared and her shoulders slumped momentarily. Recovering quickly, she said, "I've no idea what you're talking about. Now get out of my house or I'll call the police."

"You know who I'm talking about. In the mid-1990s, you married a man named Danny McCaffrey. Not long afterward, you both left Northern Ireland. You to America and Danny to the Middle East. Why is that, Kayla?"

Nadia came up behind her and said, "We know more than you think we do."

Kayla snapped her head around and with wide eyes saw the woman emerge from the darkened living room. Realizing her situation, she took a deep breath, let it out slowly and sat in a chair across from Wolfe. "I haven't seen him in a long time."

Wolfe kept the PPK close to his left hand. "Does he know where you are?"

She nodded.

"How long?"

"Six years. He used to come once or twice a year, but not since…" She paused and glared at Wolfe. "He's in the United States. That's why you're here, isn't it?"

Her question was answered with silence.

"Oh, my gawd, he's going to do it. He's finally going to do it."

Nadia asked, "Do what, Kayla?"

She turned and looked up at woman behind her. "He calls it the ultimate terrorist act."

Wolfe leaned forward. "What does he consider the ultimate terrorist act, Kayla?"

"He's figured out a way to do it."

With a raised voice, Wolfe asked again, "*Do what?*"

"Assassinate the President of the United States."

Chapter Forty-One

Kayla Callaghan's confirmation of McCaffrey's intentions provided an excuse for the Secret Service to push their way into the investigation. This basically relegated Griggs, Wolfe and Nadia to the role of outsiders looking in.

Despite words of caution from Griggs and Wolfe, two black Suburbans with government plates were parked in Kayla Callaghan's driveway. As the Kia Sportage drove by, its occupant stared at the vehicles with undue interest. After slowing almost to a stop, it then accelerated away and turned left at the next intersection.

The driver of the unmarked police car parked across the street from the restaurant owner's home noticed the sudden slowing of the Kia as it approached the house. He also noticed the driver's undo interest in the two Suburbans and then the almost panicked increase in speed as it passed. As soon as the small SUV made the left turn, the police officer started the Malibu, did a K-turn and followed.

Half a mile from Kayla's home, McCaffrey noticed the dark Chevy Malibu following. The distance between the two cars declined as the driver of the unmarked police car closed the gap. Without realizing it, McCaffrey did a rolling stop at a four-way intersection. As soon as he accelerated through the intersection, the hidden emergency lights on the car behind him started flashing and the siren whooped twice.

Knowing full well trying to outrun the police car would be a folly, he slowed and pulled to the curb. The officer who exited the police car wore a tight-fitting polo shirt over body armor, dark navy utility pants, rubber soled police shoes and a Glock 23 attached to his utility belt. As the officer approached McCaffrey's now open window, his right hand rested on the grip of his still holstered service weapon.

When he approached the window, he said, "I'll need to see your registration, insurance card and driver's license."

Looking up, McCaffrey said without his normal accent, "Registration and insurance card are in the glove box."

"Fine. Please let me see them."

After reaching into the glove box, he wrapped his hand around his Taurus 92, which he quickly pulled out and aimed at the officer's neck and head. He fired five shots in rapid succession.

In the split second he saw the Taurus in the driver's hand, the police officer's hand extracted the Glock 23. Even after suffering two fatal wounds, his automatic response caused the now-dying officer to fire two rounds into the Kia Sportage. One round struck McCaffrey in the leg and the other the passenger seat.

McCaffrey slammed the Kia into drive and accelerated the SUV away from the dying policeman lying in the middle of the residential street.

Five minutes later, with neighbors standing in their front yards gawking, first responders tried to revive the downed officer as other uniformed police personnel taped off the scene to start their investigation. Griggs and Wolfe watched from a distance as EMT's loaded the dead officer into the back of an ambulance.

Wolfe stood still with his arms folded and said, "Think they'll listen to us now?"

"Doubt it."

"Yeah, neither do I." He turned to look at his friend. "How many more officers are going to have to die before we catch this guy?"

With a sad smile, Griggs replied, "I hope none."

"Yeah, me too, but I wouldn't bet on it."

The bullet that passed through McCaffrey's right leg only struck muscle tissue. While not life-threatening, the bleeding was profuse and had to be stopped. Walking into a CVS with a blood-soaked leg would produce questions he did not need. Visiting an urgent care facility would require answers he could not provide. Using a T-shirt from his backpack, he managed to create a tourniquet, which slowed the flow of blood.

As he drove into the rural part of North Carolina, he passed numerous isolated farm homes. Noting one with laundry hanging on an outside line, he pulled into the driveway. An elderly woman sat in a front porch swing and eyed him suspiciously.

He parked the car and stepped out. Using the body of the car to hide his bleeding leg, he asked, "Sorry to bother you. I think I'm lost."

"What're you looking for?"

"Highway 64."

She chuckled. "You are lost. How'd you get so far off the beaten path?"

"Excuse me?"

Shaking her head, she stood and walked closer to the car. "You're about…"

The woman never finished her sentence as McCaffrey shot her in the chest twice. He immediately heard the barking of a large dog from within the house. Not wishing to have any passing cars see a dead woman in the yard, he dragged the body to the backyard and then parked the Kia there as well.

A detached garage located behind the house contained a ten-year-old Toyota Corolla. He left the woman's body on the dirt floor near a wall and entered the house from the back. The keys to the car were located on a peg in the kitchen. After making sure the dog did not bark anymore, he backed the Toyota out and replaced it with the Kia.

After a search of the house, he determined she was a widow and her late husband's clothes still hung in a bedroom closet. While too large for him, he managed to find a pair of jeans he could wear temporarily.

During his search he found a small sewing kit. He took this into the woman's bathroom and with the help of isopropyl alcohol and hydrogen peroxide, he cleaned the wound on his leg and sewed it closed.

Not wishing to tempt fate any further, he made a few sandwiches, brewed a pot of coffee and filled a thermos bottle found in the kitchen pantry. With this done, he drove the woman's Corolla off the property and headed toward Highway 64.

Wolfe returned to the hotel room and said, "He's disappeared again."

Nadia stared at Michael. "How long's it been?"

"Not a thing for twelve hours. He vanished after shooting the police officer."

"There's a lot someone like Danny McCaffrey can do in twelve hours, Michael."

"I know." He glanced at his watch. "It's late. Have you had anything to eat?"

She shook her head.

"The restaurant in the lobby's still open. Let's get something there. I have something to discuss with you."

Nadia finished her salad as Michael chewed the last bite of his grilled chicken sandwich. She said, "Not the best."

Shaking his head, he pushed the plate aside. "I'm really getting tired of restaurant food."

"Let's go home so I can fix us a real meal."

"I'm tempted."

"But…"

"We're not done." He sipped his iced tea and looked at her. "I've been thinking, and I believe we are going about this all wrong."

"I'm not following you."

"We always seem to be one or two steps behind McCaffrey. Why?"

She shook her head.

"Remember when we spoke to Kayla Callaghan?"

"Yes."

"She lied to us. She knows where McCaffrey is. Why did

he drive by her house with all the police presence?" He did not wait for an answer. "Because she's helping him."

Nadia remained silent as she sipped her glass of white wine.

Wolfe studied the tabletop for a few moments. "We need to know how they're communicating. My bet is via text messages or email."

"Wouldn't the police know that by now?"

"They're not acting like it. I think it's time you and I stopped counting on all these government agencies and do this on our own. We need you to get inside Kayla's computer."

"Michael, I've learned a lot from Alexia, but not how to do that."

"Then it's time we get her to show you."

Standing five-feet-nine, Alexia Gibbs was tall by Western European standards. Born in the Catalonian region of Spain to parents who did not approve of the Madrid government, she'd studied computer science at the University of Barcelona. After working for an ISP provider as a security analyst, she'd discovered a more lucrative vocation. Hacking.

During the early years of her hacking career, she had made a series of bad decisions and ended up in Mexico City's La Condesa district.

There she spent the next decade in self-imposed isolation. While keeping a low profile, she earned a meager living utilizing her computer hacking skills. During this period, she'd worn her tousled black hair short, maintained a pencil-thin physique and when in public, wore loose-fitting clothes to hide her gender. During her rare excursions into public she wore black Buddy Holly style glasses and a Chicago Cubs ball cap.

She lived alone without friends or pets. It was during this period that she made a huge mistake and unknowingly became involved with a group of Russians. Fearing for her life, she reached out to the one person she felt she could trust—a fellow computer hacker in the United States. After a daring daylight raid, she was spirited away from under the watchful eyes of her Russian nemesis by a group of FBI agents and the computer hacker. This incident changed her life.

Now married to one of her rescuers and employed by the computer hacker, she wore her black hair long and flowing. Her clothing emphasized her slender athletic body, which she maintained with the help of her ex-Navy Seal husband's habit of swimming on a daily basis. Her time was now spent doting over her son, her husband, their new house and helping the computer hacker run one of the premier go-to computer security companies in the world. But her first love remained hacking.

Alexia Gibbs smiled as she saw Nadia Wolfe on a Zoom conference call. "Nadia, how are you?" The question and pursuing conversation occurred in French.

"Fine, Alexia, and yourself?"

"I am blessed. Thomas is growing and Jimmy's new company is doing better than they projected."

"That is wonderful. Can I ask a favor?"

"Of course."

"Michael and I need your assistance." Nadia then explained the situation.

"Very interesting. Can you tell me where this computer is located?"

"We are not sure, but we can tell you where she lives."

"That will help. What about an email address?"

"We don't know her personal address, but we can give you the email address of the restaurant she owns."

"This gets better with each question. Please send the information to this email address." Alexia recited one with only numbers and letters. "Give me a few hours. I will call you when I have something."

Thirty minutes later, after discovering the restaurant's main food service provider, she used the supplier's email address to send a message with a fake invoice to the pub. Buried within the attachment was a computer subroutine that would be activated when opened. Now all she had to do was wait. Her wait lasted less than twenty minutes.

Once the subroutine found links to Kayla's personal computer, the hidden world of Kayla Callaghan and Danny McCaffrey opened up. With this accomplished, Alexia Gibbs started digging deeper.

"You now have access to Kayla's emails, text messages and phone calls. The interesting part is there are five distinct phone numbers with up to ten text messages and one phone call per number. Once they've used a number ten times, it's never used again. They never use names, but it's the same male voice on each of the calls. All of the communications have dealt with money, nothing else." Alexia paused waiting for questions.

The speaker function on Nadia's cell allowed both her and Wolfe to listen. Wolfe asked, "Can you pinpoint the location of the burner phones?"

"They're never in the same location, but they all originate somewhere between Greensboro and Raleigh, North Carolina. Except the last two text messages. The phone was headed north into Virginia."

Wolfe stood next to Nadia who sat at the small hotel room desk. He placed his hand on her shoulder. "Can you take over the monitoring?"

She nodded.

"Then let's get packed and out of here. We need to have a conversation with Ms. Callaghan."

Chapter Forty-Two

Wolfe sat at the bar of O'Dooley's Kitchen and Pub nursing a pint of Guinness. He stared at Kayla Callaghan as she avoided looking in his direction. This stalemate had lasted an hour without either person speaking to the other.

When Wolfe returned to the rental car from his sortie inside O'Dooley's Kitchen and Pub, he nodded at Nadia sitting behind the steering wheel. She immediately backed the car out of its parking space and left the strip mall lot while Wolfe typed a text message on a cell phone recently purchased at a Circle K convenience store.

"Think it will work?" Nadia took a quick glance at her husband.

"We'll know in less than ten minutes."

She parked the rental car across the street and one house down from Kayla's home and shut the engine off. Their wait lasted exactly four minutes and twenty seconds. A five-year-old Jeep Grand Cherokee pulled into the driveway of the house and skidded to a stop. The driver waited inside the SUV as the garage door opened.

Wolfe said, "Let's go."

Just as Kayla stopped the Jeep inside the garage and placed it in park, her driver side door opened and a hand grabbed her left arm. A male voice said, "Keep your right hand where I can see it."

She looked up and recognized the lean and muscular man of average height. The face was tanned, chiseled and handsome with a five-day old beard. While his physical appearance did not intimidate her, the intensity of his hazel eyes, frightened her.

"Get out of the car, slowly. Keep your right hand in sight."

As she led the man and his female companion into the house, neither spoke a word. When they were in the kitchen, he nodded at a bar stool tucked under the breakfast bar. Kayla pulled it out and sat.

"I told you the last time we spoke—I don't know where he is."

The man stared at her but said nothing. The woman went through the small purse Kayla had left in the Jeep. The black-haired female handed the Samsung cell phone she found to the man.

He held it so she could see. "Password?"

She shook her head.

"Kayla, I will ask you nicely one more time. Password?"

"No. I'm not answering any more of your questions. The last time I did, I had the Secret Service breathing down my neck for two days. I have a business to run and don't have time for this."

"Let's put it this way—we know more than you think. I

can save you from a lengthy stay in a really nasty federal penitentiary for women."

Kayla blinked several times. "What do you mean, federal penitentiary? I've done nothing wrong."

"What about in the UK? Can you say the same thing?"

She kept her stare on the man and folded her arms. "I have no idea what you are talking about."

Wolfe held up the phone for her to see. He then glanced at Nadia. "Want to tell her what we know?"

With a smile, Nadia summarized all the calls and text messages between Kayla and McCaffrey. With each sentence, the woman's ramrod straight posture seemed to slump more as she fixed her eyes on the floor and studied the tile.

When Nadia stopped, Wolfe said, "Now, what's the password?"

"O'Dooley's spelled backward, no apostrophes."

"Not very imaginative." Wolfe grew quiet as he studied the phone. After several minutes, he looked at her. "When were you leaving for Florida?"

She shrugged.

"Not a good answer."

"Day after tomorrow."

"For how long?"

Another shrug.

"Kayla, there's one thing you need to know. My companion and I are not with the Secret Service, the FBI, or any other government agency. Nor are we police officers. Which means, we don't play by federal or local police rules. Now, how long did McCaffrey tell you to stay in Florida?"

Kayla Callaghan, secret wife of Danny McCaffrey and owner of O'Dooley's Kitchen and Pub, stared at the man with the gray streaked slightly curly dark brown hair and beard. She sighed and stared at the floor. Tears pooled in the corners her eyes and leaked down her cheeks. "I'm supposed to wait for Danny. He'll meet me there and then we'll leave the United States."

Four hours later, Jerry Griggs arrived with three other men who took Kayla into custody. During their wait, Nadia worked on Kayla's computer and consulted with Alexia by phone.

At the same time, Wolfe poured through financial records of the restaurant and discovered several details he shared with Griggs upon his arrival.

Laying several documents on the kitchen table, Wolfe explained, "The restaurant originally served as a conduit for money being transferred to Ireland from ex-pats living here in the States. The original intent was for it to be short-lived, but the restaurant grew in reputation and became extremely profitable. About six years ago she started placing the profits into a Canadian bank account. Kayla has been sitting on those funds, waiting for McCaffrey."

"How much is there?" Griggs poured a cup of coffee as he listened.

"From what Alexia and Nadia have been able to determine, at one time there was over a million in the account."

"Was?"

A nod was his answer.

"How much is there now?"

"Half of it."

"Any idea where it went?"

"Into an account in the Grand Caymans."

After sipping his coffee, Griggs watched the steam rising

from the dark liquid. "Do you think McCaffrey has access to those funds?"

"At this point, no. We have access to her personal and business computer emails plus her phone. Nadia has only found one instance where she transferred money to him. That occurred about four days ago. The amount was under ten thousand and deposited in a bank here in Raleigh."

Silence fell between the two men as they stared at the documents on the table. Finally, Wolfe asked, "When's the joint meeting of Congress?"

"Joseph is lobbying the president to not ask the Speaker of the House to set one up. The Mexican President is insisting."

"You didn't answer my question."

"No, I didn't. The president has full confidence in our abilities to prevent anything from happening. He's asking for the Speaker to set up the meeting early next week."

Wolfe pursed his lips and looked at Griggs. "So, we have a week to find McCaffrey and stop him."

"I would say that's about right."

After taking a deep breath, Wolfe let it out slowly. "Go back to Washington. You understand the threat and can keep lobbying Joseph and the president. Plus, you can keep tabs on Kayla. Nadia and I will keep tracking him."

"You sure?"

With a nod, he said, "Positive. We have to assume Kayla has warned him about us. He probably even knows what we look like. What he doesn't know is we have Kayla's phone. That gives us an edge." He paused. "How long can you keep her under wraps?"

"Who?"

"Got it."

"What do we do if he calls, Michael?"

"Not sure. You don't have an Irish accent tucked away somewhere, do you?"

"I am French. The answer is no."

"I knew that. It was supposed to be a joke."

"Not a very funny one."

"Then the answer to your question is, I don't know."

"There is another problem. If he needs more money, what do we tell him?"

Wolfe shot a quick glance at her, slowed the car and found a place where he could pull over out of traffic. "What did you say?"

"The IRS has frozen her accounts. There's no money to give him."

A small grin appeared on Wolfe's face as he dialed a number on his cell phone. His call was answered on the third ring.

"Griggs."

"Jerry, I need ten thousand dollars."

"For what?"

"Bait."

Part III

Chapter Forty-Three

Uri Ben-David handed the newspaper file to the man sitting in front of his desk. The man accepted it, placed half-readers on his nose and scanned the document.

Moshe Benski, Director of Shin Bet, Israel's Internal Security Service, skimmed the report, frowned and read it again more carefully. He removed his glasses and concentrated on Ben-David. "Where'd this come from?"

"An old associate of mine."

He returned his gaze to the pages. "Do you believe it?"

"That's why I asked you to join me."

"If this is true, it could be a huge embarrassment for the Mossad."

"It could be disastrous for our country, Moshe."

The Director of Shin Bet nodded as he studied the pages once again. "Where is she?"

"Her office."

"Is that wise?"

"It is until I determine the truth. If this information was

planted to get us to distrust her, then I want to know who planted it."

"What about the person who sent it to you—could they have done that?"

Ben-David shook his head. "They could have, but they have no motive for doing so. They were as surprised as I was."

"What do you want me to do?"

"Confirm the information."

Benski stood. "If it can be confirmed, then what?"

"Tell only me. I'll take care of it."

With a nod, Benski laid the file on Ben-David's desk and left the office, closing the door behind him.

Staring at the report, Ben-David took his cell phone and dialed a number from memory.

Joseph Kincaid's forehead furrowed when he saw the number on his personal cell phone. After glancing at the time on his phone, he realized it approached midnight in Tel Aviv. He answered the call. "Good evening, Uri."

"Joseph, are you anywhere near a secure phone?"

"I can be in five minutes."

"Call mine when you get there."

The call ended and Joseph went to the basement of his home where all the secure communication gear installed by the NSA and FBI resided. At the last minute, he decided to use a laptop customized by a hacker friend of his. He opened the computer and placed his call to Uri Ben-David.

It was answered immediately.

"Thank you for calling back."

"Want to tell me what this is all about?"

"Are Nadia and Michael still pursuing Danny McCaffrey?"

His answer was a cautious, "Yes. As are the FBI and Secret Service."

"Have you spoken to them recently?"

"Uri, you're dancing around something. What is it?"

"We've had a possible breach of security here."

"Are you accusing Nadia and Michael?" His tone emphasized his disbelief.

"No—no, no, no. Nadia is the one who brought the possibility to my attention. I need their help."

"Uh…" The call went silent for a few moments. "Uri, we have our own problems over here at the moment. Can this wait?"

"I'm afraid the two situations are interrelated."

"How so?"

"While Michael and Ian McGill were in Iran, Nadia worked with Unit 8200 monitoring the cell phone communications coming out of the northern part of the country. She intercepted one phone call with a familiar voice. The voice was discussing funds being transferred to a US bank in Miami."

With the mention of money transferred to Miami, Joseph's interest grew. "Whose voice was it?"

With a slight hesitation, Ben-David said, "Daniella Weiner."

"Have the voices been compared by computer?"

"Yes, but the results are inconclusive. Certainly not good enough to accuse her of anything, let alone arrest her."

"Can you restrict her access?"

"Not without alerting her. If we do that, she might disappear."

"Well, that would prove her guilt."

"Yes, but it might create a scandal that could take down the Mossad."

"You do have a problem, Uri."

"I know. That's why I need Wolfe and Nadia. They are outsiders and less likely to spook her."

Again, Joseph resorted to silence as he contemplated Ben-David's request. Finally, he said, "Tell me what you know."

Daniella picked up on a warning sign her identity as a mole had been discovered. Certain files she used on a daily basis were suddenly no longer accessible.

The next hint came on her cell phone, which notified her someone had entered her apartment. The self-installed Ring security video would normally follow the cell phone notification. This time the video started but abruptly stopped.

She glanced at the time on the bottom right-hand corner of her computer screen and saw a time stamp of 11:13 p.m. She ended her computer session, gathered her purse and left Mossad Headquarters at 11:35 p.m. She smiled at the guards on duty as she checked out and made her way to the parking lot.

With one last look at the structure, she got in, turned the key and drove away. She did not head toward to her apartment, which she knew would now be bugged and under observation. She drove instead toward the Gaza Strip and the town of Jabalia.

Moshe Benski knocked on the door frame of Uri Ben-David's office. "We've had a development, Uri."

Ben-David looked up from his computer screen and removed his glasses. "Go ahead."

"Daniella Weiner left the building at 11:35 last night. She did not go home, and a GPS tracker placed on her car shows it in Jabalia. She's gone."

After several silent blinks, Ben-David picked up his phone and punched in four numbers. When his call was answered, he said, "I need to speak to the prime minister."

An hour and a half later, Uri Ben-David sat a conference table with Moshe Benski and the Prime Minister of Israel.

Ben-David outlined the current situation with Daniella Weiner. When he finished, he said, "Sir, we would like your permission to authorize an incursion into the Gaza Strip to bring her back for trial."

The prime minister, a tall man with broad shoulders and a paunch of equal size, shook his head. "The current stalemate with the Palestinians over our control of the West Bank could boil over if we intrude into the Gaza Strip, Uri."

"I understand that, sir. But the situation becomes more critical by the hour. Weiner knows just about everything I know."

"Are you sure she's even still there?"

Benski answered this question. "Sources indicate she is staying at a hotel near the Port of Gaza. We think she could depart at any time."

"Well, see, that takes care of the problem. Wait until she is at sea, stop the boat and arrest her. But, gentlemen, we politically cannot afford an invasion of the Gaza Strip. Take care of this quietly, is that understood?"

"Yes, sir," Both Ben-David and Benski said it in unison.

Silence filled Ben-David's armored Mercedes Benz for the first fifteen kilometers of the journey back to Tel-Aviv. Finally, Ben-David turned to Benski. "Moshe, can your source keep tabs on her?"

A nod was his answer.

"I am not comfortable trying to intercept her at sea. That will require bringing another department into this mess, which we don't need. Also, the potential of an unsuccessful operation could be even more embarrassing."

"I agree." He remained silent for a few moments. "When did she join us?"

"About six years ago…" He paused. "Oh, dear. I just remembered something."

"What's that?"

"During the time we were considering her, Asa Gerlis was instrumental in pushing her name through the selection process."

"Did he recruit her?"

"No, that might have been too obvious. I don't remember who brought her to our attention, but Gerlis became an instant supporter of Daniella's." He stopped talking, pulled out his cell phone and dialed a number. When it was answered, he said, "This is Ben-David. I need to speak with Irena Davidson immediately."

He grew quiet as he stared out the window, watching the Israeli countryside pass by. Finally, he said, "Irena, I need you to get into the personnel file of Daniella Wiener. I need to know who recruited her." Another pause. "No, I'll wait. This is extremely urgent."

Looking over at Benski, he kept his expression neutral and remained quiet. After several minutes, he said, "Yes, I'm still here. What did you find?"

Ben-David closed his eyes as he listened. "No, that's all I needed. Thank you, Irena." He ended the phone call and took a deep breath. "Gannet Tobias."

"I'm not familiar with the name."

"No, you wouldn't be. It was Gerlis' code name while stationed in Europe."

"That's not good."

"No, my friend, it isn't. Sometimes even our best efforts at security can be betrayed by bureaucratic intricacies."

Chapter Forty-Four

Danny McCaffrey swung his legs over to the floor and sat on the side of the bed. The ancient mattress springs groaned with his position shift. He had stayed in worse places, but this one ranked pretty low on the list. Finding a hotel that accepted cash and no proof of identity grew more complicated with each passing day.

The appearance of a family of cockroaches scurrying across the bathroom tile the night before had not improved his opinion of the place. After dry rubbing his face, he yawned and tried to remember the name of the town he was in. He failed.

He retrieved the cell phone from the scratched and fragile nightstand and scrolled through several news feeds. After weeks of no news about the official state visit of the Mexican President, he was surprised to finally see an announcement. Five days hence, a Joint Meeting of Congress would occur for the Mexican official to address Congress. His topic was to be about how to resolve the increasing drug problem both in Mexico and the United States.

With a smile, McCaffrey rose from the bed and hurried to take a shower.

"Bait?" Jerry Griggs asked. "Why?"

"As we discussed yesterday, we know how McCaffrey is financing himself since his overseas funds were cut off. We also know he is crisscrossing Virginia—why, we don't know. But with Alexia's help, we can now communicate with him in the guise of Kayla. I think there's a chance we can draw him into a trap, but it will cost ten thousand dollars."

"Okay, I get that. What happens when you get him into a trap and he releases the bio-weapon?"

"I need high-explosive incendiary armor-piercing ammunition for my Barrett."

"Why do you need HEIAP rounds, or should I ask?"

"Probably not."

"How many?"

"At least a dozen."

"Those things are expensive."

"Cheaper than losing the entire US Government."

There was silence on the call. Finally, Wolfe heard, "When do you need them?"

"Yesterday."

"Uh—Michael?"

"Yeah."

"Joseph was unsuccessful in stopping a Joint Meeting of Congress."

"When?"

"The Mexican President arrives Monday with his address scheduled in the House chamber at one on Wednesday."

"That doesn't give us much time, Jerry."

"No, it doesn't."

"What about the Secret Service? Are they taking this seriously?"

"Well…"

"What's that supposed to mean?"

"They've interrogated Kayla several times and each time they do, their threat assessment level declines. They do not believe one man can get past their security of the Capitol Building. Plus, since he hasn't been spotted for almost a week, they think he's abandoned the project."

Wolfe closed his eyes and shook his head. "I hope you're joking."

"Deadly serious."

"Shit."

Silence returned to the call as Wolfe stared out the rental car windshield. Nadia studied his demeanor and determined something was wrong.

Finally, Wolfe said, "We've got to go. Let me know when I can pick up the HEIAP rounds."

"I'll call you when I have them. In the meantime, stay in touch."

"Sure." Wolfe touched the *end call* icon and turned his attention to Nadia. "The Secret Service doesn't believe anyone can get past their security at the Capitol Building."

Nadia said nothing.

"I would tend to agree with them, but if one person in the world could do it, it'd be Danny McCaffrey."

"How do we find him in time?"

"That, my dear, may be entirely up to you."

Thirty-two-year-old Sarah Simpson pulled into the driveway of her grandmother's two-story farmhouse. She had not heard from the woman for a few days. While not unusual, it concerned her never the less. The feisty matriarch was fiercely independent at eighty-five, but she still needed assistance once in a while even though she would not admit it. Sarah stopped by regularly to tend to her needs.

As she stepped onto the front porch, her concern heightened. The screen door was shut, but the massive wood front door stood wide open. Her grandmother never left it open unless she was sitting in the front porch swing. With her concern growing, she rushed into the house and started calling for her.

Her only response was silence.

"Grandma, it's Sarah." She repeated the call as she searched the first floor. Approaching the rear of the house, she detected a foul odor coming from behind the door to the pantry. Concern filled her as she opened the door. The stench boiled out and she gasped at the sight greeting her. Max, her grandmother's black lab, lay on the floor surrounded by dried blood. She slammed the door shut and raced to her car.

It took fifteen minutes for Johnston County deputy sheriffs to arrive. They found Sarah Simpson's grandmother's body thirty minutes later.

Jerry Griggs answered his cell phone after checking the caller ID. "Griggs."

"Jerry, it's Bob Holston."

"Hey, Bob, how're things at the FBI?"

"Got something I want to run past you."

Griggs' eyebrows rose. "Okay, shoot."

"You asked me to keep an eye out for any car thieves surrounding Raleigh, North Carolina, right?"

"Yeah…"

"An elderly woman in rural Johnston County was found dead in her garage. She'd been shot just like her dog."

His interest piqued. Griggs remained quiet.

"There was also a black Kia Sportage there with a considerable amount of blood on the driver's seat. A bullet from a dead Raleigh, North Carolina police detectives' gun was extracted from underneath the blood."

"Let me guess—the police detective was the one parked outside Kayla Callaghan's home keeping an eye out for anyone paying too much attention to the house."

"One and the same."

"Go on."

"The Kia was traced to the hijacking of a car transport six months ago in Ottawa, Canada. The cars were fresh off a cargo boat from South Korea and had never been titled."

"I'm not going to like what you're going to tell me next, am I?"

"Probably not. The prints from the Kia were sent to us for identification."

"And?"

"No hits. But on a hunch, I sent them to Scotland Yard."

"They came back as Danny McCaffrey's, didn't they?"

"Afraid so."

"Shit."

"One other thing."

"Yeah."

"The elderly woman's Toyota Corolla is missing."

"Give me the details."

Wolfe listened quietly as Griggs summarized his conversation with the FBI. When he finished, he asked, "Have you spoken to the head of the Secret Service about this?"

"Yes, I'll get to that in a second."

"About damn time. Now give me the details on the Corolla."

When Griggs was done, he added, "Michael, this has suddenly jumped to the top at both the FBI and the Secret Service's priority list. I've been told to tell you to stand down. They'll handle it."

Wolfe laughed. "You're kidding."

"No, I'm not."

"What did Joseph say?"

"He is a firm believer in following orders."

"Bullshit. He wrote the book on disobeying direct orders. Especially if it's in the country's best interest."

"True, and he's always had the belief that a certain ex-Marine sniper cowrote the book."

"What are you saying, Jerry?"

"The package you are expecting will be delivered to your hotel tonight. Where are you staying?"

Wolfe told him.

"One other thing, Michael."

"Yeah."

"Joseph asked me to pass on a comment from the president."

Wolfe waited.

"The president said, and I quote, *Turn Michael loose and let him know we have his back.*" He paused for a brief moment. "If you run into trouble with the FBI or the Secret Service, call me."

"Thanks, Jerry."

Chapter Forty-Five

Naseem al-Nouri's anger at the woman standing in front of him increased as the morning sky grew brighter. "It was not your decision to make. You have essentially ruined years of careful planning and wasted millions of dinars because you perceived a small problem." He took a deep breath and closed his eyes.

Dressed in a traditional hijab and black thobe, Daniella Weiner rolled her eyes and considered al-Nouri with contempt. "Weak words from a man who has never placed himself in harm's way." Her hands were hidden within the folds of the robe.

"Be careful, Ms. Daniella. Your sharp tongue will get you in trouble."

She continued to stare at the Palestinian. "Where in America is the Irishman?"

Her answer was a shrug.

"You do not care where he is, do you?"

The Palestinian smiled and turned away from Daniella. "You are very perceptive for a woman."

"And you will cheat him out of the money you promised, won't you?"

As al-Nouri walked toward a window, he shrugged again.

"He will hunt you down and kill you, Naseem."

"He will not survive."

"What do you mean, he will not survive?"

He turned again to face her. "The Americans will kill him before he gets within a mile of their president. Besides, if the pathogen was not stored properly, it will no longer be viable."

"What do you mean?"

"If it is exposed to high heat for more than ten minutes, it dies."

"Was the Irishman told this?"

"No."

"Why?"

"It was information he did not need."

"So, I was only planted within the Mossad to help the Irishman?"

"No, we had many other reasons and long-term plans for you. But now those plans have been sacrificed due to your short sightedness." The Palestinian smiled. "We Arabs are an ancient people. At one time our empire stretched from the Chinese western border to Spain. It was ruled by the descendants of Mohammad. We were a great empire because we planned for the future, not for the moment. Showing the Americans their president can be targeted was only one of our goals. We want to weaken their resolve and prepare for their downfall. Once that occurs, we will pick up the pieces and the caliphate will rise from their ashes."

"You are a delusional fool." She stepped closer to the man with a fierce stare. The Palestinian backed up involuntarily, his eyes wide at her sudden approach. She continued, "Why was the money we transferred to the bank in Miami withdrawn?"

"It was discovered by the Americans. We could not afford for them to seize it."

"Where is it? Your personal bank account?"

"How dare you accuse me of that? I will…"

She withdrew an IWI Masada 9mm pistol and pointed it at his head. "Where's the money, Naseem?"

The Palestinian raised his hands to chest level, palms toward the woman. "You will never get out of Gaza alive if you kill me."

"You did not answer my question. Where's the money?"

"Safe."

She lowered the weapon. "Safe, where?"

"As you just said—my personal bank account."

The Masada rose and two bullets struck the Palestinian. One in the left eye and the other in the forehead. The body arched backward and crumpled to the floor. The remaining eye stared sightlessly at the ceiling.

Daniella walked quickly to the desk in Naseem's office and started searching for information on the bank account. She found it ten minutes later along with the password.

As the sun rose in the eastern sky, she completed the money transfer, closed the lid on the laptop, pulled the power cord from the wall and walked out of the office with it. On her way out of the personal residence of the late Naseem al-Nouri, she made sure all of the locks were engaged. Gunfire in this neighborhood was common enough she doubted anyone had paid attention. She assumed correctly.

Her car sat where she left it earlier, behind al-Nouri's residence in a back alley off the main road. Within a few minutes, she was miles from the house and the dead body lying face-up on the bloodstained tile.

The point of entry into Egypt from Gaza is through the Rafah crossing. The Egyptian government's schedule for keeping the border open or closed is sporadic. It can be open for one day, two days or seven days a week. It just depends. The only surefire consistent way into Egypt from Gaza is the old fashion way—bribery.

Daniella Weiner, using one of the many fake passports obtained during her time in Israel, smiled at the crossing guard and handed him the document. When opened, he deftly folded the currency in his right hand and slipped it into his front trouser pocket as he handed the passport back to her with his left. In Egyptian Colloquial Arabic, he thanked her and waved her through.

By the time she arrived in Cairo, she had been awake for almost thirty-six hours. She checked into the Nile-Ritz Carlton and slept until evening. Refreshed after her nap, she ate a leisurely dinner and then went shopping.

Before arriving at Cairo International Airport on the second day of her stay in Egypt, Daniella dressed in fashionable jeans, a long sleeve silk blouse and flats, similar to current fashion trends in Spain. The Arabic clothing she had arrived in, was placed in a bag from her shopping trip and deposited in a trash bin on the rear side of the hotel.

The passport she presented as she purchased her first-class seat on KLM airlines to Barcelona bore the name Sara Ruiz with a home address near the famous Las Ramblas section of the ancient city. After paying cash for her ticket, she pulled her small carry-on bag toward the security area.

Seven and a half hours later, the Airbus 330-200 touched down at the Josep Tarradellas Barcelona-El Prat International Airport. Once Daniella Wiener exited the plane, she blended into the international gathering of tourists from around the world. Her visit to the salon within the Ritz Carlton, prior to leaving for the airport, permitted her to sport much shorter hair tinted a lighter color. Wearing large fashionable sunglasses, she no longer resembled the woman who had infiltrated the Mossad and hidden in plain sight for six years.

The call from Unit 8200 confirmed a suspicion Uri Ben-David harbored, but hoped was just his overactive imagination. He replaced the desk phone back into its cradle and rubbed his weary eyes with the palms of his hand. Seventy-two hours had passed without so much as a false sighting of his former assistant. With the news just provided by the Mossad's cyber division the necessity of finding her as quickly as possible just became critical.

He stood, stretched his cramped leg and grabbed his cell phone from the top desk drawer before leaving his office. His driver picked him up at the usual spot and smiled. "Where to Director?"

"Drive around for a while, will you. I need to make a phone call."

"Sure."

As the young Mossad agent steered the armored Mercedes Benz away from the curb, Ben-David found the number he wanted and pressed the send icon. It took several moments for the international call to go through.

"Hello, Uri."

"You were right, Nadia."

"I'm sorry."

"No need to be. Now we know. Unfortunately, she has vanished without a trace."

Nadia Picard-Wolfe did not respond

Ben-David continued, "I just received a call from our friends in the Unit. Voice print analysis has confirmed the voice you thought sounded familiar to indeed be Daniella. Somehow, she determined we were suspicious of her. She left the office seventy-two hours ago and has not been seen since."

"That is unfortunate."

"There's more. After our friends knew what to look for, they searched their electronic archives for Daniella's voice print. They discovered over one hundred calls between her and the same male voice."

"Whose voice is it?

"That's the other piece of news Unit 8200 dropped on me. As you know, Danny McCaffrey speaks Arabic fluently."

"That's what we've been told."

"The male voice talking to Daniella was McCaffrey."

"How would they know each other? It doesn't make any sense."

"We're working on that. We do know that Asa Gerlis is the one who brought her into Mossad."

"She was to be my control."

"We know."

"Where did she come from?"

"We're not sure, but we think Gerlis recruited her in France."

"There's a lot of anti-Semitism in France right now."

"Yes, it has grown since the electoral successes of the

extreme right-wing National Front in the 1990s. Plus the Second Intifada, at the turn of the century, influenced even more of the French to be anti-Semitic."

"Do you think she warned him about Michael and Ian's mission?"

"We think so. However, at this time they haven't found any conversations concerning the topic."

There was silence on the call for a few moments. "Uri, the Mossad has agents everywhere. Use them. They'll find her."

"The prime minister has requested we handle this quietly."

Nadia did not respond immediately. "What's that supposed to mean?"

"He is concerned this will become a major embarrassment for Israel."

"So, you want Michael and me to handle this?"

"Yes."

"Hold on, Uri, I need to ask Michael something."

Chapter Forty-Six

Nadia muted the phone and turned to Michael, who had been listening to the one-sided conversation. "Didn't you tell me that Patrick O'Shay mentioned a rumor that Kayla and McCaffrey had a child?"

"I did."

"And that the child was delivered in Paris and given up for adoption?"

"That's what he told me, why?"

"Just a second." She returned her attention to the phone call. "Uri, there is an unsubstantiated rumor that Kayla Doolan and Danny McCaffrey had a child who was born in France and given up for adoption. No details or any proof were given, just the word of one of the IRA members who left Ireland with McCaffrey."

Nadia heard Ben-David take a breath and let it out slowly. "Do you have access to Kayla?"

"We don't, but Joseph can get it."

"Then I'll send him a DNA analysis of Daniella in an overnight diplomatic pouch. Get it compared to Kayla's."

"Jerry, we need to meet with Joseph."

"Why?"

"There's been a development we need to discuss concerning McCaffrey."

"Tell me. I will relay it to him."

"Not over the phone. This has to be done face-to-face."

"I don't know, Michael. The president has him pretty busy."

"Jerry!"

"I know, you don't ask for things unless they are critical. I'll call you back."

The small bistro in Arlington, Virginia, maintained a reputation as an out-of-the-way gathering spot for authentic Parisian food and an extensive wine list. It was one of Joseph Kincaid's favorite spots far from the DC crowd. He sat at his usual corner table in the back, waiting for Wolfe and Nadia to arrive. A glass of French Bordeaux sat in front of him as he checked the crowd for faces paying too much attention to his presence. None appeared to care.

At the precise agreed upon time of their meeting, the two operatives arrived. Joseph stood and gave Nadia a hug and shook hands with Wolfe. After the three sat and a waiter took their drink orders, Joseph said, "Okay, what's happened?"

Wolfe started, "You'll be getting a diplomatic pouch from Israel tomorrow."

Keeping his eyes on the man across from him, he took a sip of wine and remained quiet.

"Inside this pouch will be a DNA analysis."

"Of who?"

"Daniella Weiner." Wolfe proceeded to summarize the latest developments they'd learned from Ben-David.

True to his nature, Joseph remained quiet as he looked from Wolfe to Nadia and back. Finally, he asked, "You think the child adopted in Paris is Daniella?"

Wolfe nodded. "As farfetched as it may sound, Ben-David, Nadia and I do."

"Huh."

"Can you get a DNA sample from Kayla?"

Joseph nodded. "She's currently under the supervision of the Secret Service and not being cooperative."

"She doesn't have to be. She just needs to let them take a cheek swab."

The waiter returned. He set a glass of Chardonnay in front of Nadia and a dark lager in front of Wolfe. When he left, Joseph asked, "Then what?"

"Don't know, but we're working on it."

"Do you think Daniella will come here?"

Nadia answered. "I do. It would make sense. She can't go back to Israel and I am sure she's changed her appearance. I am also sure she has numerous identities she can fall back on. Ben-David can give you a list of the ones Mossad gave her. Plus, I am sure she'll have a few the Israelis know nothing about."

"That would make sense." He paused. "I'll have Jerry work on it. What about you two?"

Wolfe took a sip of his beer. "I'm tired of sitting around on my thumbs here. Nadia and I are checking out of the hotel in the morning and flying back to Missouri. We're wasting time and money. Nadia needs to work with Alexia to find out more about the adoption, if there was one."

"What about you, Michael?"

"I'll return when there's reason to do so."

A nod from Joseph was his response.

Wolfe relaxed for the first time in weeks as the Beechcraft B55 Baron cruised over the heartland of America.

Nadia's mood brightened as each mile passed beneath them. She turned to her husband, "I've been thinking about what you said to Joseph last night."

"I said a lot to him. Which part?"

"The part about an adoption."

He glanced at her then returned to his flying. "I'm having trouble with the timeline."

"Such as?"

"If Daniella is the child Kayla and McCaffrey supposedly had, she would only be in her mid-twenties by now."

"Yes."

"Plus, how did Asa Gerlis know to recruit her?"

"Think about it for a few seconds, Michael. Gerlis joined the Mossad in the early nineties, around the same time as Desert Storm. Did they ever determine where he was from?"

Wolfe shook his head. "Not to my knowledge."

"I know from information I saw when I was still with Mossad, he worked out of the Paris station during the mid-nineties."

"I didn't know that."

"He did. What if he learned about the daughter of an ex-IRA insurgent being adopted?"

"Too much of a coincidence. I'm not buying it."

"What other facts are there?"

"Until we know for sure, I'll reserve judgment."

She smiled. "Alexia is digging into the adoption records in Paris for us."

"Good. Maybe we'll know the DNA analysis by the time we land."

As Wolfe taxied the Baron toward its hangar on their Christian County property, he noticed Griggs watching them from the end of the runway. Once the plane reached its designated spot within the large structure, he observed Griggs enter the hangar and fold his arms. As the twin engines came to a complete stop, he turned to Nadia. "This can't be good news."

She nodded. "No, I would agree."

When he had the door to the Baron open, he said to Griggs, "How'd you get here so fast?"

"Gulfstreams are faster than a Beechcraft."

"What did they determine?"

"DNA of Daniella confirms she is the child of Kayla Callaghan."

"That could have been handled with a phone call, Jerry. There's another reason you're here on the government's dime."

"We have information that Daniella is already in the United States or will be soon."

"So, you know what name she's traveling under?"

Griggs shook his head. "Intercepted phone calls."

"Once again, Jerry, you could have told us that on the phone."

"The reason I'm here is that NSA recorded a cell phone

conversation yesterday. Daniella told McCaffrey about you and Nadia."

Wolfe's mouth twitched as he watched Griggs. Finally, he smiled. "I'm not intimidated by McCaffrey, Jerry."

"We know that."

"Then why did you fly all the way to the middle of the country to tell me?"

"With Canfield dead, you and McGill are the two individuals with the most experience in trying to find this guy. They want me to bring you back with me. By presidential order, you and McGill will be working with the Secret Service to stop McCaffrey." He turned to Nadia. "Joseph would like for you to work with Alexia. He believes there is something in Daniella's past we can use to either stop her or send her back to Israel for trial."

Wolfe folded his arms. "I'm not taking orders from the Secret Service."

"That's what McGill said."

"Good for him. So, no offense, Jerry, but we seem to have a stalemate here. I won't be going back to Washington if I have to take orders from someone besides Joseph."

Griggs chuckled. "You didn't hear me, did you?"

The ex-sniper did not reply.

"I said you will be working with the Secret Service, not for them. You and McGill will report directly to Joseph."

"Did you explain that to McGill?"

A nod.

"Where is he?"

He glanced at his wristwatch and then looked up. "He'll land at Joint Base Andrews in an hour."

Wolfe turned his attention to Nadia. "You good with this?"

She nodded.

Chapter Forty-Seven

Five in the afternoon at Toronto Pearson International Airport is generally one of the airport's busiest periods of the day. On this particular one, landings and takeoffs were more numerous than usual. Despite the heavier than normal traffic, Lufthansa flight LH470 landed on time. The flight's passengers departed the Airbus A330 without delays and passed through Customs and Passport Control in an orderly fashion.

Sara Ruiz, better known as Daniella Weiner, pulled a small carry-on bag behind her as she navigated the concourse toward public transportation. At the Avis counter, she handed the clerk an American Express Platinum Card bearing the same name. Despite her passport and credit card existing under a false name, the Avis clerk smiled and handed her the keys to a recent model Hyundai Santa Fe SUV.

After departing the airport's vicinity, she headed southwest toward Niagara Falls and the American border.

At the exact moment Daniella exited the Airbus A330 in Toronto, Jerry Griggs stepped off the Gulf Stream G200, followed by Michael Wolfe. To prevent scrutiny of the passengers and their cargo, the plane sat parked in a closed hangar in a secluded section of the airport. A black Suburban appeared and stopped next to the rear section of the G200. Wolfe stood at the bottom of the Gulfstream's airstairs and watched two individuals, wearing Air Force blue jumpsuits, unload the case holding his trusted Barrett into the back of the Chevy SUV.

Griggs said, "Ian is waiting for us at the hotel. We'll pick him up and head to the meeting with Joseph."

Wolfe nodded, but kept his eye on the two Air Force crewmen. Apparently, it was not their first time to handle this type of cargo as they treated it with respect and reverence.

An hour later, they sat across from Joseph in the basement of his townhouse in Alexandria. He started the gathering. "I trust your respective flights were uneventful."

Both Wolfe and McGill nodded.

"Good. Now let's get to why you're both here."

"About bloody time."

Joseph smiled at McGill. "Yes, Ian, about bloody time." He paused and opened a small laptop sitting in front of him. "I want you both to listen to a phone call intercepted by the NSA yesterday evening."

He moved the mouse to an icon on the computer screen and left clicked.

"What's the status of our project?"

Joseph said, "The first voice is Daniella, the next voice has been identified as that of Danny McCaffrey."

"Bloody stuck. I don't have access to funds."

"I've taken care of that. The original amount is now available to us."

"Good. Where are you?"

"Close. Expect me within the next twenty-four or thirty-six hours."

"Where will you be?"

"Same place we met two years ago."

"Got it."

"What is her status?"

"Not sure. Have not spoken to her for a week."

"That is not acceptable. Why?"

"Think about it, luv."

"Unfortunate."

"Yes."

Joseph clicked the icon and the recording stopped. "Very strategic, the call lasted less than thirty seconds and they both said nothing to identify themselves or their destination."

Wolfe said, "So, they've been in contact with each other before?"

A nod from Joseph. "We can now monitor the cell phone numbers."

"Let's hope so. McCaffrey has a tendency to use a lot of burners."

"NSA is monitoring the number Daniella uses since it is a foreign number. The FBI will target any number called from it."

McGill tapped his finger to his lips. "Aye, what's the name of Kayla's restaurant?"

"O'Dooley's Kitchen and Pub."

Looking at Wolfe, McGill smiled. "What would you bet that's the place?"

The ex-Marine sniper narrowed his eyes. "It would

make sense, but they both know we have Kayla in custody. Which means they'll believe we have the pub under observation. My bet is it's somewhere else." Wolfe paused. "From what Nadia has discovered, Kayla goes to restaurant trade shows once or twice a year. Let's have Nadia and Alexia check to see if that might be a connection two years ago."

Joseph nodded.

Using his cell phone, Wolfe made the call.

Thirty minutes later, Nadia gave them a possible location.

"Michael, Alexia found a reference to the North Carolina Restaurant and Lodging Association's yearly Chef's Showdown. Two years ago, her bartender won the NCRLA's Mixologist of the Year award. Kayla was in attendance."

"Where was it held?"

"Durham, North Carolina, at a renovated one-hundred-year-old tobacco barn in the downtown area. It's now a local restaurant that's famous for hosting large fundraising events."

"What's the address?"

Nadia gave it to him.

"It's a start. See if you can find anything else. Spread out three months before and three months after the NCRLA's event."

"Good idea." She paused. "Are you on speaker?"

"No, why?"

"Be careful. I love you."

Wolfe blinked several times and then said. "I will. I love you, too." It was the first time he had said those words since starting the quest to stop McCaffrey. A pang of guilt swept over him as he ended the call. He looked up at the others at the conference table. "We have a starting place."

McGill asked, "Isn't it about bloody time you and I had a visit with Ms. Callaghan, Michael?"

"That's the best idea I've heard today."

Kayla Callaghan entered the room where McGill and Wolfe sat. She immediately exhibited defiance as she glared at McGill. Her blue jumpsuit and the fact the person escorting her was a female airman confirmed Wolfe's suspicions. Her status here at Joint Base Andrew classified her as a domestic terrorist.

She turned her attention to Wolfe. "When am I going to be released?"

"Not my call."

"It's your fault."

With a shake of his head, Wolfe said, "Drop the attitude, Kayla. We know about your daughter as do the Israelis. In fact, she apparently has found her way to the States. Care to comment?"

Her reaction did not match Wolfe's expectation. Her eyes widened and she stared at him. "What daughter?"

"The one you gave up for adoption in Paris twenty-seven years ago."

"What are you talking about? My daughter died at birth."

McGill raised an eyebrow. "You don't say. Where did she die, Kayla?"

"At a hospital in Paris."

"Which one?"

"University Hospital in the 13th arrondissement."

Both Wolfe and McGill glanced at each other. Wolfe stood and left the room.

"Where's he going?" Kayla's eyes tracked Wolfe until the door closed.

"To check your story. You've lied to us so many times, we aren't inclined to believe anything you tell us."

"It's the truth."

McGill leaned back in his chair and contemplated the woman sitting across from him. Moisture pooled in her eyes as she stared at the door. "Were you and Danny married?"

"Not in the church."

"Was the child Danny's"

She studied the tabletop and slowly nodded.

"Why Paris?"

"Danny knew someone there who would help raise the child until I could get out of trouble in Ireland. After the baby died, I decided to go to the States and try to forget about my past and Danny."

"But Danny wouldn't let you, would he?"

"No, the bastard."

"What would you say if I told you there was a woman out there whose DNA makes her your daughter?"

She glared at McGill for fifteen seconds before she shuddered and sobbed uncontrollably.

McGill sat with his hands folded. "Should I believe you, Kayla? Because I'm still not quite sure I can at this point."

Shaking her head, she folded her arms on the table and placed her head there. The crying continued.

McGill heard the door open and watched Wolfe return.

"What the hell did you do, Ian?"

"Can we step outside for a moment?"

They both left the room as a female airman took their place. McGill said, "What'd you learn?"

"Her story is correct. She gave birth and the child died a day later of SIDS. But…"

"Let me guess—they didn't compare the DNA to the original child."

Wolfe shook his head. "My guess is Danny managed to have the child switched with one that had already died. Alexia and Nadia are hacking into the hospital records to see what they can learn about personnel working there at the time."

"Do you want to tell her or do I?"

"You can. I don't handle emotional women well."

Kayla became more agitated as she learned additional facts about the switch at birth. "Danny always held the death of Abigail over my head and told me how much I owed him. He blamed me for what happened."

McGill asked, "Did he explain why you were to blame?"

She shook her head. "No, at first I pushed back. Then he would scream at me, telling me even the hospital blamed me."

Leaning forward at the table, Wolfe said, "Tell me about the NCRLA's Mixologist of the Year award in Durham two years ago."

"How did you know about that?"

"Was Danny there?"

"Yes, he needed money."

Wolfe and McGill remained quiet letting her talk.

"He always needed money. There had been a fund put together for some of the Irish ex-Pats in the area who fell on hard times. Those funds dried up a long time ago. But Danny keeps telling me there should still be plenty in the kitty."

"Are you still providing funds to him?"

She tilted her head. "How did you know about the Mixologist award?"

Wolfe said, "It's not important. Did you give him money?"

She shook her head while staring at the tabletop again.

Taking a deep breath, McGill took over. "That's a lie, Kayla."

She nodded.

"So, you do give him money. Is that correct, Kayla?"

Another nod.

Taking over the back and forth questioning, Wolfe asked, "Was there a woman with him?"

The hatred in the glare Kayla Callaghan gave Wolfe caused him to instantly understand. "Who did he introduce her as?"

"An associate."

"But you didn't believe him?"

Another shake of her head. "She was half his age. It was obvious she was his girlfriend."

"That was your daughter."

Tears returned in the woman's eyes. "How…" She looked from Wolfe to McGill. "Why…"

"We can't answer that at the moment."

Kayla Callaghan started shaking uncontrollably. Wolfe opened the door to the room and said, "We're done here, airman. Could you escort Ms. Callaghan back to where she's staying?"

When they were gone and the door shut again, McGill asked, "What do you think?"

"I think Danny McCaffrey is a rabid dog that needs to be put down."

McGill chuckled. "What about the daughter?"

"I'm pretty sure she is, too."

Chapter Forty-Eight

THE NEXT DAY

Daniella sat at a small table outside a coffee shop in the concourse leading into the main Durham County library. The book in her hand sat open but unread as she waited. Occasionally taking a sip of the poorly made espresso sitting in front of her, she kept her peripheral vision trained on library patrons traversing the hallway leading into the library's main entrance.

One particular man, middle aged, wearing a tweed Irish Ivy Cap with matching scarf approached the table next to her. He did not acknowledge her presence. After he sat, he placed a shopping bag on the floor between them. Ten seconds later, he glanced at his wristwatch, stared wide-eyed at it and placed an open hand on his forehead. He stood and walked rapidly toward the building exit.

With a casual glance, she watched him walk out and then glanced at the package left behind. She grabbed it, stood and hurried after the man who left the package. Once out of the building, she walked briskly to her rental car and drove out of the parking lot.

To anyone watching a security camera feed, it would appear she attempted to return the bag. It was all a ruse.

Twenty minutes after leaving the library, she pulled into a strip mall and opened the bag. Inside were ten cell phones, each labeled with a number written in Sharpie on a piece of tape. On top of the cell phones she found a folded piece of paper with handwritten instructions. Starting in numeric order, McCaffrey would call each cell phone only three times. After which, the phone was to be destroyed and the pieces discarded.

As she read, the phone marked with the number one vibrated. She answered it immediately.

"Yes."

"Good. I take it you've read the instructions?"

"Yes."

"It was nice to see you, if only for a moment."

"There is something I must know."

Silence on the call greeted her for several moments. "What?"

"How has the package been stored?"

"In my backpack, why?"

"Has it been exposed to high heat?"

McCaffrey did not respond right away as he reviewed his journey from Calais to the US. "Yes, I hid it in the engine compartment of a high-speed boat for several hours."

"Was it hot to the touch when you retrieved it?"

"Very."

She sighed. "I was told being exposed to high heat for ten minutes or longer kills the pathogen. I was also told you were not expected to survive the delivery and even if you did, you would not have been compensated, as promised."

"And where is this individual who provided this information?"

"I made sure he could no longer sign contracts."

McCaffrey paused for a brief moment. "Good, but the other is unfortunate news."

"Yes. One more thing."

"More bad news?"

"I am no longer employed."

The silence on the phone caused Daniella to continue, "The only good news I bring is we have access to the Miami money."

"How much is left?"

"About eighty percent."

"Then it is time to leave and retire."

"Not so fast."

An irritated voice responded, "What do you mean, not so fast."

"I have unfinished business with three individuals. If you want your half of the money, you will have to assist, Father."

Deep within the mammoth NSA computer center in Utah, where computer storage is measured in exabytes, recently programed algorithms flagged a cell phone conversation containing the words, *Miami, money, father.*

The NSA supervising technician who received the notification placed the phone call into a queue for one of his support staff to analyze. When the individual assigned to review the call ran it through voice recognition protocols, alarm bells went off.

Other additional algorithms allowed the massive

computer to compare voice prints first and then keywords. Over the course of the next twenty-four hours, a disturbing pattern emerged.

In a small café off the Washington DC beaten path and far from where government elites frequented, Joseph Kincaid offered a one-page report to each of the men sitting across from him. Both Michael Wolfe and Ian McGill read the page closely.

Wolfe looked up first. "When were these recorded?"

"Within the last twenty-four hours."

"So, the Secret Service now believes the threat to the president has diminished?"

A nod was his answer.

McGill asked, "Are they still searching for them?"

Another nod, then Joseph said, "While they believe the threat has declined, they still want McCaffrey in custody. Plus, they want the bio-weapon."

"What if this is just so much BS, Joseph?" Wolfe held the page up.

"Well, Michael, that's a good question. They've consulted with a lot of virologists and microbiologists and if the bio-weapon is based on a strain of C. Botulinum, which they believe it is, there is a good probability it's inert."

Folding his arms, Wolfe tilted his head. "A good probability is not the same as the thing's dead."

McGill shook his head. "Lots of speculation and very few facts, Joseph. That's the kind of crap that gets people killed."

"I agree, Ian."

"So, what do you want us to do?"

"I don't like the comment in the first intercept where Daniella says she has unfinished business with three individuals."

With a smile, Wolfe said, "I saw that. Not sure what your concern is—it gives us an edge and a way to finally catch this guy."

"How's that?"

"Let them know where we are."

McGill smiled and nodded.

Wolfe and McGill occupied a table in the far corner of the Panera Bread restaurant near Joint Base Andrew. Kayla Callaghan, escorted by a female airman in civilian clothes, entered the establishment. When she sat, the airman excused herself and left.

"So, I'm free, just like that?"

"You were in protective custody, Kayla."

She looked at Wolfe and shook her head. "Mr. Wolfe, I have been in jails in Ireland and England. I was not in protective custody."

With a chuckle, he said, "Protective custody is a euphemism for keeping you from running away unexpectedly."

"In other words, jail."

Both McGill and Wolfe nodded.

"So, what is my new-found freedom going to cost me?"

McGill smiled. "Get a message to your ex-husband."

"I have no desire to be anywhere near him."

"That's the price of getting out of jail and getting the FBI out of your life." Wolfe stared at her. His expression grim.

She returned the stare and narrowed her eyes. "What's the message and how do I get it to him?"

"Leave that to us."

The text message that appeared on the burner phone McCaffrey currently used, arrived in his inbox at two minutes after one in the afternoon. The message was simple: *FBI knows about you. Come by the pub if you want help. K.*

How did she know the number? Was this a trap or a sincere wish to help him? The question would only be answered by confronting her. Without hesitating, McCaffrey turned the phone off and pulled both the battery and SIM card out. After flushing the SIM card down the toilet, he crushed the phone under his heel and placed the pieces in the trash can liner for later disposal.

He glanced at his wristwatch and determined he was four hours from Raleigh. The phone could be thrown out the window on the way.

Chapter Forty-Nine

McCaffrey watched the restaurant from a safe distance, parked among the throngs of vehicles belonging to shoppers at the adjacent strip mall. As the time neared nine p.m., Kayla Callaghan's Jeep Cherokee remained in its normal parking spot near the rear door of the building.

So far, there were zero signs he was being watched; there also didn't seem to be any unusual activity surrounding the restaurant. At sixteen minutes after the hour, Kayla emerged, locked the back door to the establishment and got into her Jeep. He started his car as soon as he saw the backup lights illuminated on the SUV.

As she backed out, he put his car in gear and started to back out as well. Without warning, a large black Suburban skidded to a halt inches from the car's rear bumper, blocking his path. Ten men and women dressed in FBI SWAT-style tactical gear surrounded the car with Heckler & Koch MP5 sub-machine guns pointed directly at him.

Options and escape routes swirled through his head as he stared at the guns. These thoughts drowned out the shouting from the FBI agents demanding he unlock the doors and get out. He quickly realized his options, at this point, were few. He placed his hands on the steering wheel as the agent next to the driver side window smashed it open.

The takedown lasted less than five minutes. McCaffrey was secured in the back of the Suburban just before the driver screeched the tires leaving the strip mall. A tow truck arrived two minutes later, loaded the car on the tiltable platform and drove away. By nine-thirty p.m. the lot was once again quiet as workers from the mall returned to their cars for their trip home after a long day.

Special Agent George Garcia from the North Carolina FBI Field Office stood outside the interrogation room observation window, his arms folded. He still wore the tactical gear used for the parking lot take down. He turned to Wolfe, who had introduced himself as a US Marshal, and said, "Thanks for the tip, Agent Ryan."

"My pleasure. What's next?"

He smiled and returned his attention to the subject. "Above my paygrade. But I am told he will be whisked out of here in about an hour by agents from Washington. Then he'll be someone else's problem."

Wolfe nodded, but did not respond. He knew the individuals escorting McCaffrey back to Joint Base Andrew would be FBI agents from the DC area. He turned to Garcia and offered his hand. "I appreciate your team handling this. I'm heading back tonight and will see him in Washington."

"Glad we could assist."

Wolfe left the county jail a few minutes after one a.m.

and got into a car driven by Ian McGill. As they drove away from the building, he glanced at Wolfe. "I'm surprised they took him down so easy."

"So was I."

Silence filled the car for only a few moments. McGill continued, "Any word on Daniella?"

Wolfe shook his head. "No, and that worries me. She's disappeared again."

"Think we should check on Kayla?"

Wolfe frowned. "I forgot about her. Yeah, we'd better."

By the time they parked in the modest ranch style home's driveway, both could tell something was amiss. The house was dark and the front door stood slightly ajar. Inside, chaos reigned as both Kayla and her Jeep were missing from the disheveled residence.

"We'd better let the Raleigh PD know about this."

"Yeah and Joseph."

"Probably a good idea. I'll let you handle that, mate."

After explaining the situation at Kayla's house to the cops, the two men resumed their journey toward Joint Base Andrew with Wolfe driving this time. Halfway through their trip, McGill took a call from Jerry Griggs. During the one-sided conversation, the ex-SAS man listened and only said two words.

"Got it." After ending the call, he turned to Wolfe. "Where is Allnut, Virginia?"

"Virginia."

"Smart ass. Where in Virginia?"

"How the hell should I know?"

"You're from this country."

"It's a big country and I'm from the central part of it. I've never heard of Allnut."

"Well, you'd better figure it out. The FBI team taking McCaffrey to Joint Base Andrews was ambushed there around four this morning. McCaffrey's gone and Kayla Callaghan was flown by helicopter to Walter Reed in Bethesda. She's in critical condition."

"Shit." Wolfe pulled the vehicle over and punched in a number.

―――

They met Griggs in the intensive care waiting room two hours later. When they arrived, he stood sipping coffee staring at a flat screen TV showing an old *Bonanza* rerun. He turned to them. "Never realized the plots on these old TV shows were really pretty good."

Wolfe asked, "How is she?"

"Just got out of surgery. Doctor told me it will be a while before we can talk to her."

McGill folded his arms. "What about the FBI agents?"

"One survived but died in route to the hospital."

"What happened?"

"Right now, they have few details—they'll know more when Kayla is able to answer questions. But we do know that her Jeep was involved."

―――

A tall, slender middle-aged man entered the waiting room dressed in blue scrubs and an ID badge showing his name as Alex Rivera. He said, "Which one of you is Michael Wolfe?"

"I am."

"I'm Doctor Rivera. Kayla is awake and wants to speak to you. You can have five minutes, no longer, and it can only be you. Follow me."

The doctor remained quiet as he led Wolfe through a maze of beds with multiple tubes attached to patients in various states of consciousness. The doctor turned and said, "She's still a little groggy from the anesthesia, but insisted it was extremely important for her to speak to you."

"What were her injuries?"

"Internal bleeding consistent with an automobile accident. We have it stopped, but she's going to need to stay here a few days."

Wolfe nodded.

Rivera parted a privacy curtain and nodded for Wolfe to stand by her bed. "Five minutes, no more."

Multiple tubes were connected to Kayla and her eyes were closed. He said, "Kayla?"

She slowly opened them and focused on his face. "I'm sorry."

"Nothing to be sorry about."

"She…" Her eyes drooped and she seemed to fade out. They snapped open again. "She knows about you."

He nodded. "I was aware of that. Did she try to kill you in a car accident?"

The injured woman nodded. "She claims I abandoned her in Paris. She hates me and wants me dead. I tried to explain to her I was told she died at birth. She didn't believe me and that's when she pulled in front of the SUV. I don't remember anything else until I woke up here."

Wolfe did not respond.

Kayla's eye's fluttered and she took a breath. "She told me she knows where you live."

With a concerned frown, Wolfe asked, "Did she mention why she felt the need to tell you?"

A nod was his answer, but she faded for a few moments before continuing, "She said you had to pay for exposing her in Israel. She and Danny are going to pay you a visit before they leave the country. She didn't care if I knew or not because I would be dead."

Wolfe stared at the woman as tears streamed down her cheeks and she succumbed to sleep again. He left her bedside and walked straight to Jerry Griggs in the waiting room. "I need to get back to Missouri, Jerry."

Griggs contemplated Wolfe for a few moments. "What'd she tell you?"

"They know where I live."

Chapter Fifty

As Griggs drove Wolfe to Joint Base Andrews for the waiting Gulfstream G20, he asked, "How would she know where you live?"

"I've been asking myself that question ever since Kayla told me. The only answer I can come up with is she found the information in a Mossad file before she left Israel."

"How would they know?"

"Don't know, but when this is all over, I intend to find out."

"Do you need any help?"

"Honestly, Jerry, Nadia and I can handle this better without any interference. The fact that Daniella overcame four FBI agents without so much as a scratch tells me all I need to know."

"I can find a bunch of well-trained guys more than willing…"

"No!"

"You sure?"

"Positive." He paused for a few moments. "Our house isn't as innocent as it appears."

———————

As the Gulfstream stopped on the tarmac in the private aviation section of the Springfield-Branson National Airport, Wolfe thanked the pilots, lowered the airstairs and hurried to the cargo section to retrieve his Barrett. He then jogged to where Nadia sat parked in their Jeep Grand Cherokee. After placing the rifle case in the back seat, he threw his duffel bag on top of it and closed the door. After he slipped into the front passenger seat, Nadia screeched the tires accelerating toward the airport exit.

She glanced at her husband. "Glad you're home."

He looked up from reading emails on his cell phone and smiled. "I'm glad, too. Sorry it's not under the best of circumstances."

With a chuckle, she said, "It never is, Michael. I'm still glad you're home."

Shutting the phone off, he turned to look at her as she drove. "Griggs has been sending emails to keep me up-to-date on events while I was in the air."

She nodded.

He continued. "Kayla's house was ransacked apparently by Daniella. Why no one knows."

Nadia nodded. "Was she looking for something that would identify Daniella as Kayla's daughter?"

"I didn't think of that. But it doesn't make sense. In Kayla's mind, her daughter died at birth. Why would she have anything identifying Daniella as her daughter?"

"Daniella might not have known that."

"You're probably right. Kayla told me, just before I left,

that her daughter accused her of abandoning her in Paris and that she hated her."

"Did Kayla tell her about the switched babies."

"She didn't have time. That's when she swerved into the path of the FBI suburban. Kayla lost consciousness and doesn't remember anything else until she woke up from surgery."

"How did Daniella overcome the FBI agents?"

"Griggs indicated in his emails that when the Jeep passed the Suburban it turned so that the bigger vehicle slammed into the Jeep's passenger side. That's when Kayla was injured. The accident investigators speculate that one of the FBI agents got out of the Suburban to see if anyone in the Jeep was hurt and Daniella opened fire on him. From the position of the agents in the Suburban, they think she shot each of them in quick succession."

"If the Jeep and the Suburban were disabled, how did Daniella and McCaffrey get away?"

Wolfe smiled. "Kayla told McGill and Griggs there was a small scooter in the back of the Jeep. The backseats were down to accommodate it."

"So, they don't know what they will be driving?"

Shaking his head, Wolfe said, "No. Local police are checking on any stolen vehicle reports."

"How long do you think we have before they get here?"

"Best guess, less than twenty-four hours."

"Can we be ready?"

"We have to be."

On the north side of the Beechcraft Baron's parking area, a cinder block wall with a metal door separated the space for

the plane from a two-bay garage for the Jeep Grand Cherokee. A Honda Trailmaster Challenger ATV sat in one of
the bays. The purpose of this part of the structure was
twofold. In the unlikely case of a fire in one of the spaces,
the chance of it spreading to the other would be drastically
reduced. To say Michael Wolfe was a cautious man would
be comparable to saying winters in the Ozarks are cold. It
was just a fact of nature. The cinder block wall also
provided Wolfe a load-bearing support structure for the
rooms above the hangar and garage space.

Those rooms contained an office and the heart of
Wolfe's security system for their property. In a separate
room, through a well-hidden door, lay Wolfe's arsenal of
weapons.

Nadia backed the Jeep into the empty bay and touched
the garage door opener. As the door lowered, Wolfe exited
the vehicle and walked to the north wall. Nadia followed
and trudged up the staircase to the second floor behind him.
At the top, a metal door with a heavy-duty keypad lock
blocked entrance to the upstairs rooms. Wolfe punched in
his code, a nine-digit string of numbers with three numbers
duplicated. After two failed attempts at entering the code,
three deadbolts would snap into place. Access to the office
would then only be available with a cutting torch. Something, Wolfe assumed, a common thief would probably not
have on hand.

Neither spoke as Wolfe entered the correct number
sequence and the door opened.

An inexpensive eight-foot folding table, metal chairs,
gray surplus filing cabinets, an assemble-yourself pressboard
desk from Walmart and a high-end mesh office chair
furnished the office space. On the south wall, a hallway led
to a bathroom on the right which contained a vanity, toilet

and shower stall. Across the hall stood a door leading to a large space containing a bank of security monitors for the various motion detection cameras strategically placed throughout the property.

Nadia followed him into the security room and leaned against the doorframe as he sat in front of a laptop computer. She said, "How far are you going back?"

"Five days. I'll see if anything looks out-of-place." He typed a command on the keyboard and watched as the security recording flashed before him. Five minutes later, he said, "Nothing out of the ordinary."

"Any strange vehicles pass?"

He shook his head and then turned in the chair to look at her. "Not sure that would tell us anything due to McCaffrey's habit of stealing vehicles. I only saw two pickups pass and I recognized the drivers of both. The system is now set to send a notification to both of our cell phones if any car or truck passes. We'll be able to watch live and determine if it's one of our few neighbors. If it isn't, well…"

She smiled. "I'm going up to the house. You coming?"

"I will in a few minutes. I have a few other tasks I need to complete."

After Nadia left, he returned to the Jeep to get the case containing the Barrett. He returned to the second floor and opened the door to the armory. After placing the .50 caliber rifle, by itself, on a vertical easily accessed rack, he surveyed the various weapons he had at his disposal. Nadia's Remington 700 with scope remained in its own rack adjacent to his sniper-rifle. A massive gun safe stood next to the racks with a biometric lock. He placed his thumb on the access pad and the perfectly balanced steel door swung open. Inside, he found more lethal members of his armory.

The Heckler and Koch MP5SD with its integrated

silencer and flash suppressor was designed for special forces night missions. Wolfe owned four of them. He removed two and placed them on a table across from the safe. Six magazines were also extracted and laid beside the H&Ks.

Multiple handguns in various calibers were in their cases and carefully lined up on the top shelf. He withdrew a Springfield Armory 1911 .45 ACP, three magazines and a compatible holster. He laid these on the table as well.

Stacked on the left of the safe were a dozen cases of flash-bang grenades. He withdrew four and placed them next to the 1911.

After closing the safe door, he went to a tall storage cabinet next to the safe. From within, he withdrew two 1200-yard spools of 100-lb test fishing line. The dark green color vanished when strung low to the ground in a leaf-strewn environment. Also, from the cabinet, he removed two Kevlar helmets with integrated night vision goggles.

Wolfe placed all this equipment into a heavy-duty duffle bag. He hoisted the now fully loaded satchel into the office. Glancing at his watch, he figured he could grab a few hours of sleep before doing what needed to be accomplished before dawn.

As the sun peeked over the horizon, Wolfe emerged from the wooded area south of the runway on the eastern most side of his property. The duffle bag, he carried, appeared less burdened with equipment than when he'd first entered the western tree line at eleven the previous night. With morning turning brighter, he carried the Kevlar helmet in his right hand and the duffel in his left. Sweat stained his camos and dripped off his nose.

Nadia smiled as he walked north on the runway. She had worried about him but knew he would emerge with the job complete.

When he reached the back porch of their residence, he smiled. "Anything on the cameras?"

She shook her head. "Take a shower. I'll fix you a proper breakfast."

Wolfe devoured the first omelet in seconds. Nadia immediately slid another onto his plate before he could put his fork down. She said, "Eat this one slower. You might actually taste it."

He chuckled and attacked the new one with less aggression.

She watched him as he ate and sipped her coffee. "Michael?"

Turning his attention to her, he said, "Thanks, I didn't realize how hungry I was."

"You are welcome." She took another sip of coffee. "What do I need to do?"

He paused and raised an eyebrow. "Uh…" He longed to take her to their bedroom, but decided the timing was not right. "We probably need to go over our plans."

She reached for his hand and smiled. "I saw that look in your eye. I think we have time to enjoy each other's company for a few minutes." She stood and pulled on his hand. "Come with me."

Nadia stroked her husband's hair as he snored softly lying next to her. She too had dozed after their lovemaking. After a quick glance at the digital clock on his side of the bed she discovered it as forty-two minutes past noon.

A vibration made Wolfe's cell phone dance across the nightstand. The noise startled him. "What the hell…"

She reached over him, grabbed the phone and read the notice. "Michael?"

He looked at her with an incomprehensive stare. "Wha…"

"You need to wake up."

He returned to alertness in microseconds. "What've you got?"

She handed the phone to him.

He watched the video repeat itself. His mouth twitched as he threw the covers off. "Time to get to work."

Chapter Fifty-One

"How big is the property?" Danny McCaffrey observed the rural house through binoculars. The three-year-old Hyundai Santa Fe, purchased with cash in Virginia, was parked a hundred yards west of the house on the county road.

Daniella read from the Christian County website, "His property extends another kilometer to the west and two kilometers to the south. It is basically a rectangle."

"What does the Google Earth website show you?"

"Trees start halfway to the western border and extend in an L shape to the south and then east."

"What's south of the house and barn?"

She frowned. "It appears to be a runway."

He turned his attention to her. "A runway?"

"That's what it looks like."

"Interesting. The barn must be a hangar." He paused for a few moments. "We'll wait until midnight and come in from the west."

"Good, I need a little sleep."

The first flash-bang detonated at 12:47 a.m. Wolfe, having set booby-traps in a peripheral loop around his property, knew exactly where the intruder entered his property—two hundred yards due south of the northern county road. The disorientation of the flash bang, to whomever set it off, would last for a while, depending on how close the trespasser had been to the device when it detonated.

The house was dark. Both Wolfe and Nadia wore the Kevlar helmets with built in NVGs. The interior of their home now appeared in a greenish hue through the lenses of the device. Dressed in black jeans, black thermal knit shirts, black utility vests and black camo face paint, they would be invisible to anyone without NVGs.

Wolfe said, "Okay, we know they're making their move."

Nadia nodded and started to say something when she heard a noise she could not identify. Raising one finger she whispered, "What's that?"

He listened for a second. "Shit—head for the basement."

They scrambled down the stairs just off the kitchen, making it to the basement just as the Hyundai SUV crashed through the front picture window.

Wolfe hurried to the southern wall of the basement and opened a three by three-foot panel in the wall. As the panel swung open on hidden hinges, Nadia scrambled through the opening and into the emergency tunnel leading to the hangar.

Following closely, he closed the panel and secured it from the inside. He flipped a switch and the passage became illuminated in infrared light.

During the house's initial construction, he had

contracted with a highway construction company to lay down reinforced concrete elliptical pipe from the house to the hangar. While not tall enough to stand in, the pipes allowed them to crawl on their hands and knees. Halfway through the journey, they felt the ground shake and rumble.

Nadia stopped and asked, "What was that?"

"Keep moving, Nadia, we can rebuild the house."

She did not reply but crawled faster.

Daniella backed the SUV out of the gaping hole where the picture window in front of the house used to be. She waited, keeping a low profile below the dashboard. When gunfire did not come from the interior of the home, she stepped out and tossed two satchels into the opening. Returning to the vehicle's steering wheel, she backed the Hyundai up and waited. The resulting explosions shook the structure and obliterated the front wall, causing the roof to collapse. The house became engulfed in flames moments later.

Daniella withdrew a Taurus G3 9mm and walked around the burning building.

McCaffrey lay on the leaf-strewn ground, temporarily blinded by the denotation of a flash bang. With his hearing damaged by the grenade's concussion, he did not hear the explosion at the house. The overload on his eardrums caused him to be momentarily nauseated and he leaned against a tree to steady himself. Only then, as his vision cleared, was he able see the flickering flames engulfing the house. So far, McCaffrey had underestimated Wolfe. The booby-traps had been unexpected and caused him to wonder how many more were nestled in amongst the densely wooded property.

The infrared goggles purchased at a large sporting goods store were nowhere to be found, so he carefully felt his way back out of the dense foliage. He tripped several times and completely lost his footing once.

Once out of the trees, he glanced at the sky to see a third quarter moon about forty-five degrees above the eastern horizon. This gave him enough light to navigate around Wolfe's property.

They emerged inside the hangar, directly under the staircase leading to the upper floor. Illumination came from several security lights in operation twenty-four hours a day in the windowless building. Wolfe removed his helmet and looked at Nadia. Her eyes were red, but they made strong contact with him.

She said through clenched teeth, "Where's my Remington?"

He nodded upstairs and with a grin said, "Same place it always is. I didn't move it."

"Excuse, me." She walked around him and headed toward the steps.

He said to himself, "Not sure which one of them blew the house up, but Nadia is now officially pissed. Heaven help whoever did it."

Wolfe stopped and listened carefully. Off in the distance he could hear the faint sound of a siren from a first responder. He frowned. Whoever it was would be walking into a dangerous trap. He hurried up the stairs to get his Barrett.

As he dashed up the steps, he realized McCaffrey and Daniella had split up and were attacking on two fronts, from the side of the property and a head on assault. At this point he wasn't sure what that said about their tactics, but he would keep it in mind.

———————

Daniella reached the far side of the house and held her Taurus in both hands, pointed at the burning structure. An emergency siren could now be heard approaching the house. She saw the flashing lights approach from the east and waited.

A Christian County deputy SUV pulled into the driveway and screeched to a halt. The driver stepped out of the vehicle to survey the burning structure and started speaking into his shoulder microphone.

He did not notice Daniella approach him from his left. When he did, he reached for his service weapon.

The officer died before he could withdraw his gun as three bullets struck him in the chest and head. The Israeli double-agent looked at the body without emotion and started walking back toward the hangar.

———————

Above the office on the northern side of the hangar, Wolfe had installed a crawlspace with a view of the house and the country road. The space also served as a sniper hide should the need ever arise.

Nadia arrived at the window just in time to see Daniella execute the sheriff's deputy in cold blood. With her anger growing, she calmed herself as best she could and centered the crosshairs of her Remington 700's scope on the woman's chest. The light from the burning house made her an easy target.

Without a second thought, Nadia applied pressure to the trigger and slowly exhaled. The bullet found its mark and Daniella Weiner, a double-agent planted within the Israeli Mossad by a faction of Hamas, died next to house she had just set on fire.

McCaffrey, having just circled the tree line saw everything. The sheriff deputy being shot and then Daniella dying by the hands of a sniper from the top of the hangar. More sirens could be heard in the distance and he realized if he wanted to survive to fight another day, he needed to disappear.

He looked to the west and saw the lights of a house in the distance. Armed with the second of the Taurus G3s purchased from the same sporting goods store as the infrared goggles, he stayed off the pavement and headed toward the lights.

Chapter Fifty-Two

"I thought I asked you to let Nadia and I handle this?"

Jerry Griggs smiled as he turned his attention away from the burned remains of the house. "You did. But since the Christian County Sheriff's and fire department, the Missouri Highway Patrol and the FBI are now involved, I thought you could use a little government cover."

Wolfe pressed his lips together and then gave his friend a slight smile and nodded. "Thanks, Jerry."

"Joseph has been working behind the scenes. None of this will blow back on you." He paused and looked at the leveled structure. "Sorry about the house."

Wolfe's mouth twitched. "It can be rebuilt."

"What does Nadia think?"

"She's like me—it pissed her off, but there isn't much we can do about it except rebuild."

"Does your insurance cover *Crazed Lady Terrorist*?"

With a chuckle, Wolfe shook his head. "No, my agent said he's filing it as an arson."

"Good." He grew serious. "Did anyone figure out where McCaffrey is?"

"No. I found the place where he set off one of my booby-traps. Several yards from where he fell, I found a shattered hunter's grade pair of night vision goggles. I also saw a few drops of blood on fallen leaves. My guess is the explosion ruptured one of his eardrums."

"How many flash bangs did you have hidden out there?"

Wolfe just smiled. "I forget."

"What other surprises do you have out there?"

A shrug was his answer.

Griggs put his hand on Wolfe's shoulder. "I'm staying at Joseph's place for a few days until the FBI finishes its investigation. Is there anything I can help with?"

"No, Nadia and I have a hotel suite we'll be staying at. Plus, I have a cot in my office above the hangar I can use if I need to stay here."

"I'll see you again before I leave."

The elderly man living in the isolated farmhouse had offered little resistance to the home invasion. He now lay deceased in a chest freezer positioned against a concrete wall in the basement.

McCaffrey knew something was wrong with the right side of his head. Dried blood remained crusted inside the ear canal and the only thing he could hear on that side was a loud ring. His balance was off and he tired easily.

On the positive side, he found numerous shotguns in an unlocked gun cabinet in the old man's bedroom. These he could use to mount a counterattack on Wolfe's property once all the law enforcement officials grew tired of searching for him.

It was late the following day when McCaffrey realized the money Daniella promised him was gone. She never told him its location or how to access it. This realization caused him to collapse into a lounge chair in the old man's house. Staring at a spot on the wall he did not see, he realized his hopes of getting out of the US alive, along with the money, were gone. The thought made him weary. For the past twenty years he had lived by his wits and squeaked out an existence. And again, he found himself in the same situation he had been in Ireland, broke and running from people who wanted him either in jail or dead. Only now, he was in the middle of a huge country he was unfamiliar with and nothing to fall back on.

Steeling himself to the inevitable, he started to make plans for his revenge on the man who had caused all of his turmoil.

With the multitude of investigators gone and an exhausted Nadia safely asleep in their room at the hotel, Wolfe sat before the security monitors in the room above the hangar. The first glimpses of dawn brightened the sky as he saw faint movement in a motion detection camera located at the southwest corner of his property. The shadow's movement did not resemble a deer or any other non-human creature. It was the stealthy movement of a man hunting prey.

With a smile, Wolfe stared at the monitor. "Well, well, Danny. You've returned."

Over the next hour, he monitored McCaffrey's progress as the former IRA insurgent worked his way carefully through the southern tree line. On the eastern most border of his land, Wolfe watched as McCaffrey stared hard at a security camera. The man then moved out of camera range and disappeared.

Evidence of the man's presence vanished for several hours. Close to noon, motion activated the same camera McCaffrey had stared at earlier in the day. Five seconds later, the screen went blank. Wolfe typed on the keyboard of the laptop, but the picture from that particular camera remained blank.

With a slight smile, Wolfe stood and went to the cabinet next to the gun safe. He extracted a woodland ghillie suit. After donning it, he moved to the rack where he kept his Barrett. He loaded four magazines and placed them in utility pockets within the suit. Satisfied with his efforts, he descended the stairs and walked through the door leading to the open space containing his Beechcraft.

McCaffrey's trip back to the large sporting goods store twenty-five miles north of the elderly man's home allowed him to get a high-powered air rifle and camo hunting clothing. The air rifle dispatched the camera he had spotted earlier that morning with silent efficiency and the clothing allowed him to blend into the woodland terrain. The Taurus G3 secured in its holster on his hip gave him easy to access to the weapon.

To the untrained eye, he was basically invisible. With slow and deliberate moves, he would be able to navigate through the trees with stealth.

To the eye of an experienced sniper, any movement at all would give his position away.

Exiting the hangar through a door on the south wall, Wolfe crawled to a patch of tall decorative grasses planted in random patterns for just such an occasion. His experience as a sniper trained him to anticipate his opponents' next move. Securing himself within the confines of the grass garden, he set up his Barrett and scanned the tree line to the south.

Time passed slowly as afternoon waned and the sun became obstructed by clouds on the western horizon. Late fall in the Ozarks placed the solar globe at a forty-degree angle from the southern horizon. Sunset would occur a little after five-thirty—exactly one hour away.

McCaffrey, staying well within the tree line, could see the beginning of the runway leading north toward the hangar. The bottom half of the structure was obscured by the upward slope of the land to his north.

Taking a tentative step out of the tree line, the ex-IRA terrorist kept low to the ground as he moved north in the open field. With each step, he grew closer to the top of the ridge as more of the hangar's bottom half could be discerned.

When the sun disappeared into the cloud bank on the western horizon, he could fully see the bottom half of the structure and the multiple gardens of tall grasses surrounding it. Realizing that danger lurked within any of those locations, he lay prone on the ground and waited.

Wolfe kept his attention on the Barrett's scope as he scanned the horizon for any movement. With the thickening cloud cover, twilight would arrive early, followed by a short period of dusk before full darkness. The distinct smell of rain from the approaching storm reached him when a sudden gust of wind blew through the tall grass of his hide. He knew a cold rain would soon arrive.

As the ambient light faded, Wolfe heard thunder in the distance. A typical thunderstorm for this part of the country meant a wind event would precede the actual start of rain. With temperatures currently in the fifties, a drop of twenty degrees or more could occur as the advancing cold front arrived.

Time dragged as the wind increased in velocity. Leaves still clinging to their summer hosts released their tenuous grips and swirled in the ensuing gusts. Temperatures plunged as large drops of heavy rain made contact with the ground. Having experienced these conditions before, Wolfe kept his attention trained on detecting unnatural movement in front of him.

A slight movement to the left of his scope's crosshairs caught his attention. He trained the rifle toward the disturbance and caught a glimpse of a straight line where none should be. He switched on the scope's night vision and saw the infrared outline of a human form low to the ground. He applied pressure to the Barrett's trigger.

Just as he exhaled, a blinding flash of lightning and the immediate thunderclap caused him to veer his aim to the right just as the bullet left the barrel.

With a silent curse, he corrected his aim, but the target had vanished.

The proximity of the lightning strike and the nearly instantaneous clap of thunder caused McCaffrey to flinch. When a bullet struck the ground to his left a microsecond later, he hugged the ground and immediately slithered backward.

Adrenaline pumped through his veins as his heart rate accelerated. Attempts to control his breathing failed as another lightning strike nearby had him near panic. He closed his eyes as the increasing volume of rain soaked through his clothing. He shivered involuntarily.

This is intolerable. The thought flashed through his mind as he closed his eyes. Daniella was supposed to renew his purpose. Something he had been missing for a long while. She was a kindred spirit, someone who felt political change would only occur after a violent struggle to change government and gain control of the mind and soul of the populace.

As his lifelong dream of being someone who would cause change to the world faded into the reality of what would never be, he took the Taurus out of its holster and rose. Without another thought, he dashed forward toward the death he knew would only be seconds away. As he ran, he pointed the pistol forward and started pulling the trigger.

To his utter disbelief, Wolfe observed the figure stand and start running in the heavy rain toward his location. With the yardage to the advancing target decreasing and the deluge of falling water obscuring the image, he heard bullets strike the dirt around him. As he applied pressure to the Barrett's trigger, he felt a calmness wash over him.

The rifle fired at the exact same time a clap of thunder

shook the world. This time his aim was true and a gaping hole appeared in the center of McCaffrey's chest. The fifty-caliber bullet destroyed the terrorist's heart and severed his spine almost simultaneously. The now lifeless man was thrown backward as the inertia of the bullet transferred its energy to McCaffrey's body.

A chill swept through Wolfe as he remembered a similar duel in a rainstorm with another man trying to kill him several years earlier and many miles to the east.

He lay there, as water dripped into his eyes and cascaded down his face. Exhaustion from lack of sleep and the constant stress of the past few weeks swept over him. He fought the desire to close his eyes and sleep. Finally, after wiping the rain out of his eyes, a flash of lightning revealed a hand covered in blood. Apparently, without feeling it, one of the bullets from the terrorist's pistol had grazed his head. With a sigh, he stood and trudged toward the body of Danny McCaffrey.

Epilogue

Several Weeks Later

Joseph Kincaid shook Wolfe's hand after climbing out of the dark gray Land Rover he kept on his property in eastern Christian County. They stood watching numerous individuals erecting the wooden frame of a new home for the couple. Joseph asked, "Any idea when it will be completed?"

With a smile, Wolfe said, "The builder told me with all the extras I've requested, it will take at least six months, maybe longer. We're supposed to have a wet winter so he wants to get it framed and a roof on it before Christmas. I told him I'd give him a ten-thousand-dollar bonus if he makes that happen." He paused and chuckled. "He's had a crew out here every day including weekends, ever since."

Joseph turned to Wolfe. "I haven't had a chance to tell you the bio-weapon McCaffrey brought into the US was inert."

"Then what killed all those people in Columbia?"

"The stuff McCaffrey possessed. There was a new strain

of *Clostridium Botulinum* discovered in 2013. I'm told it was the first new strain of the stuff found in forty years. Fears it would be turned into a bio-weapon have come true. The one McCaffrey had was extremely potent, but the strain is very susceptible to high temperatures. Apparently, it was exposed to extreme heat for an extended length of time. The spores in the vials they recovered from his backpack were dead."

Wolfe kept his gaze on Joseph for a while without commenting. "It came from Iran, you know."

"Yes, we were aware of that. The Pentagon, CIA, FBI, Homeland Security and the CDC are extremely worried about it."

"Did Israel's air strike destroy the lab?"

Silence fell over the conversation until Joseph cleared his throat. "They claim to have. But satellite images taken when the lab was under construction seem to indicate eighty percent of it was buried in the mountain."

"That's what Ian and I surmised when we were there."

"The air strike supposedly killed ninety percent of the scientists working at the lab. Plus, you took out the head virologist."

Wolfe studied Joseph. "Then where did the stuff McCaffrey received come from?"

"We don't know."

"Maybe they already have a stockpile. I would think someone might want to find out."

Joseph's mouth twitched. "We were thinking that might be a good job for you?"

"No."

"Why don't you think it over?"

"What is it about the word no that people in government don't understand?"

"We don't like hearing the word."

"Get used to it."

Silence once again fell over the conversation as hammers striking nails and circular handsaws cutting lumber grew louder.

Joseph folded his arms. "What extras?"

"Well—this little episode with Danny McCaffrey exposed a few flaws in my security system."

"Really? Like what?"

"The fact Daniella was able to crash a vehicle into the front of the house."

"How could you have prepared for that, Michael?"

Wolfe rolled his eyes and stared at the construction site. "Really, Joseph. You have to ask?" He paused. "Who adopted Kayla's baby?"

"I spoke to Ben-David about that. An Algerian dissident living in Paris."

"You're kidding."

"No, the woman we knew as Daniella grew up in an anti-Semitic household. The Israelis are trying to figure out if Gerlis found her and created her cover or if it was a Palestinian operation. They just don't know at this time. But they have changed a few things in their recruiting processes."

"Good idea."

"Sorry about Canfield."

"So am I. While I still didn't trust him, it was no way for a man like Geoffrey to die."

The conversation paused while both men watched the carpenters work on the house. Wolfe finally said, "Kayla told me Daniella knew where we lived. The only way she would have known that is if the Mossad has files on us. Plus,

Ben-David thought we were dead until this mess with McCaffrey started. You know anything about that?"

"Yes, sorry, that one is on me. I gave Uri a GPS location. We both thought it would enhance yours and Nadia's security. We thought wrong."

Wolfe stared at his friend for several moments. "I thank you for the good intentions. Try not to do it again."

Joseph smiled. "Trust me, I won't." Silence fell over the conversation again. Finally, he said, "Kayla Callaghan was extradited to the UK yesterday."

"Why?"

"There was a good reason she left for the US twenty years ago. Several years before the baby was born, it seems she and Danny planted a bomb that killed a number of British soldiers."

"Huh. Who escorted her back?"

"A friend of yours."

With knowing smile, Wolfe replied, "He hates that type of duty."

"Oh, he didn't mind. It seems his older brother was one of the soldiers killed in the blast."

"Ian's a good man."

"Yes, he is. He reminds me a little of you."

Shaking his head, Wolfe folded his arms. "How does he feel about taking on this task you mentioned earlier?"

Joseph turned to study his protégé. "He's onboard if you are."

"Shit."

"He said pretty much the same thing. Do you need to discuss this with Nadia?"

"Probably, if I want to stay married." He paused. "Which I do."

Next in The Michael Wolfe Saga

vinci-books.com/matterofpayback

A master bombmaker. A looming attack. A mission with no margin for error.

Danny McCaffrey has spent years selling his deadly expertise to the highest bidder. Now, he's aligned with Iran on a plan that could shake the world. Ex-CIA sniper Michael Wolfe and his wife, Nadia, must hunt him down before his next strike hits the heart of America.

Turn the page for a free preview…

A Matter of Payback: Chapter One

Mohammad Al-Qaedi lifted the explosive-laden vest onto the shoulders of Ahmed Hadid. The nineteen-year-old slumped slightly with the addition of twenty kilograms to his slender frame.

"It is heavy."

"Ahmed, to accomplish our task today it has to be."

The young Palestinian nodded. "I know."

"Make sure it is secure to your body."

Hadid pulled on the two straps and cinched them tight. A trickle of sweat leaked from his hairline toward his temple. He slipped his arms into the black ankle-length coat. As he buttoned it, Al-Qaedi placed a black Fedora on his head. Black curled sidelocks, attached to the hat, hung in front of his ears, blending perfectly with the color of his hair and beard. The young man observed himself in the mirror. "I look exactly like one of those Zionist Hasidic Jews."

"Yes, Ahmed, you do. That is the point. You will be able to walk onto the bus without anyone harassing you and then all you have to do is activate the detonator in your coat pocket."

The young man continued to gaze at his image. "Then, I will be a martyr in paradise."

Al-Qaedi nodded. "Yes, Ahmed, you will." The older man's expression did not betray his thoughts. He kept his disdain for the ignorant fool to himself.

Michael Wolfe held his young wife's hand as he escorted her to the bus station for a trip to visit her parents in Tel-Aviv.

"I wish you were going with me, Michael."

"Sara, we've discussed this numerous times, I have to work. They don't care if my wife is taking a holiday. I have to report for duty tomorrow."

"I know, but it would be nice to spend a few days together without responsibilities."

"Yes, it would."

She leaned closer to him and whispered, "I heard from my doctor this morning."

Wolfe squeezed her hand. "And?"

"I'm pregnant."

He took her into his arms and held her tight. "When you get back, we will celebrate properly. Are you telling your parents?"

"Of course. They will be excited to know they're going to be grandparents." She paused and gave him a sad smile. "I'm sorry, Michael. I sometimes forget your parents are dead."

"Me, too. They would have loved being grandparents."

The bus pulled into the station. She watched it stop and then kissed Wolfe. "I'll call you when I get there."

"You'd better."

She hurried to the bus door and waited to board. She liked to travel light with only items she needed in a backpack. Once she climbed the three steps and disappeared inside, he started to walk to their car. Wishing to see her one more time before she left, he returned his attention to the bus. She waved at him from a window in the front. When he returned the wave, a tall young man dressed in the traditional clothing of a devout Hasidic Jew passed him, heading for the bus. He noted the man sweating heavily on a cool cloudy day.

Ahmed Hadid resisted the urge to scratch the back of his neck. Sweat, plus the rough material used to construct the vest he wore under his frock, irritated his skin. The itch became so pronounced, he shivered at the same time his forehead grew damp with perspiration.

He approached the steps leading into the bus and prepared to board. His irritated neck would soon not bother him.

The sweat Wolfe observed on the Hasidic man seemed out of place and troubled him. As a trained black-ops operator, now working for the Israeli Mossad, he could not shake the sense of foreboding. He started toward the bus just as the man clad in black climbed the three steps to the vehicle's interior.

He glanced at the window where Sara sat and noticed her stiffen. His pace quickened when his wife faced the window and placed the palms of her hands on the glass. Her eyes were wide and his name frozen on her lips.

The fireball and concussion of the blast propelled him backward. His head struck the parking lot asphalt, and the world went black.

Screams and sirens dragged him back from the darkness. He witnessed the burning hell before him. Staggering to his feet, he felt a sudden despair and emptiness.

"Sara!"

Black smoke rose from the inferno. He madly dashed toward the heat and fire. Flames shot from the vehicle's shredded carcass. Shards of glass crunched under his feet as blood dripped from his forehead.

He ignored the severe ringing in his ears as he rushed toward the flames.

"Sara!"

As he got closer to the vehicle, he slipped on something. When he looked down, it was a human hand. A woman's left hand. The fourth finger bore a simple gold band with a solitary diamond. Sara's wedding ring.

A Matter of Payback: Chapter Two

Michael Wolfe handed Uri Ben-David an envelope. The Israeli commander asked, "What's this?"

"My resignation."

"Why?"

Wolfe shrugged. "It's time."

Ben-David stood and handed the envelope back to Wolfe. When he did not accept it, the Israeli let it fall unopened onto his desk. "Israel does not have time for these kinds of theatrics, Michael. We have a crisis on our hands. Do you know how many died yesterday at the Park Hotel?"

"I haven't been listening to the news."

Leaning over his desk, Ben-David placed his palms on the top to support himself. "Thirty. Thirty individuals went to Netanya to celebrate Passover. Now they are all dead. All because of a suicide bomber."

Narrowing his eyes, Wolfe's face grew hard. "I am aware of what a suicide bomber can do, Uri."

"I'm mindful of that, Michael." He straightened and folded his arms. "Israel is going into Ramallah tomorrow morning. We will be placing Arafat under house arrest. I need someone with your skills to protect our boys."

Shaking his head, Wolfe kept his eyes on the unopened envelope on Ben-David's desk and said, "Not my concern anymore."

"Is the person who planned the bombing of Sara's bus your concern?"

Wolfe's eyes rose slowly to meet Ben-David's. His expression cold. "What about him?"

"His name is Mohammad Al-Qaedi. He is Iranian. We learned his name a week ago. Our source told us he had another bombing planned. Where, the source did not know. When we did learn where, it was too late to stop it."

"Where is he?"

"Do I have your attention?"

"Yes."

"What about this letter?" He pointed to the envelope on the desk.

Picking it up, Wolfe folded it and placed it in his jeans back pocket. He returned his gaze to Ben-David. "I'll reconsider. Where is he?"

"Ramallah."

"Do you have a picture?"

Ben-David opened a file on his desk and withdrew a picture. He handed it to Wolfe. "This was taken five years ago in the Gaza Strip."

Without taking his eyes off the picture, Wolfe said, "Where do I report?"

March 30, 2002

Twenty-one kilometers north of Jerusalem, in the West Bank, lies a city called Ramallah. Within the city limits is a Mukataa, Arabic for a headquarters, built in the 1920s by the British during their occupation of the area. This particular one became Yasser Arafat's West Bank headquarters in 1996. For Operation Defensive Shield, Israeli Defense Forces occupied and surrounded the compound, basically isolating Arafat and placing him under house arrest.

Outside this compound on a rooftop nearby, Michael Wolfe and his Israeli spotter, Josef, surveyed the streets surrounding the Mukataa. Having just celebrated his thirtieth birthday without his beloved Sara by his side, he relished the thought of avenging her death.

At the young age of nineteen, Wolfe had attained the distinction of being one of the best snipers ever produced by the United States Marine Corps. Serving with distinction during the brief 1991 Operation Desert Storm, he emerged from his stint with the Marines as a decorated combat soldier. Afterward, he attended Georgetown University, earning a degree in international business management. Recruited by the Israelis to work at their embassy in Washington, he later moved to Israel, with the blessing and encouragement of the Mossad. There he met Sara Sobus, a second-generation Israeli descended from Polish immigrant parents.

Josef tapped him on the shoulder. "Ten o'clock. Five bogies with AK-47s."

Wolfe aimed his Barrett M99 .50 BMG sniper rifle toward the location indicated by Josef. The crosshairs of his scope centered on the lead Palestinian whose face and head were covered by a tactical desert keffiyeh. "What's in front of them?"

"Couple of our guys, keeping tabs on the compound."

"Do they see them?"

His spotter grew quiet. Wolfe maintained his concentration on the five Palestinians. Finally, Josef said, "No. They are sneaking up on our patrol from the rear."

Without responding, Wolfe increased the pressure on the Barrett's trigger. With the massive suppressor installed on the weapon, the rifle shot would not be heard by the men advancing on the Israeli patrol.

An enormous hole opened in the chest of the lead Palestinian. Surprise and shock triggered his comrades to abandon their quest and retreat at a full run.

Josef said quietly, "Got him."

Wolfe's mouth twitched as he aimed at the retreating men. He released another round, which ricocheted off a wall ahead of the running men. This encouraged them to run even faster.

Raising his head from the scope, he surveyed the scene. "See anything else?"

"No. Good shot, Michael."

Without a response, Wolfe returned his attention back to Arafat's compound. A man stood outside a building within the walls. Getting back behind the scope, he centered the crosshairs on the man's face. A chill went up his spine as he studied the person's features.

"Josef, there's a guy standing outside a door on the east side of the building where Arafat is sequestered. Use your scope to see if you can identify him."

"I see him." The spotter grew quiet as he scrutinized the man. "Michael, the picture you showed me this morning, I think it's him."

Wolfe did not divert his scope from the target. "That's what I thought. Radio in and let them know I have Al-Qaedi in my sights. Request permission to fire."

Studying the man, Wolfe memorized his features. He appeared to be in his mid-to-late thirties. A tan-and-brown keffiyeh covered only his head, leaving his face unobscured.

The next thing Wolfe heard was Josef saying, "Take the shot."

As he increased the pressure on the trigger, the man turned his gaze directly at Wolfe and gave him a half grin. Just as the Barrett fired, the terrorist ducked back into the building.

By May, 2002, Israeli Defense Forces no longer occupied Palestinian cities, and the number of suicide bombings tapered off. With one of their invasion's missions accomplished, Israel steeled itself for the forthcoming condemnations of its actions by the rest of the world.

Michael Wolfe reappeared in the office of Uri Ben-David. Standing at attention in front of the desk, the Israeli commander studied a report while the man standing in front of his desk waited. Finally, he said, "Once again, you managed to distinguish yourself in Ramallah. Congratulations, Michael."

With a grim expression, Wolfe said, "I had Al-Qaedi in my sights. I hesitated and lost the shot."

"That's not what I read. You followed procedures. The delay in granting permission for you to fire is what lost the shot."

"He saw me."

"You specifically, or you the sniper?"

"Me the sniper."

"So, he wouldn't be able to recognize you?"

"I don't see how. My face was behind the scope. Plus, I was over 500 meters away."

"But he knew someone was there."

"Yes."

"We have reports of him being spotted on the streets of Tehran, a week ago."

"Figures. Men like Al-Qaedi are basically cowards. They want the other guy to die for the cause."

"What about your resignation?"

"What resignation?"

"Good, kind of what I thought. Ready to track down Mohammad Al-Qaedi?"

Wolfe nodded.

"Why are you still standing there?"

Wolfe immediately walked out of his office.

Grab your copy…

vinci-books.com/matterofpayback

About the Author

J.C. Fields is a multi-award-winning and Amazon best-selling author. Many of his fourteen published novels have been awarded numerous gold, silver and bronze medals in the Reader's Favorite International Book Awards contest.

Over the past several years, many of his numerous short stories have been featured on the YouTube Podcast Fear From the Heartland, a part of the Chilling Tales for Dark Night network.

After a decade as an independent author, he signed a publishing contract with Vinci Books. Vinci Books is a world-class publisher created to offer independent authors the best of self-published and traditional publishing.

His passion for helping new authors reach their dream of publishing is reflected in his activity with numerous area writing groups and serving on the boards for the Between the Pages Writers Conference and the Ozarks Creative Writers Conference.

He lives with his wife, Connie, in Southwest Missouri.

Acknowledgments

I continued to be blessed with a dedicated team of individuals lending their talents for the purpose of making my novels as good as possible. The contents are on me, but the rest is assisted by the following:

Sharon Kizziah-Holmes, owner of *Paperback Press*, continues to be one of my staunchest supporters. She has been with me from the beginning and I am indebted to her efforts on my behalf.

To my critique group: Sharon, Shirley, Lori, Heather and Conetta, I am a better writer due to everyone's brutal assessments of what I submit.

Holly Atkinson, my developmental editor, continues to help make my novels more coherent and readable.

Shirley McCann and Tina Vyborne, thank you for your fine tuning of the manuscript, it is amazing what final read throughs discover.

Paul J. McSorley, has become both a friend and a fantastic business partner. He has lent his talents to every J.C. Fields' novel since the beginning. Due to the huge success of our audiobook version of *A Lone Wolf*, we are both able to pursue our passions full-time. He as an audiobook narrator and I as an author. While there is always a bit of sadness when I complete a new book, the excitement returns when Paul starts producing it for audio.

And again, last but not least, my wife Connie. Her

encouragement in my pursuit to become a full-time author has been unwavering. We finally did it. I am blessed to have both her support and her love. I am truly a lucky man.